DILLINGER IN HOLLYWOOD

New and Selected Short Stories

JOHN SAYLES

NATION
BOOKS

DILLINGER IN HOLLYWOOD
NEW AND SELECTED SHORT STORIES

Published by
Nation Books
An Imprint of Avalon Publishing Group
245 West 17th St., 11th Floor
New York, NY 10011

AVALON
publishing group incorporated

Nation Books is a co-publishing venture of the Nation Institute and
Avalon Publishing Group Incorporated.

Library of Congress Cataloging-in-Publication Data

ISBN 1-56025-632-X

9 8 7 6 5 4 3 2 1

Book design by Paul Paddock
Printed in the United States of America
Distributed by Publishers Group West

For Maggie

DILLINGER IN HOLLYWOOD

CONTENTS

Introduction

THE STORIES IN THIS COLLECTION reflect my relatively infrequent forays into fiction during the last twenty years or so. In that same time I've published one novel, written and directed fifteen feature films, and written fifty or more screenplays for hire (mostly unproduced, as is common in Hollywood). Getting a movie made resembles the passage of a bill through Congress (including the tendency not to resemble the original idea when it comes out the other end), and the campaign to make one takes up a lot of time. But every once in a while a story idea will come to me that seems best expressed in fiction. I feel it in words, not pictures, and steal a bit of time to try to get it down on paper. Those particular writing muscles are stiff, I think the first three or four pages stink, but force myself to keep pushing until a little bit of rhythm starts to creep in and a process of osmosis occurs, allowing me through some wall that had seemed impermeable, and I am writing fiction. The great thing about fiction, as I've often said, is that you can be God. If you want the sun to shine or three thousand troops in full combat gear to materialize, you just describe them (and do not have to worry about when they eat lunch). On the other hand, you're on your own—no composers, production designers, costumers, cinematographers, or actors to give you ideas and throw their talents into the project.

These stories, like the movies I've been involved with, cover a great range of locales and situations, and are written in styles and rhythms dictated by the subject matter. If there is a progression within them, it is one I've been unable to discover. Even the two stories—"Dillinger in Hollywood" and "Above the Line"—that both feature the first-person narrator Son Bishop, are written in a very different tone. There's a lot going on out there, and it never surprises me to see two eyewitnesses come up with widely diverging versions of the same events. What unifies these stories then is probably their origin—my constant question: If they act that way, *what can possibly be going through their heads?*

Dillinger in Hollywood

EVER HAVE ONE OF THOSE WEEKS where the TV is bust and there's steamed chicken for lunch three days in a row? It was one of those weeks, and Spurs Tatum starts in after Rec Therapy, before we could wheel them all out of the dayroom.

"Hoot Gibson held my horse," says Spurs. "I took falls for Randolph Scott. I hung from a wing in *The Perils of Pauline*. And Mr. Ford," he says, "Mr. Ford he always hired me on. You see a redskin blasted off a horse in one of Mr. Ford's pictures, like as not it's me. One-Take Tatum they called me, before the Spurs thing took."

We'd heard it all before, every time there was a Western or a combat picture on the TV, every time a patient come in with a broken hip or a busted rib, all through the last days when the Duke was dying in the news. Heard how Spurs had thought up most of the riding stunts they use today, how he'd been D. W. Griffith's drinking buddy, how he saved Tom Mix's life on the Sacramento River. It was hot and one of those weeks and we'd heard it all before, so I don't know if it was that or the beating he'd just taken at Parcheesi that made old Casey up and say how he used to be John Dillinger.

His chart said that Casey had been a driver on the Fox lot long enough to qualify for the Industry fund. I told him I hadn't realized he'd done any stand-in work.

"The bird who done the stand-in work," says Casey, "is the one they potted at the Biograph Theater. I used to be Johnnie Dillinger. In the flesh."

He said the name with a hard g, like in *finger,* and didn't so much as blink.

Now we've had our delusions at the Home– your standard fading would-of-been actresses expecting their call from Mr. DeMille, a Tarzan whoop now and then during the full moon, and one old gent who goes around mouthing words without sound and overacting like he's on the silent picture screen. Generally it's some glorified notion of who they used to be. Up to this point Casey's only brag was he drove Joe DiMaggio to the airport when the Clipper was hitched to Monroe.

"If I remember right," says Spurs, giving me an eye that meant he thought the poor fella had slipped his tracks, "if I'm not too fuzzy on it, I believe that Mr. Dillinger, Public Enemy Number One, departed from our midst in the summer of thirty-four."

"You should live so long," says Casey.

Now, I try to give a man the benefit of a doubt. With Spurs I can tell there's a grain of fact to his brags because I was in the wrangler game myself. I was riding broncs in Santa Barbara for their Old Spanish Days and this fella hires me to stunt for some rodeo picture with Gig Young in it. He says I take a nice fall.

The pay was greener than what I saw on the circuit, so I stuck in Hollywood. See, I could always *ride* the sumbitches, my problem came when it was time to get *off.* What I had was a new approach to tumbling from a horse. Whereas most folks out here bust their ass to get *into* pictures, I busted mine to get *out.* Some big damn gelding bucked me before I'd dug in, and I landed smack on my tailbone. The doctor says to me—I'm laying on my stomach trying to remember my middle name—the doctor comes in with the X rays and he says, "I don't know how to tell you this, Son, but you're gonna have to learn to shit standing up."

If they'd known who I was, *Variety* would of headlined SON BISHOP SWAPS BRIDLE FOR BEDPAN. Horses and hospitals were all I knew. Over the years I'd spent more time in emergency rooms than Dr. Kildare. So it was hospitals, and pretty soon I drifted into the geriatric game. Your geriatrics and horses hold a lot in common– they're high-strung, they bite and kick sometimes, and they're none of them too big on bowel control. 'Course, if a geriatric steps on your foot it don't take a wood chisel to peel it off the floor.

It's a living.

So Spurs I can back sometimes, though I'm sure he didn't play such a starring role in the invention of the saddle. With Casey I had to bring it up at report.

"He thinks he's a dead gangster?" says Mrs. Goorwitz, who was the charge nurse that night.

"No, he thinks he's an old man in a Hollywood nursing home. He says he *used* to be John Dillinger."

"In another life?"

"Nope," I answered her, "in this one."

We had this reincarnated character in here once, claimed to have been all the even-numbered King Louies of France, from the second right up to Louie the Sixteen. I asked how he ended up an assistant prop man at Warner's and he said after all that commotion his spirit must of needed the rest.

"I thought he was shot," says Mrs. Goorwitz.

"At point-blank range," I tell her. "They couldn't of missed."

Mrs. Goorwitz was a bit untracked by the news. She hates anything out of its place, hates waves, and many's the geriatric she's hounded to death for holding a book overdue from the Home library. She pulled Casey's chart and studied it. "It says here his name is Casey Mullins."

"Well that's that, isn't it?"

"Confused behavior," says Mrs. Goorwitz, as she writes it into the report. "Inappropriate response. Watch carefully."

The only thing that gets watched carefully in this joint is the time-punch at two minutes till shift change, but I figured I might save Casey some headache.

"Maybe he's just lying," I tell her. "To work up a little attention."

"Did he say anything else?" She was on the scent now and threatening to go practice medicine on somebody any minute.

"Not a whole lot," I tell her. "But if we breathe a word to the Feds, he claims they'll find us off Santa Monica Pier with our little toes curled up."

"This bird Jimmy Lawrence, a very small-time character," says Casey, "he had this bum ticker. A rheumatic heart condition, congenital since birth. We dated the same girl once is how I got to know him. People start coming up to say, 'Jeez, you're the spittin' image of Johnnie Dillinger, you know that?' and this girl, this mutual friend, tells me and I get the idea."

After he let the Dillinger thing out, Casey got very talkative, like he had it stewing in him a long time and finally it blows out all at once. I'd be in his room tapping the catheter bags on these two vegematics, Kantor and Wise, and it would be just me listening, and this fella Roscoe Baggs, who was a midget. Roscoe was in *The Wizard of Oz* as a Munchkin and was a very deep thinker. He reads the kind of science-fiction books that don't have girls in loincloths on the cover.

"This girl has still got the yen for me," says Casey, "so she steers Lawrence to a doctor connection who tells him two months, maybe three, and it's the last roundup. The guy is demolished. So I make him this offer– I supply the dough to live it up his final days, and he supplies a body to throw to the authorities. You could buy Chicago cops by the job lot back then, so it was no big deal arranging the details. Hard times. Only two or three people had to know I was involved.

"Well, the poor chump didn't even know how to paint the town right. And he kept moaning that he wanted us to hold off till after the Series, onnaconna he followed the Cardinals. That was the year Ripper Collins and the Dean brothers tore up the league."

"Just like Spangler," says Roscoe. "Remember, he wanted to see a man walk on the moon? Held off his cancer till he saw it on television, and the next day he went downstairs."

Downstairs is where the morgue and the kitchen are located.

"One step for mankind," says Roscoe, "and checkout time for Spangler. You got to admire that kind of control."

"Another hoax," says Casey. "They staged the whole thing in a little studio up the coast. I know a guy in video."

I told Casey I'd read where Dillinger started to run when he saw the cops outside the picture show. And how his sister had identified the remains the next day.

"He turned chickenshit on me, Son. We hadn't told him the exact date, and there he is, coming out from the movies with a broad on each arm, and all of a sudden the party's over. What would you do, you were him? And as for Sis," says Casey, "she always done what she could to help me out.

"The day after the planting we send in a truck, dig the coffin out, pour concrete, and lay it back in. Anybody wants another peek at the stiff they got to drill a mine shaft."

It sounded reasonable, sort of. And when the shrink who comes through twice a year stopped to ask about his Dillinger fixation, Casey just told him to scram. Said if he wanted his brains scrambled he'd stick his head in the microwave.

I did some reading and everything he said checked out pretty close. Only I couldn't connect Casey with a guy who'd pull a stunt like that on the Lawrence fella. He was one of the nice ones, Casey—never bitched much even with his diabetes and his infected feet and his rotting kidneys and his finger curling up. A stand-up character.

The finger was curling up independent from the others on his right hand. His trigger finger, bent like he was about to squeeze off a round.

"It's like *The Tell-Tale Heart*," says Roscoe one day. I'm picking up dinner trays in the rooms, and Roscoe is working on four chocolate puddings. They had put one on Casey's tray by mistake and I didn't have time to spoon the other two down Kantor and Wise.

"The what?" asks Casey.

"It's a story. This guy kills an old man and stuffs him under the floor-boards. When the police come to investigate he thinks he hears the old man's heart beating under the boards, and he cracks and gives himself away."

"So what's that got to do with my finger?"

"Maybe your finger is trying to blow the whistle on your life of crime. Psychosomatic."

"Oh." Casey mauled it over in his mind for a minute. "I get it. We had a guy in the can, kilt his wife. Poisoned her. At first everybody figured she'd just got sick and died, happened all the time in those days. But then he starts complaining to the cops about the neighborhood kids—says they're writing nasty stuff on the sidewalk in front of his place. OLD MAN WALSH CROAKED HIS WIFE WITH RAT BAIT– stuff like that. So the cops send a guy to check it out on his night rounds. The cop's passing by and out comes Walsh, sleepwalking, with a piece of chalk in his hand. Wrote his own ticket to the slammer, right there on the sidewalk, onnaconna he had a leaky conscience."

It had been bothering me, so I took the opening to ask. "Do you ever feel bad? About things you done back then?"

Casey shrugged and looked away from me and then looked back. "Nah," he says, "What am I, mental? This guy Walsh, he was AWOL."

AWOL is what we call the senile ones. Off base and not coming back.

"Hey, Roscoe," says Casey, "why'd this telltale character kill the old man in the first place?"

"Because this old man had a big eye. He wanted to kill the big eye."

Just then Spurs wheels in, looking to vulture a loose dessert.

"I wonder," says Casey, "what he would of done to a fat head?"

It seemed to make him feel better, talking about his life as Dillinger. Kept him up and alert even when his health took a big slide.

"Only reason I'm still percolating," he'd say, "is I still got my pride. They beat that into me on my first stretch."

I told him I'd never heard of beating pride into somebody.

"They beat on you one way or the other," he says. "The pride comes in how you stand up to it."

I went on the graveyard shift and after two o'clock check I'd go down to chew the fat with Casey. Roscoe slept like the dead and the two veggies were on automatic pilot, so it didn't make any difference how loud we were. Casey was a hurtin' cowboy, and his meds weren't up to knocking him out at night. We'd play cards by the light from the corridor sometimes or he'd cut up old scores for me. He told me about one where their advance man posed as a Hollywood location scout for a gangster movie. When they come out of the bank holding hostages the next day, sniping at the local shields, the townspeople just smiled and looked around for cameras.

He didn't have much to say on his years driving for Fox. He only hung on because of what he called the "fringe benefits," which mostly had to do with women.

"Used to be a disease with me," he'd say. "I'd go two days without a tumble and my eyeballs would start to swole up, my brains would start pushing out my ears. Shut me out for three days and I'd hump anything, just anything. Like some dope fiend."

When I asked how he'd dealt with that while he was in the slammer, he clammed up.

He was still able to wheel himself around a bit when Norma took up with him. Norma had bad veins and was in a chair herself. She'd been in the silents in her teens, getting rescued from fates worse than death. Her mother was ninety and shared a room with her. The old vulture just sat, deaf as a post, glaring at Norma for not being Mary Pickford. Norma had been one of the backgammon crowd till word spread that Casey thought he was John Dillinger. She studied him for a week, keeping her distance, eavesdropping on his sparring matches with Spurs Tatum, watching how he moved and how he talked. Then one day as the singalong is breaking up she wheels up beside him. Norma's voice had gone deeper and deeper with the years, and she filled in at bass on "What a Friend We Have in Jesus."

"All I do is dream of you," she sings to Casey, "the whole night through."

"That used to be my favorite song," he says.

"I know," says Norma.

It give me the fantods sometimes, the way they'd look at each other like they known one another forever. Norma had been one of those caught up by the press on Dillinger when he had his year in the headlines. A woman near thirty years old keeping a scrapbook. She had picked up some work as an extra after her silent days were over, but it never came to much. She still had a shoe box full of the postcards her mother had sent out every year to agents and flacks and producers—a grainy blowup of Norma in a toga or a buckskin shift or a French peasant outfit. Norma Nader in *Cimarron*. Norma Nader in *The Pride and the Passion*. Norma Nader in *The Greatest Story Ever Told*. They were the only credits she got in the talkies, those postcards, but her mother kept the heat on. I'd find Norma out in the corridor at night, wheels locked, watching the light coming out from her room.

"Is she in bed yet?" she'd ask, and I'd go down and peek in on Old Lady Nader.

"She's still awake, Norma."

"She always stood up till I come home, no matter what hour. I come in the door and it's not 'Where you been?' or 'Who'd you see?' but 'Any work today?' She had spies at all the studios so I could never lie about making rounds. Once I had an offer for a secretary job, good pay, steady, and I had to tell them 'Sorry, I got to be an actress.'"

Casey had his Dillinger routine down pretty well, but with Norma along he was unstoppable.

"Johnnie," she say, "you 'member that time in St. Paul they caught you in the alleyway?" or "Johnnie, remember how Nelson and Van Meter were always at each other's throats?"—just like she'd been there. And

Casey he'd nod and say he remembered or correct some little detail, reminding her like any old couple sharing memories.

I'd come on at eleven and they'd be in the dayroom with only the TV for light, Casey squirming in his chair, hurting, and Norma waiting for her mother to go to sleep, holding Casey's hand against the pain. We had another old pair like them, a couple old bachelors crazy for chess. One game could take them two–three days. Personally I'd rather watch paint dry.

Usually some time around one o'clock Norma would call and we'd wheel them back to their rooms. I'd park Casey by the window so he could watch the traffic on Cahuenga.

By the time I got back on the day shift, Casey needed a push when he wanted to get anywhere. He could still feed himself and hit the pee jug nine times out of ten, though we were checking his output to see what was left of his kidneys. This one morning we had square egg for breakfast, which is the powdered variety cooked up in cake pans and cut in little bars like brownies. If they don't get the coloring just right they'll come up greenish, and they wiggle on your fork just like Jell-O. Even the blind patients won't touch them. Usually our only taker is this character Mao, who we call after his resemblance to the late Chinese head Red. Mao is a mongoloid in his mid-thirties whose favorite dishes are square egg and thermometers. Already that morning a new candy striper had given him an oral instead of a rectal, and he'd chomped it clear in half. Now she was fluttering around looking for Mr. Hellman's other slipper.

"I looked in his stand and under his bed," she says to me, "and all I could find is the right one."

"He doesn't have a left one," I tell her.

"Why not?"

"He doesn't have a left leg."

"Oh." The candy stripers are good for morale, but they take a lot of looking after.

"Next time peek under the covers first."

"Well, I started to," she says, "but he was flipping his—you know—his *thing* at me."

"Don't you worry, honey," says Spurs Tatum. "Worst comes to worst I'd lay odds you could outrun the old goat."

"When they give us this shit in the state pen," says Casey, so's everybody in the dayroom could hear him, "we'd plaster the walls with it."

The candy striper waggles her finger at him. "If you don't care for your breakfast, Mr. Mullins, I'm sure somebody else would appreciate it."

"No dice," says Casey. "I want to see it put down the trash barrel where it can't do no harm. And the name's Dillinger."

"I'm sure you don't mind if somebody shares what you don't want. I mean, what are we here for?" Lately we've been getting candy stripers with a more Christian outlook.

"What we're *here* for," says Casey, "is to die. To die. And some of us," he says, looking to Spurs, "aren't doing much of a job of it."

Casey was on the rag that morning, with a bad case of the runs his new meds give him and a wobbling pile of square egg staring up at him. So when the candy striper reaches to give his portion over to Mao, Casey pushes his tray over onto the floor.

"You birds keep swallowin' this shit," he calls out to the others, "they'll keep sending it up."

Mao was well known for his oatmeal tossing. You'd get two spoonfuls down him, and he'd decide to chuck the whole bowl acrost the room. Or wing it straight up so big globs stuck to the ceiling. The old-timers liked to sit against the back wall of the dayroom afternoons and bet on which glob would loosen and fall first. So when Mao picked up on Casey and made like a catapult with his plate, there was chunks sent scattering clear to the Bingo tables.

"Food riot!" yells Roscoe, flicking egg off his fork, aiming for old oatmeal stains on the ceiling. "Every man for himself!" he yells, and then goes into "Ding-Dong, the Witch Is Dead."

I didn't think the old farts had it in them. It was like being inside a popcorn popper, yellow hunks of egg flying every which way, squishing, bouncing, coffee sloshing, toast frisbeeing, plates smashing, orange juice showering, while Mrs. Shapiro, stone blind and AWOL for years, is yelling, "Boys, don't fight! Don't fight, your father will get crazy!"

The rec therapist is a togetherness freak. They sing together, they make place mats together, they have oral history sessions together. So somebody starts throwing food the rest of them are bound to pitch in. When there was nothing left to toss, they calmed down. We decided to wheel them all back to their rooms before we cleaned out the dayroom.

"I'm hungry," says Spurs. "Crazy sumbitch made me lose my breakfast. Senile bastard."

"Shove it, cowboy," says Casey. "In my day we'd of used you for a toothpick."

"In *my* day we'd of stuck you in the bughouse. Dillinger my ass."

Casey didn't say a thing but Norma wheeled up between them, a big smear of grape jelly on her cheek.

"John Dillinger," she said, "was the only one in the whole lousy country was his own man, the only one that told them all to go hang and went his own way. Have some respect."

I never learned if she really thought he was Dillinger or if they just shared the same interest, like the chess players or the crowd that still reads the trade papers together. When Norma went AWOL it was like her mother called her in from the playground. She left us quick, fading in and out for two weeks till she gave up all the way and just sat in her chair in her room, staring back at her mother.

"I'm sorry," she'd say from time to time. No word on why or what for, just stare at Old Lady Nader and say, "I'm sorry."

Casey tried to pull her out of it at first. But it's like when we have a cardiac arrest and we pull the curtain around the bed—even if you're right in the room you can't see through to know what's happening.

"You remember me?" he'd say. "You remember about Johnnie Dillinger?"

Usually she'd just look at him blank. One time she said, "I seen a movie about him once."

For a while Casey would have us wheel him into Norma's room and he'd talk at her some, but she didn't know who he was. Finally it made him so low he stopped visiting. Acted like she'd gone downstairs.

"You lose your mind," he'd say, "the rest of you ain't worth spit."

Mrs. Goorwitz got on his case then and tried to locate relatives. None to be found. What with the way people move around out here, that's not so unusual. Casey's chart was nothing but a medical record starting in 1937. Next Mrs. Goorwitz loosed the social worker on him, Friendly Phil, who ought to be selling health food or real estate somewhere. Casey wasn't buying any.

"So what if I am crazy?" he'd say to Phil. "Delusional, schizo, whatever you wanna call it. I can't do squat one way or the other. What difference does it make if I was Dillinger or Norma was Pearl White or Roscoe was the King of Poland? You're all just a bag a bones in the end."

He went into a funk, Casey, after Norma faded—went into a silence that lasted a good month. Not even Spurs could get his goat enough to argue. He spent a good part of the day trying to keep himself clean.

"I'm on the cycle," he whispered to me one day. "I'm riding the down side."

The geriatric racket is a collection of cycles. Linen goes on beds, gets dirtied, down the chute, washed, dried, and back onto the beds. Patients are checked in downstairs, up to the beds, maintained awhile, and then down to the slabs with them. Casey even found a new cycle, a thing in the paper about scientists who had learned how to make cow flops back into cow food.

"I don't want to make accusations here," says Casey one day, pointing to his lunch, "but what does *that* look like to you?"

The day came when Casey lost his control, racked up six incontinents on the report in one week. His health was shot, but I tried to talk Mrs. Goorwitz out of it when she handed me the kit. He had a thing about it, Casey.

"A man that can't control his bowels," he'd say, "is not a man."

He knew what was up when I started to draw the curtain. Roscoe scowled at me from across the room and rolled over to face the wall. Kantor and Wise lay there like house plants. It was midnight and they'd given Casey some heavy meds with his dinner. He looked at me like I'd come to snuff him with a pillow over the face. He was too weak to raise his arms, so I didn't have to put the restraints on.

"It has to be, Casey," I told him, "or else you'll be wettin' all over yourself."

I washed my hands with the soap from the kit.

"If they ask why I done it, the banks and all," he whispers, "tell them I was just bored. Just bored crapless."

I took the gloves out of their cellophane and managed to wriggle into them without touching my fingers to their outside. I washed Casey and laid the fenestrated sheet over so only his thing stuck through. If stories about Dillinger's size are true, Casey was qualified. The girls on the evening shift called it "the Snake." I swabbed the tip of it, unwrapped the catheter tube, and coated it with K-Y.

"You been white to me, Son," says Casey. "I don't put no blame on you."

"I'm sorry."

"Don't ever say that," says Casey. "Don't ever say you're sorry. Do it or don't do it but don't apologize."

I pushed the catheter tube down till it blocked at his sphincter, wiggled it, and it slipped past. It was the narrowest gauge, but still it's a surprise that you can fit one into a man. I stuck the syringe into the irrigation branch and shot the saline up till the bulb was inflated in his bladder. I gave a tug to see if it was anchored. Casey was crying, looking away from me. His eyes had gone fuzzy, the way fish eyes do after you beach them. I hooked the plastic tubing and the piss bag to the catheter.

"I used to be somebody," said Casey.

. . .

I had a long weekend, and when I came back on I didn't get a chance to talk with him. Mrs. Goorwitz said in report how he'd been moved to Intensive Care. On my first check I found him looking like the pictures of the Biograph shooting—blood everywhere, hard yellow light. Something had popped inside and he'd bled out the mouth. He had pulled the catheter out, bulb and all, and he was bleeding down there. We put sheets on the floor and rolled him sideways across the bed on his belly so he drained out onto them. It takes about half an hour or so.

I traced him back through the medical plan at Fox and ran into nothing but dead ends. Usually I forget about them once they go downstairs, but Casey had gotten his hooks in. There at Fox I found an old fella in custodial who remembered him.

"Always taking the limos for joyrides," he said. "It's a wonder he didn't get his ass fired."

I brought the subject up at the nurses' station one night—how maybe he could of been—and they asked me how much sleep I was getting. So I don't know one way or the other. Roscoe, he's sure, he's positive, but Roscoe also thinks our every move is being watched by aliens with oversized IQs. I figure if they're so smart they got better things to occupy their time.

One day I'm tube-feeding some vegomatic when out in the corridor I hear Spurs Tatum giving his brag to a couple of recent admissions that come in with their feet falling off.

"Hoot Gibson held my horse," says Spurs. "I took falls for Randy Scott. John Wayne blew me off a stagecoach. And once," he says, "I played Parcheesi with John Herbert Dillinger."

The Halfway Diner

SOME OF THE OTHER GIRLS CAN read on the way but I get sick. I need somebody to talk to, it don't matter who so much, just someone to shoot the breeze with, pass time. *Si no puedes platicar, no puedes vivir,* says my mother, and though I don't agree that the silence would kill me, twelve hours is a long stretch. So when Goldilocks climbs on all big-eyed and pale and almost sits herself in Renee's seat by the window I take pity and put her wise.

"You can't sit in that seat," I say.

Her face falls like she's a kid on the playground about to get whipped. "Pardon?" she says. *Pardon.*

"That's Renee's seat," I tell her. "She's got a thing about it. Something about the light."

"Oh. Sorry." She looks at the other empty seats like they're all booby-trapped. Lucky for her I got a soft heart and a mouth that needs exercise.

"You can sit here if you want."

She just about pees with relief and sits by me. She's not packing any magazines or books, which is good, 'cause like I said, I get sick. If the person next to me reads I get nosy, and then I get sick plus a stiff neck.

"My name's Pam," she says.

"It would be. I'm Lourdes." We shake hands. I remember the first time I made the ride, four years ago— I was sure somebody was gonna cut me with a razor or something. I figured they'd all of them be women who'd done time themselves, a bunch of big tough mamas with tattoos on their arms who'd snarl out stuff like "Whatsit to you, sister?" Well, we're not exactly the Girl Scout Jamboree, but mostly people are pretty nice to each other, unless something happens like with Lee and Delphine.

"New meat?" I ask her.

"Pardon?"

"Is your guy new meat up there?" I ask. "Is this his first time inside?"

She nods and hangs her head like it's the disgrace of the century. Like we're not all on this bus for the same reason.

"You hear from him yet?"

"I got a letter. He says he doesn't know how he can stand it."

Now this is good. It's when they start to get comfortable up there you got to worry. We had this girl on the bus, her guy made parole first time up, only the minute he gets home he starts to mope. Can't sleep nights, can't concentrate, mutters to himself all the time, won't take an interest in anything on the outside. She lives with this awhile, then one night they have a fight and really get down and he confesses how he had this kid in his cell, this little *mariquita,* and they got to doing it, you know, like some of the guys up there will do— only this guy fell in *love.* These things happen. And now he's *jealous,* see, 'cause his kid is still inside with all these *men,* right, and damn if a week later he doesn't go break his parole about a dozen different ways so he gets sent back up. She had to give up on him. To her it's a big tragedy, which is understandable, but I suppose from another point of view it's kind of romantic, like *Love Story,* only instead of Ali McGraw you got a sweetboy doing a nickel for armed robbery.

"What's your guy in for?" I ask.

Pam looks at her feet. "Auto theft."

"Not *that.* I mean how much *time.*"

"The lawyers say he'll have to do at least a year and a half."

"You don't go around asking what a guy's rap is in here," I tell her. "That's like *personal,* you know? But the length of sentence—hey, everybody counts the days."

"Oh."

"A year and a half is small change," I tell her. "He'll do that with his eyes closed."

The other girls start coming in then. Renee comes to her seat and sets up her equipment. She sells makeup, Renee, and her main hobby is wearing it. She's got this stand that hooks onto the back of the seat in front of her, with all these drawers and compartments and mirrors and stuff, and an empty shopping bag for all the tissues she goes through during the trip. I made the mistake of sitting next to her once, and she bent my ear about lip gloss for three hours straight, all the way to the Halfway Diner. You wouldn't think there'd be that much to say about it. Then after lunch she went into her sales pitch and I surrendered and bought some eye goop just so I wouldn't have to hear her say "our darker-complected customers" one more time. I mean it's all relative, right? I'd rather be my shade than all pasty-faced like Renee, look like she's never been touched by the sun. She's seen forty in the rearview mirror though she does her best to hide it, and the big secret that everybody knows is that it's not her husband she goes to visit but her *son,* doing adult time. She just calls him "my Bobby."

Mrs. Tucker settles in front with her knitting, looking a little tired. Her guy is like the Birdman of Alcatraz or something, he's been in since back when they wore stripes like in the Jimmy Cagney movies, and she's been coming up faithfully every weekend for thirty–forty years, something incredible like that. He killed a cop way back when, is what Yayo says the word on the yard is. She always sits by Gus, the driver, and they have these long lazy Mr. and Mrs. conversations while she knits and he drives. Not that there's anything going on between them off the bus, but you figure over the years she's spent more time with Gus than with her husband. He spaces out sometimes, Gus, the road is so straight and long, and she'll bring him back with a poke from one of her needles.

The ones we call the sisters go and sit in the back, talking nonstop. Actually they're married to brothers who are up for the same deal but they look alike and are stuck together like glue so we call them the sisters. They speak one of those Indio dialects from up in the mountains down south, so I can't pick out much of what they say. What my mother would call *mojadas*. Like she come over on the *Mayflower*.

Dolores comes in, who is a sad case.

"I'm gonna tell him this trip," she says. "I'm really gonna do it."

"Attagirl."

"No, I really am. It'll break his heart but I got to."

"It's the only thing to do, Dolores."

She has this boyfriend inside, Dolores, only last year she met some nice square Joe and got married. She didn't tell him about her guy inside, and so far she hasn't told her guy inside about the Joe. She figures he waits all week breathless for her visit, which maybe is true and maybe is flattering herself, and if she give him the heave-ho he'll fall apart and kidnap the warden or something. Personally, I think she likes to collect guilt like some people collect stamps or coins or dead butterflies or whatever.

"I just feel so *guilty*," she says, and moves on down across from the sisters.

We got pretty much all kinds on the bus, black girls and white girls, Chicanas like me who were born here and new fish from just across the border, a couple of Indian women from some tribe down the coast, even one Chinese girl, whose old man is supposed to be a very big cheese in gambling. She wears clothes I would kill for, this girl, only of course they wouldn't look good on me. Most of your best clothes are designed for the flat-chested type, which is why the fashion pages are full of Orientals and anorexics like Renee.

This Pam is another one that looks good in a man's T-shirt, looks good in almost anything she throws on. I decide to be nice to her anyway.

"You gonna eat all that?"

She's got this big plastic sack of food under her feet— wrapped sandwiches, fruit, and what looks like a pie.

"Me? Oh, no, I figure, you know—the food inside—"

"They don't let you bring food in."

Her face drops again. "No?"

"Only cigarettes. One carton a month."

"He doesn't smoke."

"That's not the point. Cigarettes are like money inside. Your guy wants anything, wants anything done, he'll have to pay in smokes."

"What would he want to have done?"

I figure I should spare her most of the possibilities, so I just shrug. "Whatever. We stop at the Halfway, you get some change, load up on Camels from the machine. He'll thank you for it."

She looks down at the sack of goodies. She sure isn't going to eat it herself, not if she worked at it for a month. I can picture her dinner plate alone at home, full of the kind of stuff my Chuy feeds his gerbil. A celery cruncher.

"You want some of this?" she says, staring into the sack.

"No, thanks, honey," I tell her. "I'm saving myself for the Halfway Diner."

Later on I was struck by how it had already happened– the dice had already been thrown, only they didn't know it. So they took the whole trip up sitting together and talking and palling around unaware that they weren't friends anymore.

Lee and Delphine are as close as the sisters, only nobody would ever mistake them for relatives, Lee being blond and Delphine being one of our darker-complected customers. Lee is a natural blond (unlike certain cosmetics saleswomen I could mention) with light-blue eyes and a build that borders on the chunky, although she would die to hear me say it. Del is thin and sort of elegant and black like you don't see too much outside of those documentaries on TV where people stick wooden spears in lions. *Negro como el fondo de la noche* my mother would say, and on Del it looks great. The only feature they share is a similar nose, Del because she was born that way and Lee because of a field hockey accident.

Maybe it was because they're both nurses or maybe just because they have complementary personalities, but somehow they found each other on the bus and since before I started riding they've been tight as ticks. You get the feeling they look forward to the long drive to catch up on each other's lives. They don't socialize off the bus, almost nobody does, but how many friends spend twelve hours a week together? Some of the black girls hang, and us Chicanas can either spread around or sit together and talk home talk, but black and white as tight as Lee and Del is pretty rare. Inside—well, inside you stay with your own, that's the beginning and the end of it. But inside is a world I don't even like to think about.

They plunk down across from us, Del lugging all these magazines—*Cosmo, People, Vogue, Essence*—that they sort of read and sort of make fun of, and Lee right away starts in on the food. Lee is obsessed with food the way a lot of borderline-chunky girls are– she can talk forever about what she didn't eat that day. She sits and gets a load of the sack at Pam's feet.

"That isn't food, is it?" she asks.

"Yeah," Pam apologizes. "I didn't know."

"Let's see it."

Obediently Pam starts shuffling through her sack, holding things up for a little show-and-tell. "I got this, and this," she says, "and this, I thought maybe, they wouldn't have. I didn't know."

It's all stuff you buy at the bus station—sandwiches that taste like the cellophane they're wrapped in filled with that already-been-chewed kind of egg and chicken and tuna salad, stale pies stuffed with mealy apple-sauce, spotted fruit out of a machine. From all reports the food is better in the joint.

"How old are you, honey?" I ask.

"Nineteen."

"You ever cook at home?" Lee asks.

Pam shrugs. "Not much. Mostly I eat—you know, like salads. Maybe some fish sticks."

Del laughs. "I tried that fish-sticks routine once when Richard was home," she says. "He asks me, 'What is this?' That's their code for 'I don't like the look of it.' It could be something *basic,* right, like fried egg starin' up at 'em, they still say, 'What is it?' So Richard looks at them fish sticks and says, 'If it's fish, which end is the *head* and which is the *tail?*' When I tell him it taste the same either way, he says he doesn't eat nothing with square edges like that, on account of inside they always be cookin' everything in these big cake pans and serve it up in squares— square egg, square potato, square macaroni. That and things served out in ice-cream scoops. Unless it really *is* ice cream, Richard don't want no *scoopfuls* on his plate."

"Lonnie's got this thing about chicken bones," Lee says. "Bones of any kind, but especially chicken ones. Can't stand to look at 'em while he's eating."

"Kind of rules out the Colonel, doesn't it?"

"Naw," she says, "he *loves* fried chicken. We come back with one of them buckets, you know, with the biscuits and all, and I got to go perform surgery in the kitchen before we can eat. He keeps callin' in— 'It ready yet, hon? It ready yet? I'm starving here.' I'll tell you, they'd of had those little McNugget things back before he went up, our marriage woulda been in a lot better shape."

They're off to the races then, Lee and Del, yakking away, and they sort of close up into a society of two. Blondie is sitting there with her tuna-mash sandwiches in her lap, waiting for orders, so I stow everything in the sack and kick it deep under the seat.

"We get to the Halfway," I tell her, "we can dump it."

Sometimes I wonder about Gus. The highway is so straight, cutting up through the Valley with the ground so flat and mostly dried up, like all its effort goes into those little square patches of artichokes or whatever you come past, and after that it just got no more green in it. What can he be thinking about, driving all these miles, all these trips, up and down, year after year? He don't need to think to do his *yups* and *uh-huhs* at Mrs. Tucker— for that you can go on automatic pilot like I do with my Blanca when she goes into one of her stories about the tangled who-likes-who in her class. It's a real soap opera, *Dallas* for fifth-graders, but not what you need to concentrate on over breakfast. I wonder if Gus counts the days like we do, if there's a retirement date in his head, a release from the bus. Except to Mrs. Tucker, he doesn't say but three things. When we first leave he says, "Headin out, ladies, take your seats." When we walk into the Halfway he always says, "Make it simple, ladies, we got a clock to watch." And when we're about to start the last leg, after dinner, he says, "Sweet dreams, ladies, we're bringin' it home." Those same three things, every single trip. Like Mrs. Tucker knitting her blue sweater, always blue. Sometimes when I can't sleep and things are hard and awful and I can't see how they'll ever get better, I'll lie awake and invent all these morbid thoughts, sort of torture myself with ideas, and I always start thinking that it's really the same exact sweater, that she goes home and pulls it apart stitch by stitch and starts from scratch again next trip. Not 'cause she wants to but 'cause she has to, it's her part of the punishment for what her husband done.

Other times I figure she just likes the color blue.

For the first hour or so Renee does her face. Even with good road and a fairly new bus this takes a steady hand, but she is an artist. Then she discovers Pam behind her, a new victim for her line of cosmetics, and starts into her pitch, opening with something tactful like, "You always let your hair go like that?" I'm dying for Pam to say, "Yeah, whatsit to you, sister?" but she is who she is and pretty soon Renee's got her believing it's at least a misdemeanor to leave the house without eyeliner on. I've heard all this too many times, so I put my head back and close my eyes and aim my radar past it over to Lee and Del.

They talk about their patients like they were family. They talk about their family like they were patients. Both are RNs– they work at different hospitals but both on the ward. Lee has kids, and she talks about them; Del doesn't but wants some, and she talks about that. They talk about how Del can eat twice as much as Lee but Del stays thin and Lee gets chunky, They talk about their guys, too, but usually not till we get pretty close to the facility.

"My Jimmy," Lee says, "is now convinced he's the man of the house. This is a five-year-old squirt— he acts like he's the Papa Bear."

"He remembers his father?"

"He likes to think he does, but he doesn't. His favorite saying these days is 'Why should I?' "

"Uh-oh."

"At least he doesn't go around saying he's an orphan like his sister. I introduce her—'This is my daughter, Julie,'—right? and she says, 'Hi, I'm a orphan.' Cute."

"I used to do that," says Delphine. "Ever'time my daddy spanked me, that's what I'd spread round the neighborhood."

"So Julie says she's an orphan and Jimmy says his father works for the state."

Del laughs. "That's true enough."

"And he picks up all this stuff in the neighborhood. God, I want to get out of there! Lonnie makes parole this rotation, I'm gonna get him home and get his head straight and get us moved outa there."

"Like to the country or something?"

"Just anywheres it isn't so mean and he's not near his asshole so-called buddies."

"Yeah."

"And I want—oh, I don't know, it sounds kinda stupid, really—"

"What?" Del says.

"I want a *dishwasher.*"

Del laughs again. Lee is embarrassed.

"You know what I mean."

"Yeah, I know."

"I want something in my life I just get it started and then it takes care of itself."

"I hear you *talkin'*."

"The other night, Jimmy—now I know some of this is from those damn He-Man cartoons and all, but some of it is not having a father, I swear—he's in their room doing his prayers. He does this thing, the nuns told him praying is just talking to God, that's the new breed of nuns, right? So you'll go by their room and you'll hear Jimmy still up, having like these one-sided telephone conversations. 'Uh-huh, yeah, sure, I will, no problem, I'll try, uh-huh, uh-huh,' and he thinks he's talking with *God*, see, like a kid does with an imaginary friend. Or maybe he really *is* talking to God, how would I know? Anyhow, the other night he got that tough-guy look I hate so much pasted on his face like all the other little punks in the neighborhood and he's quiet for a long time, listening, and then he kind of sneers and says, 'Why should I?' "

We all all sort of pretend the food is better at the Halfway than it really is. Not that it's bad– it's okay, just nothing to write home about. Elvira, who runs the place, won't use a microwave, which makes me happy. I'm convinced there's vibes in those things that get into the food, and ten years from now there'll be a national scandal. Whenever I have something from a microwave I get bad dreams, I swear it, so if something comes out a little lukewarm from her kitchen I don't complain.

The thing is, Elvira really seems to look forward to seeing us, looks forward to all the noise and hustle a busload of hungry women carry into the place, no matter what it is that brung them together. I imagine pulling into someplace different, with the name of the facility rolled up into the little destination window at the front of the bus, us flocking in and the waitress panicking, the cooks ready to mutiny, the other customers sure we're pickpockets, prostitutes, baby snatchers—no way José. So maybe the food here tastes better cause it comes through Elvira, all the square edges rounded off.

She's a big woman, Elvira, and if the country about here had a face it would look like hers. Kind of dry and cracked and worn, but friendly. She says she called the Halfway the Halfway because every place on earth is halfway between somewhere and somewhere else. I don't think being halfway between the city and the facility was what she had in mind, though.

When we bust in and spill out around the room there's only one other customer, a skinny old lizard in a Tecate cap and a T-shirt, never once looking up from his grilled-cheese sandwich.

"Make it simple, ladies," Gus says. "We got a clock to watch.

At the Halfway it's pretty hard to make it anything but simple. When they gave out the kits at Diner Central, Elvira went for bare essentials. She's got the fly strip hanging by the door with a dozen little boogers stuck to it, got the cornflakes pyramided on a shelf, the specials hand-printed on paper plates stuck on the wall behind the counter, the morning's Danishes crusting over under their plastic hood, the lemon and chocolate cream pies with huge bouffants of meringue behind sliding glass, a cigarette machine, a phone booth, and a machine that tells your exact weight for a quarter, which Lee feeds both coming in and going out.

"Have your orders ready, girls!" Elvira calls, as we settle at the counter and in booths, pretty much filling the place. "I want to hear numbers."

Elvira starts at one end of the counter and her girl Cheryl does the booths. Cheryl always seems likes she's about to come apart, sighing a lot, scratching things out, breaking her pencil points– a nervous kid. What there is to be nervous about way out in the middle of nowhere, I couldn't tell you, but she manages. I'm sitting at the counter with Mrs. Tucker on one side, Pam on the other, then Lee and Del. Lee and Del get talking about their honeymoons while Pam goes off to pump the cigarette machine.

"So anyhow," says Lee, "he figures we'll go down to Mexico, that old bit about how your money travels farther down there? I don't know how *far* it goes, but after that honeymoon I know how *fast*. He was just trying to be sweet, really, he figured he was gonna show me this wonderful time, 'cause he's been there and I haven't and he knows what to order and I don't and he knows where to go and all that, only he *doesn't*, you know, he just *thinks* he does. Which is the whole thing with Lonnie—he dreams things up and pretty soon he believes they're *true*, right? So he's more surprised than anybody when the shit hits the fan."

"Sounds familiar," says Del.

"So he's heard of this place—jeez, it's so long ago—Santa Maria de la Playa, something like that." Lee looks to me for help. "You must know it, Lourdes. It's on the coast."

"Lots of coast down there."

"There's like these mountains, and the ocean—"

"Sorry." I tell her. "I've never been to Mexico."

Delphine can't feature this. "You're shittin me, " she says. *"You?"*

"You ever been to Africa?"

Del cracks up, which is one of the things I like about her. She's not oversensitive about that stuff. Usually.

"Anyway," says Lee, "he says to me, 'Baby, we're talking Paradise here, we're talking Honeymoon *Heaven*. I got this deal.' "

"They *always* got a deal," says Del.

Elvira comes by then with her pad, working fast but friendly all the time. "Hey, girls," she says, "how's it going? Mrs. Tucker?"

"Just the water," Mrs. Tucker says. "I'm not really hungry."

She doesn't look too good, Mrs. Tucker, kind of drawn around the eyes. Elvira shakes her head.

"Not good to skip lunch, Mrs. Tucker. You got a long ride ahead."

"Just the water, thank you."

Lee and Del get the same thing every week. "Let's see, we got a Number Three and Number Five, mayo on the side," Elvira says. "Ice tea or lemonade?"

They both go for the lemonade, and then Pam comes back dropping packs of Camels all over.

"How bout you, hon?"

"Um, could I see a menu?" More cigarettes tumble from her arms. I see that Pam is one of those people who is accident-prone for life and that her marrying a car thief is no coincidence. A catastrophe waiting to happen, this girl. Elvira jerks a thumb to the wall. Pam sees the paper plates.

"Oh, um—what are you having?"

"Number Three," says Lee.

"Number Five," says Delphine.

"Oh. I'll have a Number Four, please. And a club soda?"

"You know what a Number Four *is,* hon?"

"No, but I'll eat it."

Elvira thinks this is a scream but writes it down without laughing. "Four and a club," she says, and moves on.

"So he's got his deal," says Del, getting back to the story.

"Right. He's got this deal where he brings these tapes down to San Miguel de los Nachos, whatever it was, and this guy who runs a brand-new resort down there is gonna give us the royal-carpet treatment in exchange."

"Like cassette tapes?"

"Fresh from Kmart. Why they can't go to their own store and buy these things I don't know. What's the story down there, Lourdes?"

"It's a mystery to me," I say.

"Anyhow, we got thousands of the things we're bringing through without paying duty, a junior version of the scam he finally went up for, only I don't know because they're under the backseat and he keeps laying this Honeymoon Heaven jazz on me."

"With Richard, his deals always have to do with clothes," says Del. "Man come in and say, 'Sugar, what size dress you wear?' and my stomach just hits the *floor.*"

"And he brings the wrong size, right?"

"Ever damn time." Del shakes her head. "We took our honeymoon in

Jamaica, back when we was livin' high. Girl, you never saw nobody with more fluff in her head than me back then."

"You were young."

"Young ain't no excuse for *stupid.* I had one of those posters in my head—soft sand, violins playing, rum and Coke on ice, and I was the girl in the white bikini. I thought it was gonna be like that *always.*" Del gets kind of distant then, thinking back. She smiles. "Richard gets outa there, gets his health back, we gonna party, girl. That's one thing the man know how to do is party."

"Yeah, Lonnie too. They both get clear, we should all get together sometime, do the town."

As soon as it's out Lee knows different. There's a silence then, both of them just smiling, uncomfortable. Guys inside, black and white, aren't likely to even know who each other is, much less get together outside and make friendly. It does that to you, inside. Yayo is the same, always on about *los gachos gavachos* this and *los pinches negros* that– it's a sickness you pick up there. Or maybe you already got it when you go in and the joint makes it worse. Lee finally breaks the silence.

"I bet you look great in a white bikini," she says.

Del laughs. "That's the *last* time I been to any *beach,* girl."

Cheryl shows with the food and Mrs. Tucker excuses herself to go to the ladies'. Lee has the diet plate, a scoop of cottage cheese with a cherry on top. Del has a BLT with mayo on the side, and Pam has the Number Four, which at the Halfway is a Monte Cristo– ham and cheese battered in egg, deep fried, and then rolled in confectioner's sugar. She turns it around and around on her plate, studying it like it fell from Mars.

"I think maybe I'll ask him this visit," says Del. "About the kids."

"You'd be a good mother," says Lee.

"You think so?"

"Sure."

"Richard with a baby in his lap." Del grimaces at the thought. "Sometimes I think it's just what he needs—responsibility, family roots, that

JOHN SAYLES

whole bit, settle him down. Then I think how maybe he'll just feel more *pressure,* you know? And when he starts feelin' pressure is when he starts messin' up." Del lets the thought sit for a minute and then gives herself a little slap on the cheek as if to clear it away.

"Just got to get him healthy first. Plenty of time for the rest." She turns to Pam. "So how's that Number Four?"

"It's different," says Pam. She's still working on her first bite, scared to swallow.

"You can't finish it," says Lee, "I might take a bite."

Del digs her in the ribs. "Girl, don't you even *look* at that Number Four. Thing is just *evil* with carbohydrates. I don't want be hearing you bellyache about how you got no willpower all the way home."

"I got willpower," Lee says. "I'm a goddamn tower of strength. It's just my *appetite* is stronger."

"Naw."

"My appetite is like Godzilla, Del, you seen it at work, layin' waste to everything in its path."

"Hah-*haaah!*"

"But I'm gonna whup it."

"That's what I like to hear."

"Kick its butt."

"Tell it, baby."

"I'm losin' twenty pounds."

"Go for it!"

"And I'm quittin' smoking too."

"You can do it, Lee."

"And when that man makes parole he's gonna buy me a dishwasher!"

"Get *down!*"

They're both of them giggling then, but Lee is mostly serious. "You know," she says, "as much as I want him out, sometimes it feels weird that it might really happen. You get used to being on your own, get your own way of doing things."

"I hear you talking."

"The trouble is, it ain't so bad that I'm gonna leave him, but it ain't so good I'm dying to stay."

There's hardly a one of us on the bus hasn't said the exact same thing at one time or another. Del looks around the room.

"So here we all are," she says, "at the Halfway Diner."

Back on the road, Pam gets quiet so I count dead rabbits for a while and then occupy the time imagining disasters that could be happening with the kids at Graciela's. You'd be surprised at how entertaining this can be. By the time we pass the fruit stand, Chuy has left the burners going on the gas stove and Luz, my baby, is being chewed by a rabid Doberman. It's only twenty minutes to the facility after the fruit stand and you can hear the bus get quieter, everybody but Dolores. She's still muttering her good-bye speech like a rosary. The visits do remind me of confession– you go into a little booth, you face each other through a window, you feel weird afterward. I think about the things I don't want to forget to tell Yayo. Then I see myself in Renee's mirror and hit on her for some blush.

The first we know of it is when the guard at security calls Lee and Del's names and they're taken off in opposite directions. That sets everybody buzzing. Pam is real nervous, this being her first visit, and I think she is a little afraid of who her guy is going to be all of a sudden. I tell her not to ask too much of it, one visit. I can't remember me and Yayo just sitting and talking a whole hour that many times *before* he went up. Add to that the glass and the little speaker boxes and people around with rifles, and you have definitely entered Weird City. We always talk home talk cause all the guards are Anglos and it's fun for Yayo to badmouth them under their noses.

"Big blowout last night in the mess," he says to me. "*Anglos contra los negros.* One guy got cut pretty bad."

I get a sick feeling in the pit of my stomach. The night Yayo got busted

I had the same feeling, but I couldn't think of anything to keep him in the house. "Black or white?" I ask.

"A black dude got stabbed," he says. "This guy Richard. He was a musician outside."

"And the guy who cut him?" I say, although I already know without asking.

"This guy Lonnie, was real close to parole. Got him up in solitary now. *Totalmente jodido.*"

It was just something that kind of blew up and got out of control. Somebody needs to feel like he's big dick by ranking somebody else in front of the others, and when you got black and white inside that's a fight, maybe a riot, and this time when the dust clears there's Lee's guy with his shank stuck in Del's guy. You don't ask it to make a lot of sense. I tell Yayo how the kids are doing and how they miss him a lot, but I feel this weight pulling down on me, knowing about Lee and Del. I feel like nothing's any use and we're wasting our time squawking at each other over these microphones. We're out of rhythm— it's a long hour.

"I think about you all the time," he says, as the guard steps in and I step out.

"Me too," I say.

It isn't true. Whole days go by when I hardly give him a thought, and when I do it's more an idea of him than really him in the flesh. Sometimes I feel guilty about this, but what the hell. Things weren't always so great when we were together. So maybe it's like the food at the Halfway— better to look forward to than to have.

Then I see how small he looks, going back inside between the guards, and I love him so much I start to shake.

The bus is one big whisper when I get back on. The ones who have heard about Lee and Del are filling in the ones who haven't. Lee gets in first, pale and stiff, and sits by me. If I touched her with my finger she'd explode. Pam steps in then, looking shaky, and I can tell she's disappointed to see

I'm already by someone. When Del gets on everybody clams up. She walks in with her head up, trying not to cry. If it had been somebody else cut her guy, somebody not connected with any of us on the bus, we'd all be around bucking her up and Lee would be first in line. As it is, a couple of the black girls say something but she just zombies past them and sits in the very back next to Pam.

It's always quieter on the way home. We got things that were said to chew over, mistakes to regret, the prospect of another week alone to face. But after Del comes in it's like a morgue. Mrs. Tucker doesn't even knit, just stares kind of blank-eyed and sleepy at the valley going by. Only Pam, still in the dark about what went down inside, starts to talk. It's so quiet I can hear her all the way from the rear.

"I never thought about how they'd have those guns," she says, just opening up out of the blue to Del. "I never saw one up close, only in the movies or TV. They're *real*, you know? They look so heavy and like if they shot it would just take you *apart*—"

"White girl," says Del, interrupting, "I don't want to be hearin' bout none of your problems."

After that all you hear is the gears shifting now and then. I feel sick, worse than when I try to read. Lee hardly blinks beside me, the muscles in her jaw working as she grinds something out in her head. It's hard to breathe.

I look around and see that the white girls are almost all up front but for Pam, who doesn't know, and the black girls are all in the back, with us Chicanas on the borderline between, as usual. Everybody is just stewing in her own thoughts. Even the sisters have nothing to say to each other. A busload of losers slogging down the highway. If there's life in hell, this is what the field trips are like. It starts to get dark. In front of me, while there is still a tiny bit of daylight, Renee stares at her naked face in her mirror and sighs.

Elvira and Cheryl look tired when we get to the Halfway. Ketchup bottles are turned on their heads on the counter but nothing is sliding down.

Gus picks up on the mood and doesn't tell us how we got a clock to watch when he comes in.

Pam sits by me with Dolores and Mrs. Tucker on the other side. Dolores sits shaking her head. "Next time," she keeps saying. "I'll tell him next time." Lee shuts herself in the phone booth and Del sits at the far end of the counter.

Pam whispers to me, "What's up?"

"Big fight in the mess last night," I tell her. "Lee's guy cut Delphine's."

"My God. Is he okay?"

"He's alive, if that's what you mean. I've heard Del say how he's got this blood problem, some old drug thing, so this ain't gonna help any."

Pam looks at the booth. "Lee must feel awful."

"Her guy just wrecked his parole but good," I say. "She's gettin' it with both barrels."

Elvira comes by taking orders. "Rough trip from the look of you-all. Get your appetite back, Mrs. Tucker?"

"Yes, I have," she says. Her voice sound like it's coming from the next room. "I'm very, very hungry."

"I didn't tell him," Dolores confesses, to no one in particular. "I didn't have the heart."

We order, and Elvira goes back in the kitchen. We know there is a cook named Phil but we have never seen him.

I ask Pam how her guy is making out. She makes a face, thinking. I can see her in high school, blond and popular, and her guy, a good-looking charmer up to monkey business. An Anglo version of Yayo, full of promises that turn into excuses.

"He's okay, I guess. He says he's going to do his own time, whatever that means."

I got to laugh. "They all say that, honey, but not many manage. It means, like, mind your own business, stay out of complications."

"Oh."

Delphine is looking bullets over at Lee in the phone booth, who must be calling either her kids or her lawyer.

"Maybe that's how you got to be to survive in there," I say. "Hell, maybe out here, too. Personally, I think it bites." Mrs. Tucker puts her head down into her arms and closes her eyes. It's been a long day. "The thing is," I say to Pam, "we're all of us doing time."

Lee comes out of the booth and goes to the opposite end of the counter from Del. It makes me think of me and Graciela. We used to be real jealous, her and me, sniff each other like dogs whenever we met, on account of her being Yayo's first wife. Not that I stole him or anything, they were bust long before I made the scene, but still you got to wonder what's he see in this bitch that I don't have? A natural human reaction. Anyhow, she's in the neighborhood and she's got a daughter by him who's ahead of my Chuy at the same school, and I see her around but it's very icy. Then Yayo gets sent up and one day I'm stuck for a babysitter on visiting day. I don't know what possesses me, but desperation being the mother of a whole lot of stuff I ask Graciela. She says why not. When I get back it's late and I'm wasted and we get talking and I don't know why but we really hit it off. She's got a different perspective on Yayo, of course, talks about him like he's her little boy gone astray, which maybe in some ways he is, and we never get into sex stuff about him. But he isn't the only thing we got in common. Yayo, of course, thinks that's all we do, sit and gang up on him verbally, and he's not too crazy about the idea. We started shopping together, and sometimes her girl comes over to play or we'll dump the kids with my mother and go out and it's fun, sort of like high school, where you hung around not necessarily looking for boys. We go to the mall, whatever. There's times I would've gone right under without her, I mean I'd be *gonzo* today. I look at Lee and Del, sitting tight and mean inside themselves, and I think that's me and Graciela in reverse. And I wonder what happens to us when Yayo gets out.

"Mrs. Tucker, can you hear me? Mrs. Tucker?"

It's Gus who notices that Mrs. Tucker doesn't look right. He's shaking her and calling her name, and her eyes are still open but all fuzzy, the life gone out of them. The sisters are chattering something about cold water and Cheryl drops a plate of something and Pam keeps yelling, "Where's the poster? Find the poster!" Later she tells me she meant the anti-choking poster they're supposed to have up in restaurants, which Elvira kind of hides behind the weight-telling machine 'cause she says it puts people off their feed. Mrs. Tucker isn't choking, of course, but Pam doesn't know this at the time and is sure we got to look at the poster before we do anything wrong. Me, even with all the disasters I've imagined for the kids and all the rescues I've dreamed about performing, I've never dealt with this particular glassy-eyed older-lady type of thing, so I'm no help. Gus is holding Mrs. Tucker's face in his hands, her body gone limp, when Lee and Del step in.

"Move back!" says Lee. "Give her room to breathe."

"You got a pulse?" says Del.

"Not much. It's fluttering around."

"Get an ambulance here," says Del to Elvira, and Elvira sends Cheryl running to the back.

"Any tags on her?"

They look around Mrs. Tucker's neck but don't find anything.

"Anybody ever hear her talk about a medical problem?" Del asks the rest of us, while she holds Mrs. Tucker's lids up and looks deep into her eyes.

We rack our brains but come up empty, except for Gus. Gus looks a worse color than Mrs. Tucker does, sweat running down his face from the excitement. "She said the doctor told her to watch her intake," he says. "Whatever that means."

"She didn't eat lunch," says Elvira. "You should never skip lunch."

Lee and Del look at each other. "She got sugar, maybe?"

"Or something like it."

"Some orange juice," says Lee to Elvira, and she runs off. Mrs. Tucker is kind of gray now, and her head keeps flopping if they don't hold it up.

"Usually she talks my ear off," says Gus. "Today she was like depressed or something."

Elvira comes back out. "I brung the fresh-squose from the fridge," she says. "More vitamins."

Del takes it and feeds a little to Mrs. Tucker, tipping her head back to get it in. We're all of us circled around watching, opening our mouths in sympathy like when you're trying to get the baby to spoon-feed. Some dribbles out and some stays down.

"Just a little," says Lee. "It could be the opposite."

Mrs. Tucker takes another sip and smiles dreamily. "I like juice," she says. "Here, take a little more."

"That's good," she says in this tiny little-girl voice. "Juice is good."

By the time the ambulance comes we have her lying down in one of the booths covered by the lap blanket the sisters bring, her head pillowed on a couple of bags full of hamburger rolls. Her eyes have come clear and eventually she rejoins the living, looking up at all of us staring down around her and giving a little smile.

"Everybody's here," she says, in that strange far-off voice. "Everybody's here at the Halfway Diner."

The ambulance guys take some advice from Lee and Del and then drive her away. Just keep her overnight for observation is all. "See?" Elvira keeps saying. "You don't never want to skip your lunch." Then she bags up dinners for those who want them 'cause we have to get back on the road.

Nobody says anything, but when we get aboard nobody will take a seat. Everybody just stands around in the aisle talking about Mrs. Tucker and waiting for Lee and Del to come in and make their move. Waiting and hoping, I guess.

Lee comes in and sits in the middle. Pam moves like she's gonna sit next to her but I grab her arm. Delphine comes in, looks around kind of casual, and then like it's just a coincidence she sits by Lee. The rest of us settle in real quick then, pretending it's business as usual but listening real hard.

We're right behind them, me and Pam. They're not talking, not looking at each other, just sitting there side by side. Being nurses together might've cracked the ice, but it didn't break it all the way through. We're parked right beneath the Halfway Diner sign and the neon makes this sound, this high-pitched buzzing that's like something about to explode.

"Sweet dreams, ladies," says Gus, when he climbs into his seat. "We're bringin it home."

It's dark as pitch and it's quiet, but nobody is having sweet dreams. We're all listening. I don't really know how to explain this, and like I said, we're not exactly the League of Women Voters on that bus, but there's a spirit, a way we root for each other, and somehow we feel that the way it comes out between Lee and Delphine will be a judgment on us all. Nothing spoken, just a feeling between us.

Fifty miles go past and my stomach is starting to worry. Then, when Del finally speaks, her voice is so quiet I can hardly hear one seat away.

"So," she says. "San Luis Abysmal."

"Huh?" says Lee.

"Mexico," says Delphine, still real quiet. "You were telling me about you honeymoon down in San Luis Abysmal."

"Yeah," says Lee. "San Something-or-other."

"And he says he speaks the language."

You can feel this sigh like go through the whole bus. Most can't hear the words but just that they're talking. You can pick up the tone.

"Right," says Lee. "Only he learned Spanish at Taco Bell. He's got this *deal*, right?"

"Finalmente," one of the sisters whispers behind me.

"Qué bueno!" the other whispers. *"Todavía son amigas."*

"So we get to the so-called resort and he cuts open the backseat and all these *cassettes* fall out, which I know nothing about."

"Course not."

"Only on account of the heat they've like *liquefied,* right?"

"Naw."

"And this guy who runs the resort is roped off but so are we, 'cause this so-called brand-new resort is so brand-new it's not *built* yet."

"Don't *say* it, girl."

"It's just a *construction* site."

"Hah-haaah!"

The bus kicks into a higher gear, and out of nowhere Gus is whistling up front. He's never done this before, not once, probably because he had Mrs. Tucker talking with him, but he's real good, like somebody on a record. What he's whistling is like the theme song to some big romantic movie, I forget which, real high and pretty, and I close my eyes and get that nice feeling like just before you fall to sleep and you know everything is under control and your body just relaxes. I feel good knowing there's hours before we got to get off. I feel like as long as we stay on the bus, rocking gentle through the night, we're okay, we're safe. The others are talking soft around me now, Gus is whistling high and pretty, and there's Del and Lee, voices in the dark.

"There's a beach," says Lee. "only they haven't brought in the *sand* yet and everywhere you go these little fleas are hoppin' around and my ankles get bit and swole up like a balloon."

"I been there, girl," says Del. "I hear you talking—"

"Honeymoon Heaven, he says to me."

Del laughs, softly. "Honeymoon *Heaven*."

Treasure

THE OLD MAN HAD KEPT the pumps running on the day of the funeral. Ross remembered hearing them on the breeze, distantly, sweating under the jacket and tie they'd bought for his confirmation, his mother in the casket swinging slightly as the groundsman winched it down, the sound drifting through the palmettos—*ka-whump, ka-whump, ka-whump*—like the island had a heart-beat. That was the second time Digger had pulled his gang off the job.

"She's not my wife, she's yours," said Digger to the Old Man, "but there are things that demand respect."

The Old Man had brought in a gang of Cubans off the key and kept the pumps running. That time it was two months before Digger came back.

The pumps were shut off now. It was eerie, being in the house without their sound, without the vibration coming up through the floor, and as much as Ross had hated them it was worse being here in the dead quiet.

"It's the fucking Bermuda Triangle down there," Sunny had complained while Ross was packing. "Every time you come back, you can't sleep for a week." Sunny had gone down a few times with him when they first married and then washed her hands of the whole thing.

· · ·

Ross found the Old Man in the kitchen, in front of a game show on the little TV next to the sink. People were leaping up and down as colored lights flashed behind dollar signs.

"No fucking dignity," muttered the Old Man.

A host shouted out a list of jackpot prizes.

"They think it's free money. Tell 'em who was king of Poland in the First War and they give you a condo and a Pontiac." The Old Man scowled. "Ain't nothing free in this world."

A mother and daughter, still hopping, both hugged the host.

"No fucking dignity."

Ross jerked his head slightly toward the pit outside.

"So what's the story?" He hadn't expected a big welcome. The Old Man had put the J & B under the sink to pretend he was just drinking beer.

"Digger's boy pulled out yesterday afternoon. They shut down and took a walk. He knows I can't field a new crew unless I go through the Partnership, and he knows I can't do that without losing the shaky ones. Got me by the short ones."

"Did he say why?"

"Just to screw me. Punk."

"Come on. Mike doesn't do anything Digger doesn't tell him to do."

"He married that colored girl."

"I mean on the job." Ross went to the refrigerator. There was beer, the remains of a take-out chicken, a cucumber growing fuzz.

"He says he wants to renegotiate. Punk."

The smell of muck from the pit had taken over the house long ago. It had settled into the woodwork, the rugs, what was left of the furniture. When the pumps were running, there seemed to be an excuse for it.

"So you want me to talk to Mike."

"Tell him I'll bury the old bastard if he doesn't come around."

"I'm not going to do this unless you're willing to negotiate. You have to be willing to give up some ground."

"Negotiate my ass." The Old Man's eyes didn't look good— they'd lost their focus. On the TV a systems analyst from Santa Rosa tried to name the original astronauts.

"I don't see why Simkin isn't handling this," said Ross.

"You call Simkin on the phone, his meter starts ticking. You call Simkin on the phone, he has to tell the Partnership."

Ross took a beer from the refrigerator. A registered nurse tried to name the five most valuable metals.

"Mike still over by the pier?"

Platinum, Uranium—

"Over there breeding like a damn rabbit." The Old Man scowled. "Tell him to keep his mouth shut around town."

"About what?"

Silver and gold—

The Old Man looked directly at Ross for the first time. "He'll know about what."

"If I don't know anything, how the hell am I supposed to patch things up?"

Jackpot question.

"He's been saying there's nothing down there." The Old Man looked back to the TV. "That there never was."

The registered nurse named the capital of Arkansas. Dollar signs exploded in red, white, and blue.

They had turned the Treasure Chest into a Stuckey's and seemed to be doing good business. Ross saw their signs just off the causeway, and when he drove past the parking lot was full. Digger had built the Chest after Annie and poured money into it for a year, till the creditors drove him back to the pit. In that year the Old Man had used a series of journeymen drillers, mostly heavy boozers who lasted until there was another setback, a cave-in or a flood, and he'd send them packing. Digger wasn't able to admit that neither he nor Joann could cook much, and after a while the local business was as sparse as the causeway trade. Digger always overbought, unwilling to believe that the next night wouldn't pick up from the last. Fish went bad.

"The pay's the same," said the Old Man the day Digger stepped back on his porch. "We've lost five feet."

The Digger grinned like he'd never been gone. "Five feet ain't shit," he said. "I smell pay dirt."

Mike's front lawn was filled with things. Electrical things, sports things, car things, kid things. A volleyball net, a Lawn-Boy, a water bike up on sawhorses with its guts hanging down. Flamingos, the stone-cast ones, not the plastic. Two broken trampolines. Mike was in the garage working on an outboard.

"Thing won't start for shit," he said, rubbing grease from his knuckles with a rag. He jerked his head toward the cooler that sat under the tool bench. "Beer?"

Ross shook his head. "I've been by the Old Man's. I don't need any more to drink.

Mike almost smiled. "You always were a pussy in the morning, Teach."

"Where are the kids?"

"Out." Mike shrugged. "Wherever kids go."

They sat for a moment, Mike rubbing his knuckles, Ross staring at a grease spot on the floor. They hadn't really been friends for a long while.

"How long you down for, Teach?"

The nickname made Ross uneasy. Mike was the only one who still called him that, and there was an edge to the way he said it. "Couple days. It depends."

Mike nodded. "Yeah, I suppose it does."

Ross got up and looked at the things in the yard. Compared with the Old Man's place it was alive, things breeding more things, junk procreating. Digger's family, his goods and property, had swelled as the Old Man's had been whittled away.

"Like an hourglass," Mother used to sigh. "All that is ours will sift down and be theirs."

"Like a damn tick," the Old Man would grumble. "Fat with our blood."

Digger had always been on contract for straight pay, no percentage of the strike if there was one. That was the deal. Even when the Old Man had gone through everything his father had made in the Boom, and was forced to go out and sell shares to the Partnership, he hadn't let Digger in. Digger's family grew, his goods and property multiplied, but he still worked for the Old Man's wages.

Erlinda came across the lawn and gave Ross a hug.

"I see your car," she said, smiling up at him, "I think maybe you bring the family down." Mike had met Erlinda when he was with the navy in Guam. She had a pretty smile with lots of gold-capped teeth on the top left. "How you been?"

"Okay. I came down to see about this big strike."

Mike snorted. "Job action."

"Whatever it is, the water's coming up over there and the Old Man looks like hell."

Mike shrugged and went back to examining the outboard. Erlinda shook her head. "Is that why you come down?"

"Yeah. This time, that's why I came down."

"You all crazy. I go home, people never believe this shit." She went over behind Mike and put her hands on his shoulders. "You be nice to each other."

Mike fiddled with the choke, lost in thought. Ross looked away across the lawn.

"Your father's digging for gold," Sunny would tell the kids whenever Ross spaced out at home, whenever he got that dark, distant look. The kids would nod, thinking they knew what she meant.

Mike fiddled with the choke. "Digger's down from St. Pete," he said finally. "You go talk to him, Teach."

Mike had always been Jean Lafitte and Ross had always been Captain Teach and Annie had always been the governor's daughter they took turns kidnapping. She would put up a brief fight and then convert to pirate ways and go digging for treasure with them. Sometimes Mike would tie the ropes too tight and make her cry, but she was his sister and he was allowed. Ross would untie her before it was time and get caught by Mike. Then there would be water punishment.

"If I say I'll go talk to him, will you start the pumps? It's half full already."

Mike turned to face him. "What does that matter? There's nothing down there, man."

"So what? You get paid."

Mike glared. Erlinda's hands tensed on his back, as if ready to hold him down. He spoke softly. "What are you teaching now—is it history?"

"Economics."

"Okay. If you went into class one day and there's nobody sitting there and they say they'll still pay you but from now on you give your lectures to the walls—"

"That's how it seems sometimes."

"Fuck how it seems. There's nobody *in* there, right? Zip. And you're still pulling in that check, but you got to keep talking, keep teaching. What do you do? Would you go in and talk to nobody every day for fifteen years?"

Ross caught Erlinda's look. She was waiting for the answer too.

"Maybe there's something down there."

"Then *you* work the fucking dredges."

They sat in silence for a long minute. Mike went to get a beer from the cooler. Ross wished that Mike would just say fuck it, let's go fishing. His stomach was starting to do weird stuff like it always did when he came down.

"Digger's over at the Ramada with Mom," said Mike. "He told me nothing moves till the Old Man comes around."

"But what does he *want?*"

"You think he'd tell me?" There was real hurt in Mike's voice. "I'm just the man with the shovel."

· · ·

A retired shrimper named Croves had found the man with the shovel in 1910. The site was on his property and his dog had been digging there. A Professor Burnside came down all the way from Tallahassee to look at the skeleton. Croves had the sense not to move the bones much, and there was something about the clay at that level that had kept them intact. The hands had been held or bound behind the back, the skull shattered with a pistol ball. Nearby was a fragment of an iron shovel. There was a gold coin, minted in Potosí, with tooth marks in it. They matched the teeth left in the skull.

Croves brought in an old shipmate, and the digging started. They used a hand-winch system, one man in the pit filling buckets and the other on top cranking them up. The professor had found an interruption in the coral a few feet from the skeleton, a square section that had been dug and repacked. It went straight down. In autumn of 1912, Croves and the shipmate got into a drunken argument and Croves split the man's head open with a tuna gaff. He buried the man in the pit, but after a week he got drunk again and dug him back up. The county sheriff found him at one in the morning, wobbling down the middle of the road toward the pier, pushing his bloated shipmate in a wheelbarrow. He had planned a burial at sea.

Croves died from pneumonia with the criminally insane the next year. The land went into litigation that didn't end till the Old Man's father—who they called the Colonel, though he'd never been in the service—bought a quarter of the island from the state during the Boom.

The pit stood idle for a couple of years, just a local legend, a place to joke about with the Yankees who stopped on their way through the Keys. Croves and the shipmate had come to water just before their fight, fourteen feet down.

Somehow the Colonel smelled the Crash and got out of land just in time. He bought a few horses, built a hotel in Tampa, and was buried alive playing poker in Hollywood-by-the-Sea in 1926. The hurricane warnings were broadcast, but the Colonel and Duffy Shoup and two turf accountants from Miami went into Duffy's wine cellar to play it out.

"Let it blow," the Colonel had joked, "as long as it doesn't take us while I'm ahead."

The house collapsed on top of them, and it was three days' digging through the mud to find the bodies. It was impossible to tell who had been winning.

The Old Man was twenty when he took over the fortune and had failed at real estate and failed at a stable and failed with a glass-bottom boat attraction, but he had only dented the Colonel's estate and was looking for something substantial to sink his money into. His main idea was to build a hotel on the island. He hired Digger to do the foundation work, taking a chance on a young guy who seemed hungry enough to bring in the lowest bid.

They were out pacing off the site when Digger pointed out the pit. The Old Man remembered it vaguely from his father's stories and thought maybe they could incorporate some kind of wishing well into the hotel lobby– local legend, pirate's treasure, the whole bit. The winch arm was still there and Digger had some rope in his car. The Old Man, partly to show his employee that he wasn't a shined-shoes type of guy, decided he wanted to go down into the pit.

If Digger had had more rope they probably wouldn't have found it, but the rope ran out with the Old Man hanging four feet above the rain-water that had collected at the bottom, next to an irregularity in the wall of the pit. He kicked with the heel of his boot. Something hard began to take shape– a piece of wood, a cross brace. Croves and his shipmate had dug right past it, just as whoever had killed the man with the shovel wanted them to. The pit went down straight for eight feet and then tunneled away horizontally.

The hotel never happened. Anybody who took the trouble to dig such an elaborate hiding place had something valuable to hide. The university people identified the first crossbeam they dug out as Spanish oak, taken off a ship. Markings on the next one led them to guess it was off the *Delfín,* a galleon that left Potosí loaded with bullion and had been lost to either storms or pirates. The Old Man hired Digger to build a house by the site.

They'd put up the Ramada just off the causeway about a year back. Digger was in his chair by the pool reading a James Michener paperback that had gotten wet and now fluffed out like a sponge. He'd lost too much weight.

"He sends the professor," he grumbled, as Ross crossed the terrace to poolside. "He sends the doctor."

"Hi, Digger." They didn't shake hands.

"What are you now, Doctor of Money?"

"Economics."

"The old bastard won't come down from his throne in person. He sends the Doctor of Economics."

"I was just over to see Mike."

"Yeah."

"The kids weren't there, but—"

"They spend all their time outside. Suntans all year round." Digger always talked about their tans. He had never accepted that they'd come out roughly the same shade as Erlinda.

"So how's Joann?"

"She's off looking at Annie. Is this a social call?"

Ross tried to smile. "Your beef is with him, not me."

"You're wrong, son. This is families. This is the Hatfields and McCoys we're talkin."

"It doesn't have to be that way, Dig."

"The hell it doesn't." Digger plopped the book down and pushed the TURN button so his chair swiveled to face Ross.

"Water coming up over there?"

"You know it is."

Digger nodded. The muscles in his neck hung like strings. As kids they had climbed him, Mike scaling one side and Ross the other, with Annie already perched on his shoulders. He could drive a nail into a two-by-four with one whack, either hand, and pull small trees out of the ground by their roots. He'd make a muscle stand out in his arm, and all three of them would take turns punching it with their puny fists. His voice sounded like it was rumbling up from a deep well.

"This shit has gone on long enough," he said to Ross. "Tell him I want partners or he can dig out with his ringers."

It was what Ross had expected. "There's other contractors."

"None that know what Mike does. And the Old Man can't put on a new crew without going to the Partnership. He does that, and the whole thing caves in."

For Econ 101, Ross always started with Marx. It was the most elemental, and it made clear his contention that there was no pure economics, no numbers immune to the workings of culture and politics. The primitive was replaced by the feudal, the feudal by the entrepreneurial, the entrepreneurial by the corporate, and all the while a consciousness was growing among the underclass, a pit ready to yawn open at capital's feet.

"And the worker will own the workplace," said Ross.

"Halvesies," said the Digger. "I don't want the whole thing, kid, just an even split. After what I've put into that ground—"

"Dig, you've always been paid. Mike's got our couch in his fucking *living* room."

"He bought it at Kelsey's."

"After the Old Man hocked it to make payroll that last time. The guy is practically sitting on the linoleum over there. What more do you want?"

"He still owns his share. He still holds the deed. I want half." Digger's good hand tightened on the arm of his chair.

"Half of nothing is nothing, Dig."

The Digger's face drained. It was the wrong thing to say. "What about the coin?"

"The man with the shovel had it in his teeth."

"The one *we* found."

"That was a long time ago. If there ever was anything down there, they came back and got it." Ross shrugged. "And somebody dropped a coin. People drop things."

Digger watched a little girl dog-paddle across the shallow end of the pool. "I still want half."

"Digger, there's nothing down there. What's the point?"

The little girl gasped as she grabbed the edge of the tile.

"I sunk my life into that fucking pit. That's the point." Digger worked his buttons and buzzed away on his chair. Children screamed from the water.

Ross drove up to Coral Gables in the late afternoon. Mrs. Dorfman lived in a huge Spanish-style house that always had dozens of lizards clinging to the outside walls. Something about the angle of the sun. Ross found her in the back dealing with potato bugs.

"This organic spray," she sighed. "It just isn't as effective."

"Nuke 'em."

Mrs. Dorfman smiled. She was one of those women, he thought, who hadn't been attractive till late middle age. A face waiting to be sixty.

"To what do I owe the visit?"

Ross shrugged. "My father said you were in town."

"You mean there's trouble at the site." She liked to make it sound scientific, archaeological.

Mrs. Dorfman had traced the path of the *Delfín* through university libraries and museums, through historians and divers and treasure clubs, until she came to the Old Man's pit. She was the main investor in the Partnership, and she had brought most of the others in.

"When isn't there trouble at the dig?"

"Another cave-in?"

Ross shook his head. "Labor dispute."

She frowned. "Those men." She was including more than just Digger and the Old Man. "Come on inside. I'll get you something to drink."

The walls inside were covered with reproductions of old navigators' charts, educated guesses at what the New World might be. There were some coins and musket pieces in glass cases, ships' lanterns hung from the ceiling beams. There was a large case by the fireplace, empty but for the one coin the Old Man had found, waiting for the rest of the treasure. The Old Man had given the coin to Mrs. Dorfman to seal the bargain when the Partnership was formed.

Mrs. Dorfman handed Ross a dripping-cold glass of iced tea and sat with some difficulty in a deep chair across from him.

"My knees swell up," she said. "This weather."

He noticed her fingers then, twisting into arthritic claws. She seemed to be in pain.

"The water's coming up, I suppose?"

Ross nodded.

"We lose so much ground whenever this happens."

There were some pictures over the fireplace, photos of her in Egypt with her parents when she was a girl. Homely, serious, a little middle-aged woman of twelve in a pith helmet a size too big for her head, staring owl-eyed at the camera. Her parents were slightly out of focus in the background, and every time Ross came back they seemed to have faded more. But the little girl in the picture was as sharp as ever, her look at once expectant and ready for disappointment.

"I suppose it doesn't really make any difference," she said.

"Why not?"

She put her glass down. "Why does a man bury a treasure? He doesn't trust his crew. He rows to shore with a few men and tells them where to dig. Two entrances, a false one and a proper one. The false one is easy to find, but dug at low tide and angled so that if you go past a certain point and the tide comes in—"

"It fills up." Ross had heard the theory a dozen times.

"So if someone from the crew beats the captain back to the island and searches it," she continued, "they find the false entrance, the pit fills with water, and they give up. If they're smart."

"And the man with the shovel?"

"The captain didn't trust him."

"Or maybe the man with the shovel *is* the captain." Ross smiled at his thought. "Maybe after they dug the hole the men decided the hell with this, bumped the captain off, and took the treasure. A labor dispute."

Mrs. Dorfman wasn't smiling. "Either way we've wasted our time."

"What about the coin, though? The Old Man found it after he'd dug past the flooding point."

Mrs. Dorfman rose slowly and crossed to the case that held the coin. "It came out in the sluice. There's no way of telling what level it washed from. People drop things."

Mrs. Dorfman had bought the house in Coral Gables to be near the pit. When she was back in Maine she called once a week to see how the dredging was coming along. "It's not the treasure," she had always said before. "I just want to know what happened. Who dug the hole. Why. I just want to know."

"Digger wants half of my father's share," said Ross. "Either that or Mike stays out."

Mrs. Dorfman shook her head. "Why come to me?"

"You have to approve any change in share status."

"Your father doesn't have much left to give half of."

"How much?"

"Eight percent."

The last Ross knew, he'd owned a third.

"What happened?"

"He was sick. The drinking, not eating well—there were hospital bills. He had to sell shares."

"Did Digger offer to buy?"

"For twice what your father got for them. Some sort of mutual fund."

Mrs. Dorfman made a face. "They don't care about treasure. Just dollars and cents."

There was a shifting blush of gold on the old woman's cheek as she looked down into the case. Something about the angle of the sun. There was a cross stamped on one side of the coin. On the other side was a strange design, like a one-winged bird.

"Do what you can," said Mrs. Dorfman. Her attention seemed to have drifted, as if Ross had already driven away. "If he won't give it up—well, there are things we'll never know."

The old man was drifting behind scotch when Ross got back to the house.

"She wanted me to pull out!" he shouted, as Ross came in. "To give up. Said she was going to leave me."

It was the famous story of the coin again. The TV had regressed to black and white, playing a *Honeymooners* episode.

" 'It's a dream,' she'd tell me, 'a dream that will bury us all.' "

The Old Man paced from the kitchen to the living room and back, talking to the walls. He had started before Ross stepped in, past needing an audience.

"It was a bright morning. The night before, she'd said, 'This is it, James. I'm taking the boy.' "

Ross opened the beer. When he got this way the Old Man always referred to him as "the boy," as if the little boy of those days had drowned and been buried and Ross the adult was some new, strange person.

"There was a rattle in the sluice. Soto—it was Soto's in his first year on the crew—he ran over with it. Grinning like a little boy with that big gold tooth up front that he had."

The Old Man was smiling now, a hazy far-off smile.

"Mary was on the porch with the boy." He was almost whispering, rapt. "And he runs up and opens his fist and there it is. He gives it a bit of polish on his shirt and there it was like the day it was minted, gleaming like that big gold tooth in his grin." The Old Man was oblivious to the TV, oblivious to Ross sitting at the kitchen table. He paced, trying to make it come back.

"It killed her," said Ross.

"She stayed," said the Old Man. "She saw it wasn't only a dream."

"She died in a year," said Ross, "from the damp. From the pit. Her lungs."

"Like the day it was minted," said the Old Man. "Gleaming."

Ross sat on the fork of a backhoe parked at the edge of the pit. Swarms of night bugs zipped around the yellow antivandal lights over the dredgers. The edge of the pit was only a few yards from the house now, opening like a mouth, wider every year. A pole marked where the original hole had been. Now they were excavating the whole stratum, quarrying for treasure. The pit would swallow the house in a year. Ross heard water sounds from the base of the center rig. It was coming up. Like blood into a wound, seeping. Healing what had been cut into. He remembered the last time he'd sat here with the pumps not running. After Annie. That long ago.

Giant moth shadows, thrown from the yellow lights, flapped across the surface of the pit. Ross imagined the pirate. He looked different from when Ross imagined him as a boy, no more Fairbanks grin, no more parrot on the shoulder. Ross saw a tired man with a three day growth of beard. People were after him, people wanted to hang him. His men were simple killers. He was walking into a small clearing in the palms followed by two men carrying a chest. One was a sailor, a runaway slave with big crooked teeth and huge arms. A man you could climb. The other was the pirate's son.

They dig for a long time, the sailor and the son, while the pirate watches, forehead knotted, lost in thought, occasionally listening toward the beach for the threatening splash of an oar. The men come out of the hole. They hoist the treasure up on ropes— it sways slightly, like a coffin poised to winch down into a grave. They begin to lower it, hand over hand, then the pirate decides and tells them to stop. They put the chest on the dirt next to the hole, puzzled. The sailor is the pirate's friend, the one man of all the crew he trusts to bring this far.

"This is yours," the pirate says to his son, tapping the chest with the toe of his boot. He opens the chest and takes two coins from it, new coins fresh from the mint at Potosí. The son feels sick in his stomach. A breeze rustles the palm fronds overhead. His father drops one of the coins into the hole.

"This is for those who come after me," he says.

There is a pistol in the old pirate's hand, the hammer pulled back, straining, a cold ball of metal aching in the chamber. The old pirate hands the other coin to the sailor, his friend.

"Put it in your mouth," he says.

The sailor puts the coin between his big crooked teeth. The pirate has him kneel with his forehead touching dirt. He gives the son a piece of rope.

"This is yours," he says. "This is what you have to do."

The son ties the hands of the sailor, his father's friend, behind his back. He has climbed this man. His stomach is like a hammer pulled back, aching for release.

"This is what you have to do."

The sailor's big crooked teeth dig into the soft gold as the ball smashes through his head.

Parrots, hundreds of them, scream and wheel overhead as the shot echoes. The son's stomach is like the parrots in flight, screaming.

"This is yours," says his father. "This is for you."

The Old Man watches as the son fills the hole, finishing with a small mound over the murdered sailor and his shovel. The Old Man and the son each take an end of the chest and walk out of the clearing with it. Parrots, unruffling, settle in the palm fronds overhead.

Ross sat and watched moth shadows flap on the surface of the pit. It was what he did as a boy when his mother and the Old Man were fighting in the house. It was something he did a lot of nights. It was how he found Annie.

When he came inside, Ross found his father asleep with his face on the kitchen table. The TV was crackling, stuck between channels.

They'd been playing pirates near the pit, which wasn't allowed, trying to find the treasure, and Mike told Annie she couldn't come. She said she'd tell if they didn't let her. Mike made him tie her to a tree, tight. They snuck down into the pit, poking sticks into the wash where it was sucked up into the sluices. It was fun for a while. When they untied Annie they told her they'd seen something under the water, something like a wooden chest, and tomorrow they'd pull it up and she couldn't come and they'd be rich and she'd be poor. Just to tease her. She cried. Ross wanted to say she could come, Ross wanted to marry her when they got big, but Mike was watching, and if he was nice to Annie without permission he'd get the water punishment. Their mothers called them to dinner.

Ross gave the Old Man a gentle shove.

Moth wings flapping over the pit. The pumps beating like the island's heart. Something pale white gleaming in the water, floating.

Ross shoved harder. The Old Man moaned.

They'd found a possum drowned in the pit once. Ross came down to poke whatever this was with a stick.

He got the old man awake. His eyes weren't quite focused but he was awake. "He wants half," said Ross.

Annie was floating in the water. Face down, the way they floated in the bay looking for fish in the rocks. The Dead Man's Float. She was face down, floating gently, looking for buried treasure.

"He wants half of your share. You're going to give it to him."

The Old Man's eyes swam into focus. "But this is for you," he said. He always said that when he was backed into a corner. "What will be left?"

She sagged like a rag doll in Digger's arms when he waded out of the pit. The trooper wanted to fish her out with a tuna gaff, but Digger went in. Night bugs clouded around, drawn by the gleaming of Annie's wet skin in the yellow light. Pit water running from her hair made a winding trail in the dirt, a dripping line between Digger's huge footsteps that Ross followed in the yellow light, his stomach like the Dead Man's Float. And then the pumps went off, like the heart of the island had stopped, and he could hear a breeze in the palm fronds, could hear the trooper's radio squawking like a parrot, could hear the dark, soothing water sounds from the pit.

"What will be left?" said the Old Man to Ross. "What can I leave you?"

"You can leave me alone," said Ross.

He saw the curio shop on the way out of Simkin's law office in Key West. It wasn't much from the outside– THE TREASURE TROVE burned on the side of a fake sea chest spilling over with costume jewelry, a skeletal shark's jaws hanging over the entrance. Inside were mostly things that said SOUVENIR OF KEY WEST, made from glued and lacquered seashells. The Old Man had always pointed the place out as a clip joint on their trips to town when Ross was a boy. He felt funny being inside for the first time.

The proprietor was blind and had a parrot on his shoulder. A second glance revealed that the parrot was plastic, covered with real feathers, fastened to the man's shirt with wire hooks. The man had three days' worth of white stubble on his face and a spacy, unsettling grin. He looked like Blind Pew in the Wallace Beery movie.

"I've got what you want," he said, cocking his head to listen as Ross wandered into the room.

"What do I want?"

"Whatever it is, I've got it." The old man smiled. "Just look around."

There were rubber sharks and alligators. There were crates of citrus and pecan candies and frosted glass pitchers with flamingos etched on them. There were table clocks and mirror frames encrusted with shells, there were whole green sea turtles mummified in lacquer. There were Seminole handicrafts and T-shirts with wisecracks on them and postcards of bare-breasted blond girls holding oranges that said CHECK OUT THESE BEAUTIES! There was a glass case with coins and artifacts from Spanish wrecks.

"I can open that case for you if you want," said the old blind man from behind the cash register. He stood facing in the opposite direction.

"Sure."

He navigated through the cluttered aisles of tourist junk without bumping a thing.

"How do you keep people from stealing?"

The man's smile was crooked, something unsettling about it. "Sparky keeps an eye on things." He nodded to the parrot on his shoulder.

"Sparky doesn't look too lively."

"Used to have a real one, but who wants bird shit runnin' down their neck all day?" He pulled something on the bottom of the parrot.

"Arrrk!" it squawked, mouth stiffly flapping open and shut. *"Pieces of eight! Pieces of eight!"*

Ross picked up the gold coin that had caught his eye as the man stared into space next to him.

"Used to have two of those," said the blind man. "Sold the other back in 'fifty-six."

There was a cross stamped on one side and on the other a strange design, like a bird with one wing.

"There was only one run at Potosí with that design," he said. "It went out with the Silver Fleet, and most of it got to Spain. They lost one or two to weather, one or two pirates. Galleons. So that's a rare little item you've got there."

Ross held it up so it gleamed in the morning light slanting through the display window.

"I got a book back there by the register'd tell you what the market is for it, but for you"—the man's grin as he swung his head toward Ross seemed knowing, insinuating—"for you I could do a deal."

The eyes of the plastic parrot seemed to drill into Ross as he thought. He turned away and there was a monkey made of coconut halves staring up at him pleadingly. A mass-produced scroll on the wall showed panicked sailors leaping from a ship that was battering itself to pieces on a lighthouse rock. The coin burned a little in his palm, still hot from the sun magnifying through the glass cover on the display case.

"I never seen another like it," said the blind man, "but for the one that went in 'fifty-six. Sold her to a treasure hunter who came in off a drunk and paid flat cash. A man with a gleam in his eye."

It didn't take long for them all to sign the papers. The hardest part was for him and Mike to lift Digger onto the porch in his chair. Digger's muscle had gone to something else, and he was dead weight. Not much was said. Simkin left the boilerplate out and just explained the dollars and cents to Digger and the Old Man and Mrs. Dorfman. Mike and Ross stood on the ground below the porch, ready to leap in if there was any last-minute trouble from their fathers, but the old men were subdued. Mrs. Dorfman had an annoyed frown on her face the whole time. She looked more frail away from her museum of a house.

Ross took a last listen to the breeze in the palms and then heard the dry scratch of his father signing the agreement. Digger nodded to Mike and Mike waved to Soto. The pumps shuddered and sighed and then plodded back to life, *ka-whump, ka-whump, ka-whump.* Simkin had a bottle of champagne, but no one wanted to share it with him. The Old Man stayed at one end of the porch watching the pumps, and Digger sat in his chair reading the agreement line for line. Mrs. Dorfman sat signing a dozen proxy copies as Simkin drank alone. Mike and Ross wandered toward the pit together.

"You remember the year Mickey Mantle was so hard to get?" said Mike. "The card?"

"Yeah. They must've printed a hundred for the whole damn country and every kid in America was trying to complete his collection. I think it was 'fifty-six."

"No," said Ross. "'Fifty-six was the year my mother almost left. The year they found the coin."

"Later, then. It was like there was nothing more precious in the whole kid world than that baseball card. We had everything but him, and we kept buying the gum and we'd get doubles and triples and quadruples of guys."

"We had like twenty of Jerry Lumpe."

"And those kids came down from Jersey—"

"Massachusetts—"

"—on vacation. And they had one and they hated the Yankees. And there was someone that they wanted, that they needed to complete their favorite team."

"Warren Spahn."

"The Braves, right. So we had that big trade."

"With Annie in the middle."

Mike nodded his head. His crew was checking out the pumps, lining up the spill from the pit over the sluices, just in case something was floating loose. That's how they'd found the last one. "With Annie. It must have been 'fifty-seven then, before Annie." Mike had never said her name to him since the night. Not once.

Ross missed Sunny and the kids so much his stomach hurt. He didn't know what he'd tell her about the coin. "We put Warren Spahn in her left hand," he said, "and the Massachusetts kid put Mickey Mantle in her right, and she made the switch."

"A regular ritual," said Mike. He looked back up at the porch. They were all still there. "It didn't mean shit, kids with a piece of cardboard, but it was like this holy ritual."

A man with a gleam in his eye, the blind curio dealer had said. Didn't have the book value in cash, but he made promises. "It's for the wife and boy," said the treasure hunter. "It's for the future."

Mike shook his head as if clearing it. "Me and Erlinda are going to drive up north with the kids."

"You should stop with us," said Ross. Their wives had never met.

"Yeah, that would be nice."

They looked into the water on the surface of the pit, puckering as the pumps sucked away below. Ross wondered if it could get lost forever down there.

"Digger wrote out a will last week," said Mike. "He put my kids in it. He's stopped calling Erlinda 'the colored girl,' so we have dinner now and then. He told me at dinner how they were in the will, then he sprung this thing about shutting down till your old man came across with a piece."

"Christ."

Ross's stomach was tight, waiting. It could be any time, minutes from now or weeks from now. He wasn't sure it was the right thing to do, but now it was done. People dropped things.

"I don't know if the will thing was to bury the hatchet or to make me go along with him. Like I give a shit about owning a piece of the pit."

Ross had asked the blind man where he had gotten the gold coins in the first place. "There are things we'll never know," said the blind man.

"You should plan to stay a couple of days when you come up," said Ross. "The kids would get along."

The pumps were beating regularly now, dark water spurting into the sluices. The ground throbbed with their rhythm.

"You ever think what Annie would have been?" Mike said.

Ross nodded. "I think about her all the time."

Mike looked at him then, unguarded. "Me too."

Ross hadn't expected it quite so soon. There was a shout from the sluices and then old Soto running, faster then he'd moved in years, toward the house. When they got there he was holding it up to the light, holding it up to the people on the porch. Digger had wheeled close, and the Old Man and Mrs. Dorfman leaned over the railing on either side of him. Old Soto, grinning toothlessly, held it up and did a little dance of excitement in the mud at the foot of the porch. He'd given it a good rub on his shirt and it was there in his brown palm, a cross stamped on one side, a strange design, like a one-winged bird, on the other.

Ross could feel Mike beside him. Mike was pale, shaking his head. Digger said something about pay dirt and the Old Man said something about a dream and Mrs. Dorfman wanted to examine the markings. There was color in her cheeks now, maybe from the excitement, maybe something about the angle of the sun. Ross looked from the coin to the eyes of the old people on the porch.

Gleaming.

Peeling

"MUDBUGS COMING!" CALLS BIG ANTOINE, like he always does when he dumps them onto the table. Little Antoine, his father, used to have to step on a box to do it, but Big handles a twenty-gallon can like it was a slop bucket. Big sweats a lot, even more since he took over running the place and tries to be courtly.

"Good to see you ladies working so nice," he'll say, hurrying through, wiping his face with the towel he carries around his neck. "Y'all looking exceptional today."

They don't look up unless it's something special. Even when he dumps, crawfish spilling out red and steaming onto the shiny steel table, a new hill of legs and feelers and black-bead eyes, the women keep their faces in it, peeling. Big Antoine always has two cans on the fire. The one with the corn and onions and potatoes mixed in the boil is for the straight-up orders, two pounds or five on a round metal tray, peel 'em yourself. The other can, the women got to pull the tail meat out for the bisque and the gumbo and the étoufée and the po-boys.

"Tour bus just come up," says Antoine, shaking the can out. "Gonna keep you ladies busy."

It is Ophelia and Vinie and Pearl and the new girl, LaTonya, and Li and Jasmine around the table, Vinie and Jasmine at opposite corners. They reach in and sweep a new little pile from the mound in the center.

"*Écrevisse, exercice,*" says Ophelia, who still speaks French at home and likes to rhyme.

"Man make me hot, the way he sweat," says Jasmine.

"Ought to lose him some blubber."

"Nuh-uh." Jasmine raises her eyebrows the way she does when informing them of the latest scientific findings. "Man carry that much weight into his age, worst thing he can do is lose it. Like a drinking man, past a certain point going dry will just *kill* you."

"It depends on what the fat is *made* of," says Pearl. "Cajun man like Antoine, it's all butter fat. Everything they make is one stick of butter this, two stick of butter that. He want to lose weight, all it is he got to leave out that butter. It just melt away off his hips. But you take a man like Clarence Toussaint."

"Butcher-man Clarence?"

"That's him. That man is *wide* and he's *solid*. Boys he grow up with call him Mudslide, 'cause he open his belt this big black belly come rumblin' out—"

"*Mudslide.*"

"—and that is solid pork-chop fat. Man could run the marathon race every morning, eat on bean sprouts and water like them fashion ladies do, but that fat is going *nowhere*."

"*Et qu'est-ce que c'est cela?* What this hanging over your chair?" says Ophelia, and the others giggle. Pearl is big, big and thick-armed and strong-coffee-colored.

"Beignets," she says, taking no offense. "Which is mostly lard. Got a serious liking for beignets."

"It's not the lard that kills you, it's the sugar," says Jasmine. "You breathe that powdered sugar down your lungs, choke you right to death."

"That's no lie."

The conversation dies there and they are quiet awhile, peeling. Wet tearing sounds, tossing the meat to one side and the carcass to the other. They don't have a radio because Big Antoine says it interferes with his *Greatest Cajun Hits* tape for the customers whenever the door swings open.

"Chank-a-chank," says Ophelia when the accordian sounds pump in, "*neuf à cinq.*"

They are shucking crawfish like this for five minutes before Vinie finally says, "Beer."

"What?"

Vinie usually has the last word, reacting after the fact to topics already filed and forgotten, as if she needs the time to consider all the possibilities.

"Beer. That's beer fat the man's lugging around. You ever see him put anything else in his mouth?"

Most of Big Antoine's trips through are to the cooler for another can of Dixie. On a busy day he'll do two six-packs.

"Man drink beer all day, never pees."

"How you know that?"

"Girlene is looking right at the customer bathroom all day long, tells me she never see him go in." Girlene is the red-faced cashier down from Slidell. "And we know he can't *fit* in the employee bathroom. Man is made of beer."

"Beer and worry," says Pearl.

"He didn't worry," says Vinie, "he wouldn't squeeze through that doorway."

Vinie is small, with wispy gray hair and light brown eyes and wrinkled butterscotch skin. She wears glasses low on her nose and peers over them to the crawfish. She has a delicate way of peeling, quick and light, and is the only one without at least one bandaid on her fingers.

The new girl is wearing eight. On her first day, Jasmine laid it down to her.

"Antoine got but two rules," she said. "No cursing allowed, and you got a cut you put a Band-Aid on right away."

By noon the new girl's hands were raw and bleeding.

"You'll get used to it," said Pearl, being nice. "And then your hands will toughen up some."

"I don't want to get used to it," said LaTonya. "I want to get a real job."

The others all smiled then.

"This ain't real enough for you?"

"Girl wants one of those six-figure jobs."

"You find one, girl," said Pearl. "Don't give up on it. Don't be like us old-timers."

"*Sans rêve,*"—Ophelia shrugged—"*pas de grève.*"

LaTonya had her hair braided African style, which the others all admired but said they could never do themselves. The new girl was the only one of them under fifty, except maybe Li, who was some kind of Asian and hard to figure.

"Me and my sisters had us some braids when we were girls," said Jasmine, who wore makeup to work and a wig with straight bangs made of some plastic that gave off oily rainbow highlights when the sun slanted through the little high window about four o'clock every day.

"You had to have some *length* to do it, but we Cherokee on my mother's side and we all had long black hair."

You can still see how pretty Jasmine was some forty–fifty years ago, with her high cheekbones and hazel eyes.

"She gonna tell us about Pocohontas again," says Pearl.

"That wasn't her name." Jasmine has this way of talking sometimes, like she's dealing with small children. "All I'm saying is, it run us some *time*, dealing with them braids. I admire a young woman take some care with her appearance."

"I do it while I watch TV," says LaTonya. "It keeps my hands busy."

"You get some babies," says Ophelia, "you forget about your hair. *Les enfants n'arrêtent pour rien.*"

LaTonya looks to Vinie, who usually does the translating.

"She's telling you enjoy it while you can," says Vinie, "'cause them kids will run you to the *bone.*"

Mostly they work in silence, hours at a time, pulling off the heads, ripping legs apart and squeezing the tail meat out with thumb and forefinger, stripping the blue-black vein when it's big enough to see. Pearl hums to herself sometimes, pretty churchlike pieces of songs that make her face crease with feeling. Pearl is the only Baptist among them and asks detailed questions of the others about nuns. Do they get their monthlies, do they take baths together, is there a special kind of underwear? Pearl is good for hours on the subject of nuns, and Ophelia likes to tell her wild stories. The new girl still gets mixed up and will put the meat on her left and the husk on her right and swear and then apologize to Jasmine. Li never says anything and peels with seamless intensity, staring at the crawfish as if there is a story they might reveal. When the silence is finally broken, it is as if they have all agreed to speak at once, their talk like rain held too long in heavy clouds.

Jasmine usually starts it.

"There isn't no manner you can endure 'gainst the ways of the Devil," she says.

"Speakin' for yourself," says Pearl.

"It's envy wakes the Devil up."

"Envy—"

"Got you a house, got a job, got a man? Devil wants a *taste* of that."

Vinie sighs, shakes her head. "Here it comes," she says quietly.

"We gonna hear about *him* again," says Pearl.

"La même histoire."

"Had me a man name of Lucien Beaucoup," Jasmine continues.

"Don't start." Vinie doesn't look up, but her hands are still.

LaTonya feels the tension and looks around– older women, church women, women her mother's age, maybe even her grandmother's.

Jasmine pushes on. "Pretty-lookin', sweet-smellin', churchgoin' man. Good to his mama. Worked him a job on the shrimp fleet, out of Delc'm—"

"She's bringin him back."

"He was a young man then, just over with his schoolin.' Come round the back of my house, three nights out of four, and he *sings*. Wouldn't knock on the door, wouldn't wait up for me on my path to school,

wouldn't tell no brags to the other boys. 'Cause he *shy*, see, and *respectful.*
Not like what they got today."

"Not at all."

"Little tiny boys with them big bold eyes. Impertinent."

"Lucien Beaucoup," says Ophelia, into the rhythm of it now.

"That's right, *Lucien.*"

"Singing out back."

"Out back of my house whilst me and my sisters was helpin' our mam
with her mending. Three nights out of four."

"My mam took in mending too," says Pearl, coming in strong to head
the story off. "Washing, mending, leatherwork. Could sole up some
shoes. Learnt it from Papa 'fore he was kilt in France."

"What's he doing in France?" asks LaTonya.

"He was in the World War. The first one."

Vinie smiles. "You that old, Pearl?"

"This is after. He walked through that war thout a scratch on him.
Come back home. Five–six years pass, he gets a letter from some woman
in France."

"White woman," says LaTonya.

"That's what they got there, mostly. She say he's got him a little
daughter he left behind– she needs him. He gets his money together,
books a ride on a ocean liner. Goin to bring that little girl back."

"Her mama too?"

"He didn't know 'bout that. Left my mam on the dock, carryin' me
inside her. She knew it but hadn't got to tellin' him yet."

"Went off to France."

"Went off to France. Town name of X. That's how you say it, like 'X
marks the spot.'"

"Got a ticket to X—"

"Walk down the main street, go to the address, knock on the door,
door opens– French girl papa standin' there. Bam! Put a bullet smack in
my papa head. Laid him *out.*"

"Lord."

"French girl papa had had her write that letter. So my mam took up with Mr. Lester when she heard. Mr. Lester was behind all my brothers and sisters that come after."

"And you never seen your own."

"Not but a picture. Big handsome man in a uniform. He was a cobbler, and he left my mam with some knowledge of it. She always tell me the story when she working on some shoes."

"Wonder what happened to that little French girl?" says LaTonya. "With her papa dead on the street and growing up 'mongst all them white people."

"Little French girl cost me knowing my own blood," says Pearl, flicking tail meat onto the counter. "She can *fry*."

The women are peeling, thinking about the French girl, when Jasmine starts to sing.

> *Jolie fille, jolie fille*
> *Écoute-toi ma chanson.*

She closes her eyes, pulling their attention back.

> *T'es la reine de la ville,*
> *La lumière et le son—*

She looks at them.

"That's a *fais do-do*," says Ophelia to LaTonya. "'Bout how pretty this girl is to him. Queen of the world."

"That's what he sing," says Jasmine, "three nights out of four. My sisters look up from the mendin', tease me something terrible. My cheeks would take color, my fingers trippin' all over each other. Only thing worse was the nights he wouldn't come. Those nights my ears would hurt from listenin' for his voice out back."

Jolie âme, jolis yeux
Tellement douce et gentille—

She sings:

T'es la reine de mon coeur
La raison de ma vie.

"Don't hear that kind of song no more," says Ophelia, after a moment.

Pearl waves a crawfish in her hand as she talks. "Now they all got they own radio station, carry it up on their shoulder wherever they go, rattle the walls with that noise they put in their ears. Most of em is deaf to a normal voice." She realizes, turns to LaTonya. "No offense, darlin'."

LaTonya shrugs. "S'not *my* music."

Jasmine raises her voice a little. "Lucien Beau*coup*. Church-goin', sweet-singin' man. He come for *me*."

"It's the same old story."

"All set to marry us at Mary Star of the Sea Church, down in Guidry Parish."

"Same sad story."

"We was *meant* for each other."

"Like beans and rice."

"Only the other one come between—"

"A snake in the garden."

"With her yellow eyes—"

"Watch it, now."

"And her hot nasty words—"

"Careful."

"The other one that come and wrecked up my life. Not 'cause he would have looked at her twice. But 'cause she worked the Devil on him. 'Cause she traffic with the dark spirits."

Vinie stands suddenly and walks off into the employees' washroom.

Pearl and Ophelia slowly push their chairs away and then Li and La Tonya join them, standing and stretching. Vinie is the one who asked Antoine for the five-minute break, so she gets to decide when to take it. Jasmine, tight-lipped, keeps peeling.

One by one the women go in to wash and dry their hands. Li leans against the wall with her arms folded across her chest, eyes unfocused. She never speaks in English, though she seems to understand a little. Pearl mutters about her feet, shifting weight from one to the other, and LaTonya massages her fingers. She worries about the cuts, wondering if they'll ever heal, one scab peeling off and another starting to form. Vinie is serious about the five minutes, watching the second hand on the big clock on the wall, poised over her chair, then sitting back down on the click. She figures they should be honest, since Antoine gave it up without a fight.

"I don't see any problem in it," he'd said. "Long as my mudbugs keep coming."

Jasmine is frosty when they all sit around her again. She holds her chin tilted as if rising above pain or insult. The other women seem to ignore her.

"Might gonna rain pretty soon," says Pearl.

"Be a flood in my yard, *s'il pleut,*" says Ophelia.

"You living down by the water these days?"

"*À côté du lac.* Little bitty rain, I got to walk ankle-deep to hang the laundry out, take it two days to drain."

"I'm up on a hill now," says LaTonya.

"Us, too."

They work awhile, Pearl humming and rocking as she peels. Vinie breaks it.

"I come through the flood of 'thirty-five," she says.

"That were some high water."

"My mam was workin' for a man name Buster Petite," says Vinie, "lived over in Placquemine. Had the rheumatism in both his legs, sit up all day in this rocker chair, waving his cane, yellin' out orders. Kept my mam on the run from the minute she set foot in that house till the minute she feed him his hot milk in bed at night."

"*Ma mère ne bouge pour bruit.* Always tell her people, 'Case you didn't hear, M'sieur Lincoln freed the slaves.'"

"You got to train 'em," says Pearl. "Most of your white folks is capable of learning, long as you got *patience.*"

"Like Antoine."

"Big Antoine is *nothing*. You remember his daddy?"

"Little Antoine a holy terror in his day. We had some *wars* with that man, God rest his soul."

"Amen."

"This was other times," says Vinie. "White people was outa control in them days." She turns to Li. "You maybe weren't here, Miss Li, but that's the truth."

"She don't understand you, Vinie."

"Sure she does."

Li doesn't acknowlege that they're talking about her.

"Woman is from Vietnam. Talk that goulash."

"That's a food, not a *language.*"

"I heard her talk it once, sound like goulash to me."

"Yo, Miss Li, you from Vietnam?"

"She from someplace worse than here, I bet."

"Don't be mean. Where you from, miss?"

Li just looks at them, either not comprehending or pretending not to.

"See? She don't even know that."

"So what happened to Buster Petite?" asks LaTonya.

The women all look at the new girl.

"These young ones always in a hurry," says Jasmine, breaking her silence. "Got no patience a-tall."

Vinie sighs. "Mr. Petite see the first rain comin', he says it won't amount to spit in a windstorm. But my mam knows different. She seen the yard animals actin' up, yellow dog eatin' dirt, chickens walkin' backward, house cats with they tails low. But the old man says his legs tell him no, and they don't ever lie."

"My knees just fill up, ever it's gonna rain," says Ophelia.

"My ankles start to hurtin'," says Pearl.

"Mr. Petite wouldn't let my mam pull him outa there. Water's up to the top of the porch, leakin' in under the front door, he still says it's just a shower. He runs that cane under the arms of his rocker and grip hold and says, 'Here I sit, come hell or high water.' The windows bust through then and mam grab me up and run into the attic, us and Buster Petite's fifteen house cats, all of 'em jumpin' on us and diggin' in with they claws, tryin' to push close."

"Hell or high water," muses Pearl. "Nothin' on earth more stubborn than a old white man."

"Man has that many cats," says Ophelia, "you got to *wonder.*"

"Them cats in Mam's hair," says Vinie, "up my back, yawlin' and scratchin' and all the while Buster Petite downstairs yelling like he's in a rumpus with the Devil. 'Get back!' he yells. 'Get back, dammit, this *my* house!' There was banging then, and we look out the little attic window and see it's telephone poles, tore loose and come running by in the flood-water. Levee broke under and there's all manner of things afloat, and we can't hear no Buster Petite anymore."

"Man sound nasty," says Pearl. "I hate to hear a man yelling out orders in a house."

"*Les blancs de ma mère* had a buzzer for a while. I'd be down in the quarters with the others what worked for them. Sound go right up my spine, everytime they push it."

Pearl and Vinie nod. Antoine blasts through and then crosses back out with a cold can of Dixie sweating in his hand. Cajun music pounds in, fading as the door closes behind him. Jasmine hasn't given up.

"You ever hear the sound of a woman had her heart pulled out of her?"

"Uh-oh."

"Listen what come to life," says Vinie.

LaTonya looks around and sees that the others have resigned themselves to whatever is coming next.

"I had me a man name of Lucien Beaucoup," says Jasmine.

"I heard that name before."

"That man was *devoted* to me. Promised to hold me up like the night holds the stars."

"You hear violins playin'?"

"But there was another woman laid her greedy eyes on him. Woman that traffic with the dark spirits, woman stoop to gris-gris cause she couldn't catch a man no other way."

"Gettin' personal now."

"First she take the egg from a black hen, write my name on it backwards, and throw it clear over my house. Make me burn with a fever. My eyes swole up tight, skin prickle like it's a million ants crawlin' on me." She wiggles her fingers around her neck and makes a face. "Then she take a cock rooster and bury him up to his neck in the yard, so's he can see but he can't move. She let another rooster into the yard. First he have at all the hens, and that buried rooster comb fill up with angry, then he peck the buried rooster's eyes out. She cuts that comb full to burstin' with angry off and hangs it in a frog-leather pouch between her titties. Next day she pass Lucien Beaucoup on the lane, says, 'Mornin', Mr. Beaucoup,' all honey-voiced and cow-eyed, but he pay her no mind 'cause she's ugly as warts on a dog. After he pass she write his name in the dirt and spit on it and circle it nine times walkin' backwards, holdin' on to that cockscomb. Next morning she see him on the path, she don't say a word but he fall like a shot bird right down into her arms. Charm had *worked.* That moment I broke from the fever, sweat gone *cold* on my body, and I sensed I'd lost him forever. I set up a wail then, my sisters say it chilled the blood and sent the hound runnin' under the house to hide. Done pulled the heart right outa me."

There is a long silence. LaTonya is unsettled by the passion of Jasmine's telling, her hands frozen over her tiny pile of crawfish.

Pearl notices. "Can't 'spect you to keep up with the rest of us," she says gently, "but you got to *try*."

"Sorry." LaTonya plunges her hands back in.

"It's just Antoine, he sees six women in here, he dump six women worth of mudbugs on the table."

Landry, the day cook, comes in then to shovel up the tail meat they've peeled and take it back to the kitchen. Landry reports on what people are eating.

"Boudin's not moving," he says. "Dirty rice just sittin' there. They all went for the blackened fish." He makes a disgusted face. "Must be from out of state."

The women hold to their rhythm when he's gone. LaTonya's heart always sinks a little when she sees her morning's work disappear as if it never existed. It's fifteen minutes before Vinie speaks.

"He just give up on you," she says simply.

Jasmine frowns. "Somebody talkin'?"

"He got tired of sittin' outside your window all night, waitin' for you to decide. He went to find him a live woman."

"I feel a bad wind, like somebody *talkin'*."

The two women keep their eyes on the table, fingers flying.

"Got tired of you protectin what didn't nobody else *want*. Give it up for a bad idea."

Jasmine slaps down wet tail meat. "How you know that?"

"'Cause Lucien *told* me, is how! I live with the man fifty years, you don't think he *talk* to me?"

LaTonya has never heard Vinie raise her voice before. The two women lock eyes across the table for a moment, then look away.

Jasmine mutters, just loud enough for the others to hear, "My mama's day they'd have hung you for a witch."

Vinie works this in her head a moment, frowning, building an answer. She doesn't get to say it.

The first thing Li shouts is more like an animal cry than language. The rest, as it comes out, is loud and passionate and singsong, harsh and deep one moment, climbing to an airy whine the next, Li looking to each of them for confirmation as she rails. LaTonya sits staring next to her, pummeled by the sounds, feeling loss and betrayal and deep anger behind them. Li's neck is taut, face darkening, her wiry body straining to wrench the words out. She holds a crawfish tight in her fist, crushing it as she pounds the table for emphasis.

She doesn't stop so much as run out of breath. The storm is over as suddenly as it began, and Li sits looking into the center of the crawfish pile. Big Antoine pokes his head in.

"Something the matter, ladies?"

"Not a thing, Antoine."

He nods at Li. "She's not peelin."

"She does 'em faster than us," says Pearl. "Ever little bit she's got to stop and let all us catch up."

Antoine shrugs. "Long as that meat keep coming." He wipes his face with the towel and goes back out.

"She does that sometimes," Pearl tells LaTonya. "No saying what sets her off."

"She had a hard life, *la pauvre*," says Ophelia. "You can see it in her face."

The older women sigh.

"Gonna rain."

"Feel it in my knees."

"Feel it in my ankles."

LaTonya watches Li's hands as they slowly come to life, ripping heads, peeling. "What happened to the old man?" she asks.

"Old man?"

"Old man. Buster Petite."

"He *drownded*, girl," says Vinie. "What you think? That were the flood of 'thirty-five, couldn't no old man in a rockin' chair sit through that."

LaTonya nods. "Your mother must have been relieved."

"*Relieved?* Child, you ever seen someplace after the floodwaters run off? She had to *clean* that house. Only thing made her happy in the whole business was when the water got up under the attic window and she throw Buster Petite's cats out, one by one, and watch 'em float away. I helped her catch them. Cats near clawed my mam to death."

"Some folks say," says Jasmine, "whoever kill a cat gonna hear it wailin' every night the rest of their life."

Vinie glances up at her. "I sleep fine," she says. "Sleep like the *dead*."

Toward quitting time, LaTonya's thumb splits open.

"Damn," she says.

"No cursing," says Jasmine.

Pearl puts the Band-Aid on it. "You just sit it out till five, darlin'," she says. "We give Antoine plenty crawfish today."

"I'm not pulling my weight."

"You got plenty years to run past us."

"Not if I can help it."

"Might be you *can't* help it," says Vinie. "Don't want you thinking that way, but it might be an actual fact. I been here some twenty-five years."

"*Vingt-trois, moi.*"

"Me too."

"I went to school," LaTonya protests.

The older women smile.

"Well, child, I guess you got no problem."

When the women get up to wash their hands and gather their things Li sits, staring at the remaining crawfish. Ophelia touches her shoulder.

"*Viens avec nous, mon ti,*" she says. "Whatever it is weighin' on you, it's all in your head now."

But Li is still there when the night women come in to take their places, peeling.

Keeping Time

THE OWNER ISN'T AROUND SO there is only an old man to help Mike with his kit. Each time Mike hands him another case from the van he examines it, then nods and goes 'Uh-huh' as if he's taking inventory. The old man is lanky, with maple-colored skin and eyes huge and soft behind thick lenses.

"Got to deal with the mess," he says, when it's all inside, and leaves Mike to set up alone.

The kit is pretty simple these days. Only two rack toms, floor tom, couple cymbals, the bass he just bought, and the snare he's had forever. Mike looks to the back of the room where the old man is cleaning. The distance throws his time off, a gap between the push of the broom and the sweeping sound. Mike tightens the head on the snare. Need the firepower.

It is a club he hasn't played before, though *club* is an exaggeration. A former grange hall with a makeshift bar, plywood sheet laid on shipping pallets for a stage. The stage is against the wall, which is better acoustics and always makes Mike feel more secure. The time outdoors in the storm with Blood Source, when he tumbled back into the ooze below the bandstand, neither the players in front or the rain-soaked headbangers in the field noticed he was gone till his solo came up.

He's played worse.

If the janitor doesn't stick around for the first set he'll be the oldest person in the club. Bet on it. The last show, keeping time under the new girl's vocal and looking out at the children in their torn clothes, washed in the red light, it sat on him hard.

The time he was keeping brought a picture to him, like it always did. This time he was breaking rocks on a chain gang, not a soulful, swinging Sam Cooke kind of scene but something nasty and tired where each heavy-armed chop was another day off his life. It sat on him hard and heavy and he looked out at the kids in the red light and thought "Am I boring *them* or are they boring *me.*"

"Man, you were *buried* in that groove tonight!" Joey said at the motel later. "Thought we'd have to call nine-one-one."

And later still, the phone call to his kid on the Coast, the long stretches of dead air between them that Mike wanted to fill with drumming, screaming, something. 'If it's too loud, you're too old,' said the kid at the mixer board who'd kept creeping the volume up all night.

There was a time he'd be wired already, adrenaline pumping, just setting the kit up. Attack mode. Showtime. Standing on the edge, waiting for the music to give him a nudge.

Mike's hands lie palm down on his thighs, dead meat.

The janitor comes up with a full dustpan to dump in a cardboard box next to the stage. He smiles at Mike. "Mr. Time," he says, eyes flicking over the pieces of the drum kit. "Mr. *Rhy*thm."

The old man chuckles to himself as he turns back to his work. Mike sighs and sits into the kit, rolling the sticks around his fingers to limber up. There was no time to practice before the gig last night or the night before. It seems pointless sometimes, a drummer with half his chops could sit in on most of the songs and nobody would notice, but by now it's a habit. Mike starts with simple paradiddles, bringing the tempo up very slowly, and the old familiar picture comes– knuckles taped, stroking the speed bag at some dingy boxers' gym– *pa*-pa-pa-pa *pa*-pa-pa-pa *pa*-pa-pa-pa

Easy combinations, barely breaking a sweat. His right foot starts to work the bass drum in—*boomp*—like a solid shot to the body. Then he's up on the ride cymbal-doing little featherweight dance moves.

Cheechee-chacha-cheechee-chacha-cheechee-chacha-cheechee—jumping rope cross-handed, starting to feel better in a mindless way, approaching a groove, and the few times the old man comes up looking like he's going to throw down some story about his lumbago Mike drives him away with power fills, punishing the crash cymbals with a knockout flurry till the janitor is back across the room. Back to the basics, then, but faster.

Faster.

Faster.

(Warp speed on the snare, the sound pulsing as the single chops roll together, cymbals giving it some outline, bridges cracking before a flood.)

When he was a kid Mike practiced on pillows. It would bug his parents without giving them the noise to protest and built up his wrists and hands, so that when he got on real heads they just *flew*. There was a kid down the street whose father bought a new car every three years and the kid had a Slingerland set in his garage that he never used because he was time-deaf. Mike worked hard keeping on the kid's good side and maybe once a week he'd get to pull the garage door down and go at it. The drums had been in his head since he was eight and he'd keep time with his hands on the back of the seat in the old Dodge till his father noticed and wrenched the dial from Duane Eddy to Perry Como. By the time he was thirteen he was sneaking off to play with older kids in a band called the Squires, getting to show off on *Telstar*, which they used as their theme song. They only knew six or seven songs but played them at great length and great volume and it was *thrilling*.

Mike is sailing somewhere over a hundred-twenty beats a minute, working the whole kit, when he realizes one of the toms is flat and he has to stop. The old man is there in a moment, the same little smile fixed on his face.

"What you call your band?"

"You never heard of it."

"Maybe I have." It is a sweet smile but it feels like he's looking for an opening. Mike hits the tom, listening.

"Orpheus Descending," he says.

The old man shakes his head. "Never heard of it."

"We're new."

The old man nods. "How bout you? You aint so new. Know your way around them drums, too. Spect you been with somebody else I might know."

"The Squires," says Mike, adjusting the head. He notices that the old man's fingers on both hands are curled with arthritis. "The Mudhens, Blood Source, the Krypton Kowboys, Natty Weasel, Zenophobe, Cheese in the Mail, Junior Birdmen, Bonesteel, Dislexia, G-Force—"

The old man looks at him without expression.

"I spent fifteen years in something called Faith. Fella named Jay Kelly put it together," says Mike, feeling grumpy.

"Never heard of them neither," says the old man. "Somewheres you learned to play, though."

Mike takes it as a compliment and lays down the intro to "Paint it Black." Everything is in tune. Mike goes back to his chopbuilders, running off five-stroke rolls and trying to ignore the old black man staring at him with magnified eyes.

Faith was the one that broke his heart. They started out doing covers, all of them just kids, but Jay could write and sing a bit and they all could play and the music was just exploding in so many directions and there was always a gig someplace. Jay called it hillbilly funk but it was really a little bit of everything, which was one of the reasons the record companies nibbled but never bit.

"Eclectic," the A and R guy would say. "You people figure out what you're doing, let me know."

"We're playing music," Jay would say. Jay was born with a chip on his shoulder and liked to insult record brass. "When you feel like recording some, let *us* know."

They had an old school bus painted like a gila monster that the bass player, Elsewhere Evans, would drive from gig to gig, wearing a leather fringe vest and a Ralph Kramden hat. He was the only one of them not doing serious drugs, pulling numbers on stage that left Jay shaking his head.

'The laws of gravity do not *apply*,' Jay would say and Elsewhere would give that big-eyed look like he just realized there were other people on the planet. They always left time for at least one state police pullover on the way.

They built up a bit of a following, sharing bills with groups that got contracts, got famous, crashed and burned. But Faith stayed where it was, playing clubs and small auditoriums, getting tighter, always talking about producing their own album when they saved enough money. They came very close.

Girlfriends came and went. People in other groups started to cover some of Jay's stuff in their live acts. They played Germany for six months and everyone got the flu. They came back and nothing had changed.

"We play music," Jay would tell them, at the end of one of their long bus-ride debates. "That's what we *do*. The other stuff, recording, being on a fucking TV show, whatever, that's something else. It's advertising." He made the word sound like an unnatural sex act. "You want that, there's other bands."

There wasn't too much to think about, really, no reason to keep track of passing time. Mike was making a living playing the drums, travelling and sleeping late and getting high and getting it on with pretty girls and hooked deep into the music, cutting time into whatever pieces he wanted and jolting them back through the people in the room and it was thrilling with a regularity that made him understand the junkies he'd meet on the road, thrilling in a way the hawks from the record labels and the session geeks could never fathom.

But they all hung on Jay like children to a moody father– loving him and resenting him like children, giggling behind his back but following blindly. Jay booked the gigs, Jay held the money, Jay wrote the songs, and in the last years, Jay drank himself to sleep most nights. When Roach was facing serious time in Louisiana, Jay sold his publishing rights to pay for the lawyer. They had a killer demo of "Heart of the Eagle" but then a British group covered it and went to Number Five and that was gone for them. Jay turned yellow, his liver shot, and he started with the delusions. People were following them everywhere, mysterious people out to steal the music from him.

"We travel in a bus painted like a gila monster," Mike pointed out. "Makes an easy target to follow."

"They're in my *head*," said Jay, humorless. "They're stealing it straight from my *head*."

They sold the bus to a day-care center in Arkansas to pay for his funeral.

Losing Faith seemed like a relief at first, but nothing replaced it. Eleven bands in seven years since then, and each time out he had to work a little harder to find the thrill. Sometimes he'd connect with a song, start to feel it deep again and realize he'd been in a fugue for weeks, playing on automatic pilot, just getting through the night.

Mike launches an assault on the snare and cymbals, sweating now, grinding his teeth, ending with a vicious chop to the crash. He lays the sticks across his lap, the sound still ringing out onto the corners of the room.

A pair of bartenders are puttering behind the counter now. Neither looks old enough to drink. The janitor stands watching Mike for a long moment, silent, seeming to sense his mood and waiting till it settles.

"I used to be Guitar Slim," he says finally. "One of the o*ri*ginal Guitar Slims."

Mike lets the statement hang. The old man pronounces *guitar* like *sitar* and holds up his bony claws. "Wouldn't think it to look now, would you? These fingers could *sing*."

"It's nice," says Mike, "that you been able to stay in the music business."

The old man winks behind his thick lenses, then sits at the edge of the stage facing away from him.

"What you call a drummer that break up with his girlfriend?" he asks.

"I don't know."

"Homeless."

Chok. Mike hits a rim shot, smiles.

"I wasn't but a boy when I started," says the janitor. "Caught the tail end of the swing bands. They stuck me off to the side on a little stool. Horn player was the *man* then, Louis Armstrong, Harry James—got all the girls hangin' on 'em. I'm hooked in, even get a little solo now and then, but it's a Charlie Christian kind of thing, you know. Po*lite*. I come into my own with the jump bands—Wynonie Harris, Louis Jordan. That was *fun*."

As the old man talks Mike lifts the sticks and sets them to a light little shuffle, soft on the hi-hat. He sees tap dancers, two stringbeans marking time up on their toes, twin-looking guys with million-dollar smiles that flash steady all through their number, sixty-four, count-em, sixty-four teeth—making it look easy.

"I'm still off to the side, see, but I get to shout in on the chorus and you're more part of the *story*, right? Bouncy. They had me hooked up to a little amp but I'm all bouncy and clean on it, nothing heavy, you bend a note and that bandleader—Kirby Wentwood was our man, flipped his hair around like Cab Calloway—he be on your *case*. And then, I can't recall just when, it turned into something else. I believe I was in New *Aw*lins."

Mike leans on the bass and snare, rattling off press rolls, pounding the second four hard—

"That's right," says the old man, nodding his head in time, "New Awlins. Always something cooking down there. I hooked up with a bunch called Maurice and the Moonbeams. Maurice played boogie woogie piano– folks was calling it *rock and roll*."

Mike gets onto a backbeat, playing soft and steady the way he does under the vocals, stamping out lengths of time.

"Now the guitar is still second fiddle, so to speak, and I been holdin' it in for *years*. I come up in East Texas, see, and those old men play some gutbucket there, that's what I come up hearin. Their guitar is up front, bottle-neckin', moanin', and wailin'—but that's all *blues*, which is considered Uncle Remus music by the youngbloods. So I'm playing my ax with T-Bone Walker in my head and lead on my fingers, sittin' on it, holdin it back like a jockey that got a bet on a different horse."

The old man lays his twisted hands on his knees as he talks. Mike plays even softer.

"Them early days, doing bars about the South, it was Maurice on his piano and the sax man that got to wail. Sax man was an older gentleman, name of Carlyle. I mean old. Man claim he heard Buddy Bolden play when he was a boy. And he was *fat*, Carlyle. He could blow, too, but in them days the habit was your sax man got up on the bar counter and walked while he wailed. Wasn't no bar owner lettin' Fat Carlyle get up and bust his wood, so what he'd do for solos was lie on his back and kick his legs up in the air and *honk*. Carlyle could get 'em goin', too, people dancing, going crazy while he's on his back and Maurice is standing up slamming them eighty-eights, the bass player—this is upright days—he's tipped his bass on its side and he's standing on it slappin notes and the drummer is hacking away and here's me in the corner piddlin' my little chord changes, trying to stay out of the *way*."

Mike does a series of fills, crossing hands, hitting everything in sight. The old man waits him out.

"Uh-huh," he says, when Mike eases back into his groove, "it was *rockin'*. But most nights I felt like I was listening instead of playing. Then this one gig we got . . . where was it?"

The old man closes his eyes, trying to remember.

"Alligator, Mississippi," says Mike.

"That's right," says the old man. "Miz-*sip*pi. Carlyle gets down on his back for this number we took off on and he plays his ass off, them fat old legs kicking up in the air, but when it's done he don't get *up*. He *can't* get up. Man lies there on the floor for the rest of the set, even plays the change-of-pace solo on "Deep Purple" flat on his back. Set ends and it take three of us to get the man up and into a chair. "Boys," he says, "I think I popped my string."

"Well Carlyle is *out*, he layin' in traction like a whale up on a beach but we got to keep giggin'. Some of these old boys owned bars in them days if you don't show they come after you with *heat*. Next night we're in some other place, some other town, and we come to that number and there's no sax, right? There's no Carlyle. And that's when I step forward."

Mike drops everything but the bass drum, hitting solid fours with his foot. He sees the club. The patrons and players are separated only by cigarette smoke and there's beer on the floor and a ceiling fan blowing pest strips and people are ready to bust through, booze and frustration and Saturday-night longing bright in their eyes and this skinny maple-colored kid steps up with wires bolted to his guitar and a tiny box of an amp on a chair.

"I played what the sax man played," says the old man. "Only I played it on my guitar. There was a *hole*, see, and I had to fill it. I'm slidin' the notes, bendin' 'em around, playing blues riffs and harmonica runs and Sunday preacher hallelujahs and it's all squawkin' out that box of mine and it's starting to distort—but in the *mood* right?—and I can feel the people are with me. I can't *see* 'em, 'cause my eyes was already poor and I don't have my glasses on and it's smoky, but I can feel the floor bouncing and people shouting and Maurice he's laughing over at his piano and I go till I burn that amp *down*. Maurice takes over then, banging keys with his forehead and elbows and I step back into the smoke with my ax and I'm drippin' sweat and my whole body is shaking like my heart is still wired to that guitar. I'd been floatin' in the womb for eight–nine years and that night I was *born*."

The old man turns so Mike can see his face.

"You dig what I'm saying, right?"

Mike nods. He's broken a sweat himself now, and his palms are starting to tingle the way they're supposed to.

"After the gig, guy come up and says 'Young man, you play just like Guitar Slim.'"

Jay had a tape of Slim, singing "The Things I Used to Do," and they'd listen to it in the bus at night. Highway pictures—headlights swallowing white line, lonely road opening up before them.

"I hadn't heard of the man. Them days it was all new, there wasn't this music television. Rock and roll was outlaw music– you had to go *find* it. This man works for a fella who owns clubs back in Texas and he says how Guitar Slim got him a number everybody wants to hear, got a new way of playing, and there's only one of him and lots of folks got money they'll lay down to see him. There was maybe a half-dozen fellas out on the road being Slim already, and this club owner wanted me to open up a new territory."

Mike treads water, dragging on the cymbals.

"Maurice told me, 'Son, you got a shot at some serious coin, you *jump* at it.' Maurice never had no head for business, he's just playing along, you know, 'cause it was fun and he met lots of women. That man went to women like a dog for gravy."

"So I hit the road in East Texas as Guitar Slim. Had a couple fellas behind me, they could play some, and we did a good show for the people. Some of them Slims couldn't play and they wouldn't last a night, and some wasn't so *Slim*, see, and maybe they had a little bit of a following under they own name and they be found out, but if they could *wail* with that guitar people would forgive 'em. I had Slim's number down cold and folks say I even looked like him, though I never met the gentleman. Man took sick and died young.

"Once I got past the Slim part of the set that stage was *mine*. I had all these ideas and feelin's to work out, and the people was with me, and the music, Lord, it just *carried* me in them days. Sometimes people would get so het up, they'd lift me on their shoulders and pass me around, I be playing on my back floatin' across the room on a sea of hands and some-times they bring me out onto the street in them dusty little towns and I'd play out there. Had to keep making the cord to my amp longer."

"The things used to do," Mike sings softly, *"I can't do them things no more."*

"Guitar Slim days," says the old man, smiling. "That was some ride."

"They ever find you out?"

"One night in Corpus. Some fellas bring they grandfather up to me in between sets, man is six years older than *dirt*. He look me up close with his old yellow eyes, poke his boney finger into my chest, and says 'You is a *lie*, boy. I known Slim since he's drinkin' Mama's milk and you ain't *him*.'

"I had me some attitude 'cause of how well the music was going, so I just look at him steady and say 'That's *Delta* Guitar Slim you talkin' about. I'm *Tex*as Guitar Slim.'

"Old man give me one of them nasty Methusalah looks and humphs and says 'Well long as we got that *straight*, boy,' and his grandsons ease him away. Man, I played my country ass *off* that night. I out*Slim*med myself. People dancin' on they chairs, out in the street, pretty women sweatin' all through their dresses and I'm chasin' the music in *deep*, digging down into it, gettin' hold of them blues notes and turnin' 'em every way but *loose*."

Mike sits back against the wall and starts to play on his thighs. Something is working in his wrists now but he doesn't want to drown the old man out. Over the years he's felt the music move down from his head to his hands and feet, first as if the muscles were remembering, then as if they were doing the thinking, making the music happen on their own.

"That easy money come when you're a young one, you just pour it away like water. All of a sudden I was *somebody*, see. Before, the fellas in the band would have all those names for me– 'Four Eyes,' 'Perfessor,' or else 'that big-eyed boy with the guitar.' But now I was Guitar Slim, I was the man they come to *see* and I was growin' up and runnin' wild at the same time. Good part of a year I carried that man's name, and I like to think I done my best for it."

Mike rocks as he plays, hands to sticks to thighs and back in a closed circuit, "How'd it end?"

The old man shrugs. "Something new come along, how it always does."

The old man is silent for a long time, looking down at his hands. Mike goes back up on the skins, as light as he can play. There have been flashes with this new band, and sometimes he thinks it's really going to happen. Joey can write and play lead and occasionally his music is surprising, but he can barely shout on key. Lenny, his asshole buddy from grade school, is a butcher on the keyboards but Joey won't cut him loose, the bass player is solid on his six-string, chasing Lenny off his line, and now Joey's gone and hired this girl, Deathstar, who dresses like the women in the X-Force comics and wears five-inch nails with black polish. Her voice is on the rough side of Melissa Etheridge, heading fast for Tom Waits-ville. Every band he's been with that hired a girl singer has self-destructed within months. Somebody starts fucking somebody or stops fucking somebody or else she starts getting noticed and suddenly you're her boys and the whole thing starts to suck. It happens even with the nice ones. At the moment there's a tension between her and Joey that's good for the music and Mike doesn't mind being the scoutmaster too much. They're kids and have no sense of time.

When he met Joey they'd just lost their drummer, a tubercular-looking kid who played with his shirt off and chased after the groove without ever catching it. His mother made him quit.

"Be nice to have an older guy sit in," said Joey. "Keep us in line."

Now when one of them gets lost or is off to the races Mike will go find him, drumming louder and rock steady, reeling him back. Now and then there's a tempo battle but Mike can always win, taking off and leaving them behind. You want to play fast? You don't have the chops. Lenny will try to hang with him for a while but Joey gets it and just stops playing, letting Mike kick it out and then dial it back down.

"Don't fuck with Mike," says Joey to the others. "Man will burn your fingers *off*."

All Deathstar ever says is that he plays too loud when she's singing.

Mike excuses himself and goes to the pay phone. Somehow he's gotten to be the responsible one in the band and Joey sleeps all day and forgets to put in for a wake-up call.

The phone rings eight times before he picks up.

"Yo."

"It's Mike."

"Right. Mike. What time is it?"

"See that thing next to your bed with the numbers on it? That's a clock."

Mike hears the superhero say something in the background. She doesn't sound happy. He closes his eyes.

"Hey, wow, we'll be over," says Joey. "How is it?"

"Mr. Ed used to live here."

"Right."

"Where's Lenny?"

"Said he was going to the mall."

"What mall?"

"There's always a mall, man." Joey is vague when he's just awake, the way Jay used to be when he was deep into hash.

"Well the van is over here with all the stuff. All you have to do is show up."

"Haven't missed one yet."

When Mike gets back to his kit the old man starts in like he never left.

"Got into a jazz thing next."

"Uh-huh."

"Played behind Purvis Lee."

"Don't think I know him."

The old man smiles. "Yeah, Purvis done his best to stay out of the light."

Mike starts to three-quarter the beat, wandering dreamily across the bar, setting up a loose dialogue between the snare and the cymbal.

"We're playin' cool jazz in the Deep South, which means we splittin' hot dogs four ways. Purvis Lee Quartet, and I got all the rope I need to hang myself. Purvis can deal with anywhere I want to go with my guitar, long as it's laid back and—you know—*cool.* Didn't like to hear the same thing twice. Caught the drummer practicing once, like you doing? Says, 'Man, you work your shit out on *stage,* that's what I'm payin' you for.' Drummer say 'Payin' me? Since when you call this chump change *pay?*' You don't want to fool with no drummer. You ever hear 'bout some musician put his hand to murder, nine times out of ten it's the drummer did it."

"If I wasn't a drummer," says Mike, deadpan, "I'd be a serial killer."

"How you know when the bandstand is level?" asks the old man.

"How?"

"The drummer dribbles out of *both* sides of his mouth."

Chok. Booom.

The old man rubs his legs with the heels of his hands. "Played with Purvis six months, had six different drummers. Hard man to please. Didn't like audiences neither. He had me around to play guitar whilst he put his horn down and go look ugly at the payin' customers. If there was white folks out there it put him in a terrible mood. 'This is *our* music,' he'd say. 'What they hangin' around for?' "

Mike smiles and closes his eyes, playing "Take Five." The music teacher at his high school lectured them on how jazz was real music and rock was just noise. The JDs would make fart sounds and he'd say 'See? Just *noise.*'

"First it was *our* music, then it was *my* music, like he owned the whole thing. Finally he got into some kind of Buddha thing, start off the set with this chant he done—'Hiya, hiya, hiya, nyang, nyong, nyang'—like them bald fellas in the robes on the corner? Got to be too much for me."

"You don't own music," says Mike. "You just get to ride it for a while."

The old man nods. "You ever see pictures?"

Mike lays his sticks on the snare.

"Pictures?"

"Like while you're playing."

"Yeah," says Mike. "All the time. Some of em come back a lot and others might just show up once."

The old man stands up and stretches. "There was a long piece Purvis would get into—Lord, whatever else about the man, he could *play.* Blow his soul out through that horn. This piece was kind of classical sounding, elegant, and I'd kick back while he's off on it and I always got this picture– slave days, early slave days, and we're in some rich white folks' house and they got a grand *piano.* French lookin' people, use it to play minuets and whatnot, so it's probly New Awlins. Always somethin' cookin' in New Awlins. And there's this boy, house servant, all dressed up in his servant vines only he's *bare*foot, right? Not the way it would be maybe but how it always showed in my *pic*ture. Every time he passes that piano he gives it a look. His people was musical, had all kinds of pretty African instruments, but not like this white folks' machine. All that gleaming wood, them ivory keys.

"He's a little scared to go near, 'cause the white folks own it. He seen what they do with it. Anyhow, in my picture, one day this boy look around to see that nobody is about and he sits on the bench. Little bit of a thrill just to do that. Spreads his fingers and lays them out on the *keys.* Feels a buzz coming up through his fingertips. He starts high and goes low, hittin' every one of them ivories, black and white, and when he gets to the end he *knows*, see. Boy has all this music inside of him and he looks at that piano and thinks Lord amighty I could do some *damage* with this."

A kid in his early thirties wearing an expensive jacket and jeans strolls in like he owns the place. The old man is suddenly across the room, puttering with the broom in his claws. The kid doesn't seem to notice him, and comes up to Mike.

"You Joey?"

"Mike. Joey's on his way."

The kid nods, indicates the room. "How you like it?"

"Tough to say till I hear the sound system."

"I got tired of law," says the kid. "Me and a buddy went in on it."

Mike picks up his sticks and starts to mark time with rim shots. "Can always use another place to play."

"These kids got shit for ears," says the owner. "If you haven't been on MTV for*get* it."

"We haven't been on MTV."

"You the one was with the Steve Miller Band?"

"Jay Kelly."

"J. Geils?"

"Kelly. The band was called Faith."

"Oh." Disappointed. "Who else were you with?"

Mike tries to gauge the owner's exact age. "Natty Weasel."

The owner grins. "*Reggae*. Right. No problem, mon. You opened for Third World."

"UB 40."

The owner winks, raps his knuckle on one of the toms. "We open in fifteen, get some college kids tonight. You sure your people are gonna show?"

"Always have before."

The kid nods, chewing his lip. "How about VH-1? They put the older groups on that."

"We haven't recorded yet."

"Oh. Well, the guy who recommended you saw you somewhere, said you were good."

Mike starts in with the paradiddles again, tattooing the snare.

"You get some people in here," he says, looking away languidly as his sticks bite into the kit, "and we'll wipe the floor with them."

When the owner goes into his office the old man returns. "I owned a club once," he says.

Mike eases off.

"I didn't really *own* it so much as it was in my *name*. Money man had him a prison record, couldn't get a liquor license. The Jack of Spades, over in San Antone. Music every night, pour you an honest glass of scotch. Made us up a house band, I fronted them for twenty years. The Extrordinaires."

"Twenty years."

"That's right. Till I started having problems with my fingers."

Mike is feeling better. MTV my ass. He looks to the rear door, wishing the others were there. He wants to play. He wants to take the college kids who are beginning to trickle in and nail them to the wall, wants to see what Joey and Deathstar will be up to tonight, wants to whip that sorry keyboard player's act into some disciplined time. He plays simple straight eights, slamming the back beat home. If I keep playing this long enough, the thinks, people will come with guitars and some rock and roll will happen.

Sure enough, Joey and the bass player, Kevin, wander in past the old man as if he's not there and set up their amps. They never talk much before a show, some kind of pregame jitters keeping them inside themselves. Mike keeps pumping.

The old man is up on the stage now, watching the room.

"You got children?" he asks, raising his voice a notch.

"Got a son," says Mike. "In high school. Wants to be a rapper."

"I got five by my proper wife. Then there's one I don't know much about."

Kevin has his bass plugged in and lays down a chugging line under Mike's beat. The college kids chat, yell hellos to each other. Beer circulates in pitchers.

"This gal I met early on when I was Guitar Slim," says the old man.

"We had us a night. Set her rockin' from the stage and rode it all the way to her bedroom. Indian-looking gal, brown skin and straight hair."

BWARANGGGGGGGG!

Joey hits a chord and there is a shriek of feedback. He monkeys with his amp.

"Near the end of my run, I'm back in the same town and there she is, got a biscuit in the oven.

"'Mr. Slim,' she says, 'you gon' be a father.'

"Like I said, I had some attitude then, so I says, 'Won't be the first time,' all mannish-like and hard, even though it's not true. I wasn't ready for no gal to put salt on my tail, father or no.

"'You got a wife?' she says.

"'Two of 'em.'

'Well, you stay famous, I'm gon' bring him to see you.'"

Joey makes a little run on top of them, sustaining the high note and making it weep. Deathstar walks in wearing her Spandex rig, and the college boys perk up. She grunts to Mike, still sleepy-eyed under her thick mascara. A kid who looks like he's twelve and writes his own computer programs sits in at the tiny mixing board. Joey points to himself and jerks his thumb up, then to Mike and jerks it down. The kid starts pushing faders.

"It was a boy?"

"That's how the word come back. Never seen that gal again. Didn't go lookin' for her, neither. Be about your age now."

Mike shrugs. "The way it goes sometime."

Lenny shows up and starts booping and beeping the different settings on his keyboards, off in his own galaxy.

"Only thing trouble me now," says the old man, "is the boy don't know who his father really was. Probly got him some old-time rock and roll book, open it up, and there he see Guitar Slim, the dead and buried one. Only the man is a forgery, see, 'cause I'm his real blood."

"Probably a number of kids left behind by all those Slims running around."

"Probably is."

"You know mythology? Like Greek mythology?"

"Venus and Mars and all them?"

"Right." Mike has to speak up loud to be heard. Deathstar is clearing her throat over and over, something from the TB ward, and the others are still tuning. "You know how the big cheese, Zeus, is always changing into things to get it on with women—a bull, a swan, a shower of gold—"

Joey does a skittering little solo, notes flashing clean and fast.

"That boy's father is a power chord in the key of C."

The old man grins. "That's right," he says. "And when he come out the womb, he had STRATOCASTER stenciled on his back."

"And when he cried—"

"When he cried, he cried the blues. Made the crow weep in the cornfield."

"The music came out of your amp—"

"And went right through that gal. I was just the vessel."

"A guilty bystander."

"That music take form inside her, and it come out a child. With a song in his bones." The old man shakes his head, sighs. "Still, would of been nice to see him grow up."

The players are groping toward each other now, rallying around Mike's backbeat, and the kids are starting to look over toward the stage as if something might happen, the guys checking Deathstar out and the girls watching Joey. Mike smiles, thinking about what's coming. "No prisoners," Jay used to say every night before they kicked in. It gives him a chill to remember.

No prisoners.

The old man senses it building. He brings his gnarled fingers up to his forehead in a salute as he starts to drift from the stage.

"Mr. Rhythm," he says, almost yelling.

"Uh-huh." Mike locks eyes with the old man, holding on, close to the edge.

"Mr. Time."

"That's right."

"You do some damage with them skins, hear?"

Then Jay screams and the music carries them away.

To the Light

"THAT'S JUST THE MUCUS PLUG," Annie says to the sister. "Tell her not to worry about it."

"I don't know the word for that."

"*Tapón de moco?*"

"She doesn't speak Spanish."

Annie spent six months working at a clinic in Honduras but never learned any of the indigenous languages. People would cover their mouths and giggle whenever she'd try a phrase. Her Spanish was okay, occupational, but most local people were shy or didn't speak it, and the doctor was an old stoner from Frankfurt who quoted Mothers of Invention lyrics as he worked.

"Vat is ugliest part of your body?" he would muse while stitching up a machete cut on some expressionless campesino's hand. "Some say your nose, some say your toes—I sink it's your mind. *Ja?*"

"*Yo soy partera,*" Annie learned to begin, and immediately the women would cut her some slack, confiding things they wouldn't tell Dr. Fritz. If she'd met the girl before and there were no portentous signs, the Indian midwives might let her sit and watch the way they did it. "*Está de dar la criatura a la luz,*" they would say, just before the birth. "She's going to give the baby to the light." The phrase made her imagine the baby's first impression as something warm and fleshy, like a candle flame seen through the webbing of your fingers.

This girl, the mother, is small and copper-colored and has a broad Indio face. She is scared tight, balled up against the wall on a steel cot in a barrackslike room with a half-dozen other beds evenly spaced. Underneath the beds are cardboard boxes filled with personal belongings and suitcases closed with duct tape and polished Sunday shoes, the walls above them busy with pinups and family photos and various saints being mortally afflicted. The girl has on only a checked red shirt, her stained underwear and sweatpants tossed on the floor. She tries to cover herself with her hands but can't reach all the way around her belly.

"Can you ask her how close together the pains are?"

"She says she has them one after the other."

"Very close together?"

"Yes."

It isn't a good setup. No medical history, no hospital backup, a first-time mother who can't communicate, water already broken well before Annie got there, stranded out in the middle of nowhere. Annie tries to pump a little confidence into her smile, patting the girl, the mother, on the leg. She's not comfortable being touched.

"Tell her I'm going to look now. To see if the baby is coming."

The girl moans through tight lips, watches with a trapped-animal look in her eyes as Annie positions her legs and feels on the outside for a shape. It's low, very low— she hopes the hard mass up top isn't the head. The last thing we need.

"Have her relax as much as she can."

At least the sister, the boyfriend's little sister, doesn't seem too freaked by the whole thing. She wears glasses that she adjusts by squinching her nose and leans close to see when Annie does something, like she's watching a science experiment at school. Junior high? It's tough to say for sure, they're so little and they mature so early. The boyfriend out on the porch looks barely old enough to drive, but he navigated the country roads at breakneck speed without putting them in a ditch.

Annie spreads her fingers to gauge it. Eight, possibly nine centimeters. Nearly wide open.

"Damn."

"Something wrong?"

"No, it's fine, it's fine. I was just hoping we could get her to a hospital first."

The membrane of the cervix has thinned out, the body fully engaged in the pelvis. Ready to pop. Annie touches the bit that is starting to push through. It isn't the head.

The mother says something in a panicky voice. The sister answers back.

"What?"

"She's afraid she's gonna explode."

Annie chooses her words carefully. "Tell her nobody has ever exploded. But if she wants to help the baby she's going to have to push now, not try to keep it in."

The boyfriend's sister translates. Annie looks to the few instruments laid out on the sterile sheet from the kit. If the head was presenting she could stall a bit, give her a gulp of tequila, and hope the ambulance got there quick. No such luck.

She hadn't even wanted coffee. Driving up to join Thomas at the cabin, needing to talk to him about the article, her heart still racing. She had to get off the road, and there was the diner she'd passed by for years and never gone in, pickups and battered station wagons out front, SE HABLA ESPAÑOL sign in the window. Just sit and stop shaking and try not to think about what she'd read.

Annie scoops a gob of lubricant onto her finger, picks up the plastic bottle.

"I'm going to do something to make her poop."

The sister giggles. She has dimples and a nose that starts high on her forehead, wears a windbreaker with the Nike logo on the breast pocket, and has her bangs moussed up into a claw in front. Totally Americanized and too cool for her own good, like a thousand others Annie has seen hanging at the mall in front of Everything for a Buck.

"We're going to need all the room we can get. Grab a sheet, something that doesn't look too gross."

Annie helps the girl onto her side and eases the tip of the bottle in, squeezes gently. She makes a fist, hoping the girl understands.

"Hold it in a sec. Hold it—hold it—hold it—"

The sister comes back with a threadbare sheet.

"Spread it out under there. That's it. Now"—she looks to the girl and opens her fist—"let it go."

The sister repeats, and the girl lets go.

"Good. Very good. Now you—Zora?"

"Zoila."

"Zoila. Fold it, fold it—wipe there—now go throw it somewhere out of the way. Wash your hands and bring me some more."

"Sheets?"

"Pillowcases, towels, whatever's clean."

"This isn't our house."

"Whose is it?"

"Our uncle lives here with other men. They working now."

"We'll clean up after, don't worry. Tell her she's doing great."

Annie washes the girl with the antiseptic soap again, washes herself up to the elbows, and changes gloves. Only one pair left.

She always tries to avoid the crime stories because they get her so upset. Children killing their parents. Children killing each other. But sometimes she can't help herself and Thomas makes fun of her.

"There's an experiment they do at Yerkes with baby chimps," he told her one time. "You get a bunch of them in a cage, then you throw in a sack of rubber snakes."

"Rubber snakes?"

"Chimps are hardwired to freak if they see a snake, even a rubber one. But they're also hardwired to be curious. So they open the sack right away and totally flip– hair standing on end, shrieking, showing their gums—"

"Like you at the cabin when the shower goes cold."

"I don't shriek, I cry out in anguish. Anyhow, they throw the sack in a corner, stomp on it a few times, and for five or ten minutes they're whimpering, hugging each other—classic post-trauma behavior. But before you know it, they're back at that sack, opening it up for one more peek, like kids watching a horror movie through their fingers."

"You're saying I'm hardwired."

"I'm saying you get enough drama at work. You shouldn't be looking for more in the newspaper."

It wasn't the photo—another skinny boy with his shirt off, with his tattoos and shaved head, dead-panning between a pair of Snohomish County detectives. The headline, EVERETT MAN HELD IN DOUBLE MURDER, was generic, and the text—teenager and his girlfriend found shot in her apartment, indications of drug trafficking—she usually wouldn't get to the second paragraph, the paragraph that always began with the suspect's name: "Dylan Kletter, 25, resident of Everett, was charged today with two counts of homicide in connection with the—"

She did the math. There were so many Dylans now, but what—1976? That was the year, wasn't it?

"Now," she says to the sister, "when the contractions come—you know the word for contraction? "

"What is it?" Zoila lays a pile of pillowcases on the edge of the bed.

"Like a big muscle spasm. Like—"

"It hurts and it squeezes?"

"Something like that. When those come I want her to push her stomach out, not clench it in."

The sister translates.

At first Annie thought somebody in the kitchen had cut themselves—the waiter asking if anybody was a doctor, her thinking she might have something useful in her kit in the trunk of the car. Then the boy, the father, almost mute with anxiety in front of the bubbling stock pots, the waiter saying Yes, we called the state police and the regional hospital, but couldn't you go check on her till they got there? It wasn't so far.

"*Sí*," she confessed. "*Soy partera.*"

She'd assisted Rose at least a dozen times before her first solo, mostly out at Rainbow's End before they started growing hemp and got busted and then restructured themselves as a lesbian carpentry collective. But when it came time to be the one in charge, she didn't feel ready.

"You can't learn any more just watching," said Rose. "You'll do fine."

"But this girl—her baby—"

"Keep your heart chakra open," Rose told her. "And listen to your fingers."

Annie demonstrates, placing her hands behind her thighs. "Okay, we're going to try it when the next one comes. Put your hands here."

"*Así*," says Zoila, assuming the position as well.

"Tell her to breathe slowly when it comes, but not deep. Push that stomach out and open up."

The girl grunts, clenching her eyes and mouth shut, butt muscles knotting. Sweat rolls down her temples.

"That wasn't quite what we need. Listen, are she and your brother married?"

"Not yet."

"But they want to be?"

"Yes."

"Get him in here. He needs to talk to her."

"To say what?"

"Have him tell her how much he loves her, that he wants to get married as soon as they can."

The sister just looks at her.

"I mean it. Go."

Annie had met a few of them later– children of friends who grew up in

Seattle, strangers who stopped her on the street and pushed a reluctant boy or girl forward. "Do you know who this is?" But most were just out there, doing what people do, living their lives. She'd lost exact count, but it was around three hundred.

Ruth was there for the first one. Watching, silent, letting Annie run the show. In the back of an old mail truck painted every color in the spectrum, a hippiemobile that smelled of brown rice and incense. The guy had a ponytail and kept stepping out to smoke a joint.

"Never blow weed in your own ride, man," he said. "Pigs'll sniff you out."

The boy comes in, stiff, blank-faced. He sits on the edge of the mattress. His sister speaks to him in Spanish. Annie turns her head away, and shuffles the instruments while the boy dutifully says what he says to the girl on the cot, taking her hand, barely audible. She can sense the girl loosening a bit, can sense a flow that wasn't there before.

The girl speaks to the sister.

"She asks if he can go now. It makes her embarrassed."

"He can go."

Annie has gotten used to them being there, shallow-breathing in unison, fiddling with video cameras, interjecting factoids half-remembered from their birthing classes. The girl seizes up with another contraction, crying out sharply and jerking her head from side to side. The boy hurries back out to the porch.

"Tell her to keep her eyes open, to keep her mouth open and loose, and make a sound like this." Annie chants a deep sonorous *Ommmmmmmmmm.* "Have her try one now."

The girl makes a noise.

"Looser with her mouth. She has think about opening herself, making herself as wide as she can. She has to push from here, not squeeze down there."

The girl does better with the next one, and even better with the one after that. It's a breech for sure, but at least a complete breech, the rubbery little buttocks beginning to crown. The girl isn't dilated as wide as would be nice and there's no chance of a C-section in this half-assed set-up, but things could be worse. Not much, but they could be.

The mother, the first one, was blond and pale and didn't want to push.

"It'll come out when it's ready," she whined. "We don't need to be aggressive."

Annie smiled but shook her head. "Out in Nature," she said authoritatively, "animals always push."

"Really?"

"That's what Nature wants. If you don't push we have to pull it out with forceps. Like these big salad-tong things?"

"Major bummer," said the father, who told them his name was Wasatch, though the blond girl kept calling him Brian during her contractions. "That would bite the Big One."

Annie rubs oil on the girl's perineum. "She has to be especially loose here," she tells the sister. "If it hurts a little she can't tighten up."

Annie can feel the back of the head clearly from the outside now. It's going to be about timing. Timing and luck.

"So. Zoila. You speak three languages."

"I think so." '

"English, Spanish, and—what is it?"

"Zapoteca. From my grandmother."

"You pick apples too?"

"When I'm not in school."

The girl has another contraction and Zoila, getting into it, breathes with her.

"You've seen this before."

"On television. They make more noise."

The girl pushes again, and this time a drool of thick black meconium squeezes out.

"Open the packet there—that one—and wipe that stuff off."

"What is it?"

"What newborns have for poop. Careful."

The girl contracts again. Annie pushes the head down from the top to keep it flexed. "That's it– push—push—push—"

The sister speaks along with her, leaning close to the girl's ear, cooing to her in the soft Indian language.

"That was great. Tell her she's my hero."

Zoila giggles.

"Tell her."

Zoila translates, and the girl gives Annie a shy smile through her tears. Annie props the syringe as quickly as she can. Better a cut than a tear. The sister is watching every movement.

"You giving her a shot?"

"Just a little anesthetic. I'm going to have to cut down here."

"To make her bigger."

"That's right."

"It should come with Velcro. You know that stuff—like on sneakers?"

"Velcro."

Zoila demonstrates, miming with her hands. "If we had it down there, when the baby comes you just pull it open, makes that little noise, get the baby out, then put it shut again."

"You may have something there. Tell her this will sting."

The only mother she'd ever lost had been a quick and easy delivery but then she started hemorrhaging and Dr. Chatterjee and all his arsenal of equipment at St. Alban's weren't enough to make her stop. Bonnie something. She'd been really excited because her baby was coming on Gandhi's birthday.

Annie flicks the needle in, eases the plunger.

"You live up here?"

"We come back every year."

"So you're—?"

"Illegal." Zoila shrugs. "My brother is always scared about it, but I go to school and nobody says nothing."

"It's good you keep going to school."

Zoila points to the scalpel. "You going to cut her with that?"

"When the anesthetic takes hold. Give it a chance to numb."

Zoila brightens. "Now we'll all be Americans."

"Why's that?" A half an inch, maybe a tad more. Straight down, keep the blade shallow. No big thing.

She points between the girl's legs. "'Cause it's gonna be one, and we're related."

The girl contracts, her perineum going white, Annie supporting it with her fingers.

"Not yet, not yet."

The girl seems to be past her panic now, eyes intense, focused inward. Between the contractions she whispers something to herself, rhythmic, like a prayer she knows by heart.

They had wanted to keep the placenta.

"What do you want it for?"

"We thought we'd bury it and plant a tree on top," said Wasatch.

"A peach tree." Cindy was trying to nurse her little boy but kept poking him in the eye with her hardened nipple. "So some day he can eat fruit that was fed by his own—you know—afterthing."

"Peaches don't grow up here."

"Cherries, apples, whatever."

"You have a cooler?" Rose asked them, filling out the paperwork. They'd debated about what Wasatch called "the whole labeling trip" but finally agreed to have her write in his last name. Kletter with a *K*.

"Got that old Eskimo there."

"'Cause it won't keep for long. You think this truck smells funky now—"

"Gotcha. Keep a chill on it."

• • •

Annie watches Zoila for a moment, into it now, holding the girl's hand and waiting for the next bit of action. "I'm gonna want you to put those gloves on," she tells her. "You saw how I did it before?"

"You didn't touch the outside with your fingers."

"You know what a *partera* is?"

"That's you."

"You think you'd like to be one someday?"

"How much does it pay?"

Annie laughs.

Zoila jerks her head toward the girl. "I'm never doing this, neither."

"Having a baby?"

"Some girls I know, it's all they can talk about. And look at her."

She'd stopped trying to share the pain a long time ago. Coming home after with her muscles sore, hands shaking—it didn't help. Now it was just a place they went to and she tried to slide them past it, get them not to embrace the pain but to detach from it by concentrating on other things.

"It will be over pretty soon."

"And then you have six more. You got kids, missus?"

"No."

"*Palabra?*"

"Really. I don't." People think it's strange, and she tries not to be touchy about it. The postman only delivers, she tells them sometimes. He doesn't keep the mail.

"How come?"

"Just never got around to it." She stretches the perineum tight. "So what do you think you'll do with your life?"

"You know who Christina Aguilera is?"

"*I Turn to You.*"

Zoila grins.

"Will you sing it for us?"

"You kidding me?"

"No, it will really help. Sing it like it's a lullaby."

Zoila sings. She has a pretty voice. Annie makes a quick cut, presses a sterile pad on top of it.

"Do you get your period yet?"

Zoila shakes her head no without a break in the song. Younger than I thought.

"You know what it is, though?"

Zoila nods yes.

"Ask her if she has any of the napkins you use for it." A lot of the Mexican girls, the ones from the country, won't use tampons.

"She got some in her bag out in the car."

"We're going to need them."

Zoila heads outside, singing the second verse. Annie pats the girl on the thigh.

"You're doing great."

She looks at her watch. With the breeches you want to get them out quick. She slides a finger in, finds a tiny foot, hooks it.

"Ready? Push—push—push—"

Once Thomas took her to the Institute to watch a dolphin give birth in a glass tank. It was smooth and liquid, a spurt of cloudy water, the baby with its dolphin smile already fixed as it wriggled free, and Annie unable to hold her tears.

"That's what it should be like for us," she said to Thomas. "Totally in the flow, almost weightless, just a tiny change in temperature and then the light above."

"Silhouetted with circling sharks."

"I mean it. Fighting gravity, water to air—what's that about? The pain seems so pointless."

"Bigger brain, bigger cranium. Our heads evolved faster than our pelvises. Pelves."

"You're such a geek."

The mother dolphin maneuvered under the baby and gently pushed it to the surface for a blow of air.

"No sense romanticizing the animal kingdom. Incompetent mothers, fratricide, eating their own young—"

"Stop."

"You'd never make it in a baboon troop," said Thomas, putting his arms around her. "Too much empathy."

Zoila comes back with two sanitary napkins still in their wrappers.

"Unwrap them and then put the gloves on. Things are going to start happening fast."

Annie gets the other leg out with the next push.

"*Ay, mira,*" says Zoila, seeing, "*es un macho!*"

She tells the girl, who starts to cry and smile and crane her head down to see. Annie feels the cord, gets a finger around it. A pulse. Definitely a pulse.

The article said he'd shot the teenager five times, in the living room, then kicked in the bathroom door and shot the girl, who was hiding in the tub. Once, in the mouth. The suspect's parents weren't mentioned. At the arraignment, the article said, the suspect showed no emotion.

"There's so much of that black stuff."

"It gets squeezed out."

"Will he swallow it?"

"A bit."

"*Qué asco.*" Zoila makes a face and carefully works her fingers into the first glove. "Isn't the head supposed to come out first?"

"Usually, yes. But if they really want to be with us, they find a way."

"*Venga, Manolo,*" Zoila says, to the feet sticking out. "We waiting for you."

"That's his name?"

Zoila gets the second glove on. "Uh-huh. Manuel."

The last baby she'd delivered for a migrant had been a Brittany. Brittany Ramirez. The girl pushes again. Annie places Zoila's fingers on the perineum. "Just support this, nice and easy."

"Really?"

"She won't mind. Go ahead."

Annie pulls gently on the little body, from the hips, pressing on the head from outside. The navel clears, the cord tight. Annie tries to turn the body slightly, looking for slack.

"*¡Que linda!*" exclaims Zoila. "It's all like purple and blue."

"That's the umbilical." This is where we could lose him. The cord wrapped, oxygen cut off.

"What turns into the belly button."

"Right."

"We had it in Life Science, but they only showed us drawings. My hands are getting dirty."

"That's not important now." Annie realizes she is sweating though it isn't hot in the room. The fucking ambulance is lost somewhere. She'll get an earful for leaving her mobile phone at the clinic again.

"We are no longer living in the Dark Ages," Dr. Bannerjee will sing at her. "We must embrace technology."

The girl gives an enormous grunt and pushes hard. The right shoulder slides out. The cord is loose again. Zoila talks rapidly to the girl, cheer-leading. Annie reaches under and works her finger into the baby's mouth and pulls. It's going to be really tight and the circumference is less with the chin down.

"Just a couple more now. Tell her."

Zoila translates, wiping damp hair back from the girl's face with her free hand.

"His other arm is stuck behind his head, and I have to turn him some on this push. Be ready to move your hand."

"Is he breathing in there?"

"Not yet."

"You have to spank him, huh?"

"Not unless he's bad. Ready?"

The girl cries out and lifts her hips off the mattress as she pushes. Annie pulls the arm free. Another push, veins bulging in the girl's temples, her face the color of dried blood.

"He's here!"

"Almost." Annie uses the ear syringe to suction the baby's mouth and nose, his eyes still hidden behind the cervix. "Last one, honey. We're almost there."

The baby squirts out the rest of the way, Zoila giving a little yip as she catches it.

"Careful, he's slippery."

"Oh, my God, oh, my God!"

"Get that towel around him." Annie clears the airway with the syringe, strokes the baby's spine. He starts to take color.

"Is he okay?"

Toward the end, Wasatch only paced on the outside, smoking dope and shaking his head, muttering "Gotta stay mellow, gotta stay mellow," over and over. He poked his head in for a moment just when Cindy, the mother, was screaming and blowing snot from her nose and emptying her bladder onto the Navaho blanket beneath her all at once.

"Gnarly gig, man," said Wasatch, and wandered away again.

The baby came out face up and needed a lot of starting. Annie with her mouth over his mouth and nose, blowing rhythmic puffs of air into him as Ruth massaged his legs and arms. Then Annie felt it in her fingers just like Ruth said she would, a heat, a something different starting in his chest and flowing outward, insistent new life on its way into the world.

His face wrinkled like an old monkey's when he cried. Annie was crying too, tears rolling off her nose.

"You've got yourself a little boy here."

"He's gonna be Dylan," said the mother. "For the first name? We thought that would be really cool."

The baby makes a few coughing sounds. Annie takes him from Zoila, holding him face down. He starts to cry.

"*¡Ay, qué bueno!*" cries Zoila, giggling, and starts talking rapidly with the girl. The mother.

Annie goes through the Apgar– heart rate okay, breathing deep between cries, muscles responding. Pretty damn good, considering.

"Can she hold him?"

"Down low here. There's more to come." Annie clamps off the cord, waits for it to change color. "Tell her the baby is fine."

"He really is?"

"*Palabra.*"

Annie slices the cord and checks it– three blood vessels, no problem. She has Zoila press a sterile pad to the perineal cut till she's ready with the sutures.

She needs to be with Thomas, to do the math with him. She needs his rational arguments, his icthyological metaphors. The girl in the tub, the article said, was three months pregnant.

The boyfriend sticks his head in. "*¿Llegó?*"

"*Ven a ver,*" calls Zoila proudly. "*¡Es un varón!*"

Annie turns the baby boy to put drops in his eyes. His face is still glistening with birth goo, his nose flattened, his eyes enormous black holes in the sudden light, registering shapes without names. The boyfriend is by the mother now, trying manfully not to cry, talking to her softly.

Annie moves her head close to whisper to the baby.

"Glad you could join us," she says. "Be good."

Casa de los Babys

ASUNCIÓN BREAKS YESTERDAY'S TORTILLAS into the egg she stole from work, then scrapes the coated pieces into the dented skillet. She balances the skillet over the little fire, waving smoke from her face with her free hand. The smell wakes Blanca and Eusebio, who complain of the cold like always and skitter out behind the *choza* to pee. Asunción takes the forks out of the plastic bag hung by the window and pokes another scrap of packing crate into the fire.

"We're going to sing today," says her sister, lying back on the pallet they share to pull on her uniform skirt. "All of the different classes."

"*Qué bueno.*" Asunción left school in the middle of the year she was Blanca's age, so she never got to do the singing.

"How like a bird with wings of fire," Blanca sings tentatively, but the rest of the lyrics escape her. Eusebio takes his fork and begins to eat from the skillet.

"It will be better if you wait."

Eusebio just looks at her, chewing tortilla. He never listened to Mami when she was alive, and he doesn't listen to Asunción now. He squats with his feet on a piece of cardboard covering the cold floor, his too-small shoes joined by the laces and hung over his shoulder. Blanca has orders to deliver him to his classroom so he won't go running with the ones who stay in the colonia throwing stones at dogs and breaking into houses but complains it isn't her fault if her brother is a *travieso*.

"Take care of the fire," says Asunción to her sister, before she joins the march outside, "and do your best with him."

There are dozens, then hundreds of people walking through the sandy streets of the colonia, all in the same direction, men and women joined by girls and boys just old enough to work. More than half peel off toward the *fábrica,* and a few dozen turn right to the bottling plant. Quiroga's van bumps past the ones who continue, stopping for whoever can pay ten centavos for a two-mile ride to the buses.

A girl is selling coffee and *pan dulce* from a cardboard box at the interchange. The sun is just beginning to pry the cold fog from the highway as thousands of them—chauffeurs and gardeners and waiters and maids and nannies and street vendors and security guards, the Army of the Underpaid—crowd into exhaust-belching buses with the sweet long-suffering face of poor Milagros from *En Casa Dividida* emblazoned on the side. Asunción and her *compa* Socorro turn it on in every room they are about to clean and try not to vacuum during the scenes where Don Vicente's youngest son Güero sneaks into the servants' quarters to tryst with Milagros. Asunción is squeezed far to the rear, standing over the hot engine and trying not to let the exhaust smell overwhelm her.

The bus winds down the side of the mountain into the lake of smog that covers the city. Sometimes, when she is standing near the front, Asunción can see through the tangle of tall buildings to the rolling waves of the harbor. Socorro lives by the docks and is always after her to take the van with her to the beach, but she has nothing to wear and is afraid the waves might sweep her away. The sound of them is nice, though, punctuating the long hours at work, rumbling just beneath the traffic noise from Calle 6 de Julio.

Vans and buses own the city streets at this hour, a few manic taxis careening around them, morning-weary herds of seamstresses and grill cooks and masons and carpenters and shop clerks and mechanics and laundry workers and gas station tire inflaters dispersing at each major intersection. They roll through the *mercado,* vendors just starting to set up their stalls, the driver jamming on the brakes and honking as three boys in dirty T-shirts are chased across his path by a cursing one-eyed man waving a plastic Virgin of Charity. Asunción can sit for the last twenty minutes, closing her eyes till the next-to-last stop.

"*Joven*," says the woman in her late fifties who sits across from her, touching her maid's uniform and nodding at Asunción's. "Which one do you work at?"

"Posada Santa Marta."

"Ah, la Casa de los Babys." The woman smiles. "Do the mothers leave you tips?"

"Not so many tips," says Asunción. "But if you need diapers it's a paradise."

The cars were full up so Pito had to wait till the last pass of the patrol, then sneak into the back of the mercado stalls with the Garza brothers. The ones where they sell fruit are full of flies, so they look for the stand where the old *tuerto* sells *retratos* and madonnas and paintings of Christ with glow-in-the-dark eyes. If he finds you still asleep there in the morning he chases you, but he's so slow that the only scary part is his bad eye, a bluish, filmy thing with the eyeball looking off in the wrong direction. Sometimes there is an errand to run for a vendor and some money to be made, but mostly the police come early and chase them from the mercado. You can buy a spray bottle for fifty centavos from Rufino Torres who works for Don Pardo the Trash King, but Pito only has ten so he rents one for the day from one of the older boys who says he'll break his arm if he doesn't bring it back. This morning the tuerto chases them in front of a bus that has to jam on its brakes, but they dance away from him through the traffic.

"Tuerto! Tuerto! Tuerto!" they yell at him over the whizzing cars and buses. "Go fuck yourself!"

Little Garza is whining 'cause he got a spider bite sleeping on the floor of the stall, but Big Garza tells him to shut up. They pick up rocks to throw at the dog packs, more for fun than protection though Big Garza has puncture scars where one bit his arm and wouldn't let loose. They station themselves on Independencia, where three-way traffic merges by the statue of the soldier on the horse and the signal lights are slow. A driver can have his windshield washed, see acrobats and fire-eaters perform, buy Chiclets, cookies, toys, sunglasses, newspaper, or hear complete ballads or rap songs, all before the light goes green. Women with babies strapped on work the line, peddling corn-husk dolls or religious medals, a boy in his teens walks on his hands and collects donations with his toes. Once Pito bought balloons from Rufino Torres and crammed them into the behind of his sweatpants, waggling the oversized butt at motorists in time to whatever was playing on their radios, but they like that better when little girls do it.

La Posada Santa Marta is five blocks from the embassy and two from the beach. There is a cool blue-tiled entrance from 6 de Julio to the lobby, where Señora Muñoz supervises the daily routine and reads three newspapers with a toaster-sized TV playing *novelas* on the counter beside her. The building wraps around a courtyard with a fake-marble fountain and a few small tables for breakfast and pre-dinner drinks. A cat with a damaged ear stalks the courtyard garden, prancing with moths or cicadas or the occasional small lizard in its mouth. There are three tiers of rooms with balconies overhanging, red bougainvillea draping the stucco walls and wrought-iron railing. A satellite dish tilts sunward above orange scallops of tile roof. The windows and doors are Moorish, round portals alternating with square, elegant assymetry throughout the building. On the other side of the fountain from the garden is a shallow swimming pool. A very old man and his grandson start each morning by skimming dead palm fronds and lamp-crisped insects from the surface. The water, in the hotel's shadow most of the day, is very cold.

Gustavo is on the night desk, still reading his mysteries when the first deliveries are made to the kitchen, holding his place with his finger when

Señora Muñoz relieves him so he can find it on the long bus ride home. The *recamareras*, Belkis and Ximena and Flor and little Socorro and Asunción, prep their carts in near silence. Ignacio, the breakfast and lunch cook, lays out his equipment and starts the boys cutting fruit, while Rubén sets the tables for the mothers.

There are other guests—commercial travelers, some tourists passing through to the ruins, relatives of local families around the holidays—but the mothers are always there, a constant supply of them that Señora Muñoz chooses to house on the second floor.

Skipper comes through first in her bathrobe, ordering a complicated array of juices on her way to the pool.

"Una loca," says Rubén, shaking his head as he does every morning, hearing her gasp as she enters the frigid water.

"Breaststrokes right through the ice cubes," mutters Leslie, settling in across from Gayle. "Must be the Aryan blood."

"Her people are mostly Swedish. Lutherans." Gayle smiles at Rubén. *"Buenas días, Rubén."*

"Muy buenas días, Señora." The dining room walls are busy with scenes of rural harmony– scattering chickens, barefooted harvesters, boys with big hats and small burros. Rubén, who takes the breakfast orders, wears a selection of sorbet-colored guayaberas and speaks solicitous English. "And will the ladies be taking something liquid this morning?"

"Café solo," says Leslie, rubbing her eyes. *"Muy negro, muy fuerte."* Leslie speaks fluent Spanish with a pointedly American accent, as if everything she says is in quotes.

"And why not?" says the waiter with a slight bow.

"The fruit plate *por favor?*" asks Gayle. "And a *jugo* of orange?"

"Hoo-go," says Leslie, "not Jew-go. Gimme a break here."

"You're so good at it."

"I studied it in college, you didn't."

"But you've got an ear. I just sound like some old cracker."

Gayle has been rubbed hard by life. Her eyes are ten years older than the rest of her and she thinks visibly before she speaks, voice measured and wary of passion. She lost a lot of sleep in her party years and hasn't caught up with it yet.

"Jugo de naranja, café solo, plato de frutas," says Rubén, backing away. "It will arrive suddenly."

"Look at her out there."

Sparrows flit in through windows open to the courtyard, vigilant for crumbs. There are bamboo torches and a bug zapper at night, and the fountain is turned off at ten. Only Skipper braves the pool, swimming metronomic laps, praising the lack of chlorine. The others watch her from the dining room, having discovered that sitting at the outside tables adds an hour to breakfast.

Nan's voice precedes her into the dining room.

"The children are so adorable," she is saying. "You just want to bake them some cookies and give them a bath." She strides in with Jennifer in tow. "Morning, ladies." She waves. "Our water sprite in her element?"

"Building her calorie debt."

"Wouldn't I love to have one of those." Nan sits with Jennifer at a table nearby.

"Eileen coming down?"

"We knocked," says Jennifer. "She said she wasn't hungry."

"Gal's been missing a lot of meals."

On her first day at the Posada, Eileen apologized for not sharing. Family of nine kids, she said, you had to guard your food while you ate it. When the others order a little of everything at a restaurant, Eileen gets her own entreé and focuses on it, hunching over the food till she's eaten at least half.

"She's on a budget—Eileen."

"I'll say. Woman gives two centavos to some little beggar boy, and it goes in that notebook of hers."

"Well, she doesn't bitch and moan about the prices like some people."

Nan gives Leslie a look. "Bargaining is a respected part of the culture here. If you don't complain they take advantage of you."

"It's already five times cheaper than at home—you got to knock them down even further?"

"If the offer is too small, the merchant will not accept it."

"More wisdom from the little red book." Leslie has dissed Nan's guidebook before. "What's it called again, *The Bargain-Hunter's Guide to Third-World Countries?*"

"Eileen doesn't bargain. She shops but she never buys."

"She's freaked out about how long it's been," says Leslie. "Her job."

"She's at the university."

"In clerical."

"It's still a university." Nan rarely asks a question, her voice nailing each sentence with a flat certitude sure to overwhelm the faint of opinion.

"But she's not a professor," says Leslie as her coffee arrives. Rubén lingers, always amazed to see her drink it without sugar.

"So?"

"Professors can bug off for months at a time. A sabbatical, whatever. But in clerical, she's probably losing pay."

"She said her husband's between jobs," ventures Jennifer.

"Unemployed."

"She said he's between—"

"I asked her what his next one was going to be, and she said he hadn't found one yet." Leslie's voice seems to be smiling dryly even when she's serious. "That's unemployed."

"So somebody lied for them." Nan studies the menu, though it hasn't changed since they arrived.

"Or he got laid off after the application went through," says Gayle.

Nan fixes Rubén with a look. "You suppose the fella back there could do a pair of eggs over easy? So they're not runny but they're not scabby on both sides either?"

"I will order it done."

"And bacon? Crispy so you break it, you don't tear it?"

"We will attempt to comply with this, Señora."

"And no beans on the plate."

"Fruit plate for me," says Jennifer.

"They're Catholic," says Nan, putting the menu aside. "That might make a difference here."

"If somebody stipulates the kid has to be raised Catholic, yeah."

"They can do that?"

"Why not?"

Jennifer shrugs. "You'd think, under the circumstances, they'd just be happy to—"

"Beggars can't be choosers," says Nan.

"Something like that."

Gayle turns her fruit plate so the pineapple faces her. "Maybe faith is different. They make exceptions."

"You must have told them that you'll raise yours up in your sect."

Gayle smiles sweetly at Nan. "Religion," she corrects. Gayle has the husky voice and sharp cheekbones of the recently ill and a network of broken blood vessels beneath her skin. Her hair is brownish and tortured into a wiggly perm, her skin dry and peeling from the sun. When she smiles it is heartfelt and weary, like a swimmer emerged from a long and dangerous crossing.

"And that child's parents," Nan continues, "have no say in the matter. They gave that right up when they gave up the baby. Why should Catholic have anything to do with it?"

"I bet there are nuns involved," says Leslie.

"I haven't seen any."

"There are." Gayle fishes through her handbag. "Where they keep the babies. In my Polaroid—see? That's a nun behind the woman holding Consuela."

"Awww, look at her! "

"Is that your name for her or theirs?" asks Nan.

"It's *her* name."

"That she was given—"

"By the birth mother, yes."

"Consuela."

"We plan to change ours to Henley," says Jennifer.

"Your husband's name."

"Uh-huh."

Leslie deadpans her. "So they'll call him Junior."

"Henley Junior."

"You know they can't say their *j's.*"

Jennifer has three small frown lines on her forehead, the only wrinkles on her face. "You're making fun of me."

"No, really, it's genetic."

"Don't be mean, Leslie." Gayle takes her role as peacemaker seriously. She goes to the AA meetings at the cinder-block Evangelista church near the mercado and listens to the alcoholics confess their lives in Spanish. She ignores the words and understands it all.

"It'll be 'My name is Henley Yoonyer,' " continues Leslie.

"I was more worried that the other children where we live can't pronounce *Julio.*"

"They could learn."

"I'm not interested in having our son be a test case."

Nan looks to the doorway. Nobody else is coming down. "She stopped coming to dinner, you know."

"Eileen."

"Eileen."

"Room service?" wonders Gayle.

"There's no tray outside her door in the morning. I think she just can't afford to eat."

"Well, we should treat her, then." Every night Gayle lays her own currency out on the bed and counts it, does the conversion, calculates how many more days she can hold out.

"Gayle's right," says Jennifer. "We should."

"But not make it too obvious."

"They stall much longer, we'll all be skipping dinner," says Leslie. "You can tell little Henley Yoonyer how you sacrificed."

Gayle pokes her. "You're terrible."

"Pregnant women wait nine months," says Jennifer. "I don't suppose we should complain."

"Yeah, but they don't have to lie on a beach, or drink rum Collinses—"

"Or go shopping every day."

"But their babies are *theirs*," Nan declares. "One hundred percent."

Leslie steals a bit of papaya off Gayle's plate. "Genetic," she mutters. "Big fuckin' deal."

It's important to pick them up even when they aren't crying. They need to eat and to sleep and be warm, and they need some *cariño,* some tight warm holding and a loving voice, or they won't grow. Doña Mercedes never carries more than one at once, unless they are born twins and have a chance of landing in the same home. She doesn't have a system. It's more of a feeling, a kind of ache in the air around their crib– this one needs to be held now. She can't remember names anymore, and those are likely to change when they leave, so she calls them *pequeño* or *pequeña* depending on the sex and tells them what's out there waiting for them.

"You're going to drive a car, mi pequeño," she says, holding the little one upon her huge shelf of bosom, "a car that has its very own *casita* attached to the house that your parents live in. Your teeth are going to be shining white and perfectly even."

She doesn't tell them the scary things, the things that make her shake her head and mutter a *bendición* when she sees them in the movies and TV shows from up north. They'll discover those soon enough– the gangsters and wild Indians and drug parties and the serial killers lurking in every neighborhood. But life is not so wonderful here, either, and maybe they'll be fortunate, find a home far away from the danger.

"You will learn to read and go to a beautiful school with the *yanqui* children." Doña Mercedes talks to him softly, even after his eyes begin to roll and his body slackens. "You will eat as many hamburgers and fried potatoes as you wish."

She gently lays him down, pulling the coverlet up tight to his cheek, then lifts the girl who is kicking her legs rhythmically in the crib beside him.

"*Tranquila, tranquila, mi pequeña,*" coos Doña Mercedes, bouncing the baby slightly as she moves toward the patch of sun that slants across the changing tables at the back of the room. "You are the luckiest of girls. You will sleep in your own room and learn to speak Inglés on a telephone with no wires."

There is an energy at this hour, as if the whole room is a single living thing, a squirming mass of pure need. One of them babbling loudly sets another kicking, which reminds another he is hungry, and the wailing flares up throughout the room, raw souls just released from Heaven bumping into each other without focus or form. Doña Mercedes lays the little one on a changing table and carefully strips off the sodden diaper, tossing it into the wheeled cart that is already half full, then lifts her by the heels and begins to clean all the doughy cracks with a washcloth. Her *abuela* came here way back when the sisters ran it and there were no yanquis desperate enough to steal off with a brown baby, her abuela poor and hungry from the mountains, walking straight from the paupers' field where they buried her second-born, holding her hands under her breasts and saying one of the few things she knew in Spanish.

"*¿Pecho?*"

And the sisters, sweetly disapproving, said that yes, she could be a wet nurse there till her milk gave out, and it didn't for twenty years. Mercedes' mother always said she and her brothers and sisters were so tiny 'cause they only got what was left after the orphans had drained Abuela, but of course all of the relatives were tiny and brown and made to work very hard and eat very little in the stingy mountains they came from. Her mother stayed to work there too in the years when the breast was replaced by the bottle and the powder, the babies more colicky, redder and scrawnier, a few lost to disease whenever the city's water sat too long and too shallow. Mercedes grew up playing with orphans, feeling their longing and contempt when she left every night with her mother, watching the city swallow them up when the sisters said they were too old and had to make room for the next batch. By the time the Ministry took it over, the foreign adoptions were starting, picking out only the lightest-skinned and healthiest at first and then growing till only the damaged ones remained unchosen now, the ones you could tell from birth would never look right in the beautiful school, eating fried potatoes and speaking Inglés on a telephone with no wires.

"Así, mi pegueña," says Doña Mercedes, as she powders the baby's bottom. *"Un culito seco."*

They took one away this morning, told Doña Mercedes to get it ready and bring it out front. It should be a joyous moment but she is never sure, some days feeling like a delivering angel, other days like a bullet searching a battlefield. The empty crib will be filled within the week, the room will stay alive, noisy, needy, but it always is a bit of a loss to her, seeing a little one leave the only place she knows they'll be safe.

There are two, three, four other women pacing with babies in their arms when she returns to the crib. The sisters work in the city these days, talking to the young girls, arranging for clinics and counseling, but they don't handle the little ones anymore. There are little ones coming in drug-sick from addict mothers, SIDA babies who won't last six months, babies that in her abuela's time would not have been saved, would have been tucked into a little hole in the paupers' field and prayed for on their saint's days. Once or twice a year one will come in who was found in a trash heap– infected, underweight, barely able to whimper. Doña Mercedes makes sure these get more than a couple of rides a day, get to feel the beat of a caring heart against their bodies.

"Mi ejército," she calls them sometimes. *"Mis bravos."* Her army of tiny

souls waiting to travel to a foreign land and try to survive there, waiting for their number to be called, their future to come for them with plastic diapers and a list of vaccinations to be suffered. She tries to imagine them in their new lives but can never see a face, only a sense that it is less crowded, quieter, a bit colder. "You've sent a regiment out there over the years," Dario likes to tease her. "At least a couple battalions."

"She's so good at it, so natural," her family members say. "It's a tragedy she never had her own."

"Or just became a nun."

But Dario had only shrugged back when she asked if he wanted children, and a shrug was not enough. There is no shortage in the world. "Why should I add to the crowd?" she likes to tell them if it comes up. "We've got so many we're giving them away."

There are six of them, women separating and regrouping as they wander through the mercado. Pito drifts in their wake, watching the bags. The youngest one, tall with all the blond hair, is the most careless and leaves hers beside her, laid on top of whatever merchandise she is poking through. It is a multicolored mesh bag she must have bought from Tacho the Bag Man and you can see everything she has crammed into it, which is mostly things Pito would have a hard time selling on the corner by the statue. She keeps her wallet jammed into the front pocket of her shorts and smiles and shrugs apologetically to the vendors if she walks away without buying anything.

Another one has short hair and one of those belly packs you don't even try to fool with, her elbows up to hide her hands when she counts out *reales* for a purchase. She picks things up and scowls as if it is their fault for not being something she would ever want. This one buys a rag doll and then spends a lot of time by Sánchez the carver's stall, asking the prices on his dogs. Sánchez is famous for his dogs and wears dark glasses that give him the look of a blind man even though he can see perfectly well. Sánchez buys his stock from the shop on Calle Victoria and has learned only enough carving to rough out the body of a misshapen buffalo as the *turistas* pass by. He puts bandages on his fingers and has only one of every design on display out on the table. *"Mis hijos,"* he says to the turistas. "These are my children. It is difficult to part with them." The short-haired woman haggles for ten minutes before she buys a trio of little wooden dogs.

One pair stays together the whole time, coming back twice to the tuerto's stand to point at the crucifixes and retratos of the Virgin. *Compañeras.* One is older and looks a little beaten up for a turista, and the other dresses strangely. They laugh a lot. The one with the strange clothes doesn't even have a bag. She carries a painting of Jesus driving a mini van full of haloed worshipers under her arm and keeps stopping to jam her feet back into her pink flip-flop sandals like they are too big for her.

Another one looks a little like the Valkyrie in the comic books the Garza brothers steal from Estrada's *farmacia,* with muscles in her arms and legs and a tan that looks like it goes everywhere. She mostly plants herself by the old *india* who sells shriveled herbs from the mountains and asks in inglés what each is for. The *vieja* can only point to one pile of crumbling leaves or another and then touch the part of her body it cures. All the indios in the sierra have worms, so most of it is probably for the stomach.

The last one is the most promising, wandering a little farther than the others, her wallet riding high in the mouth of the leather bag she hangs over her shoulder. Pito never lets her out of his sight, looking for an opening. Getting the thing in your hand is the easy part. Getting away with it without the turistas or the vendors or the guardia (who stroll through the aisles flushing out beggars and *ladrones*) catching on to you is the hard part. The woman has reddish hair and seems interested in books, picking up the thin ones with pictures like the comics but with harder covers and more writing, the kind the little ones who go to schools are carrying when they pass him in the morning.

Pito is edging closer, a step and a reach away, turning books over in his hands as if he is interested in buying one, when the woman says something to him. The woman turns and sees him and holds up the book she has been looking at and says something to him.

Pito always starts with *"¿Americano?"* and, if they say no, *"¿Deutsche?"* and if no he tries *"¿Svenske?"*. The Japanese stay in big groups and don't give anything, so he hasn't bothered to learn any phrases. If you sit by the Americans and they don't get up right away, they'll try to practice their Spanish and smile and ask you questions. Pito never asks for anything until they get up to go, and sometimes they give him loose change or what's left of their lunch without his asking. Once, when he hooked some tourists, Flaco Peña and Migas and another kid from the docks came and hung close till Migas was able to lift the lady's pocketbook. Later Pito tried to get them to share the money but they wouldn't. A couple times when it was men alone they were *maricones,* but he was afraid to go and do things with them. The kid they call Rulos says he gets them to take out their money first, then grabs it and runs, but the older ones all say he really sucks them. Rulos got caught stealing spray paint by the cops, ran out of Gordo's store and right into a pair of them, and they slapped his ears so hard he can't hear much anymore. The joke is his nickname should change to Cómo because whenever you say something to him he puts a hand to his ear and says *"¿Cómo?"* The cops will mostly leave you alone if you stay away from the tourist hotels and the restaurants in the Barrio Dorado. The only time they caught Pito they turned him upside down to empty his pockets, but he wasn't carrying drugs or money so they let him go.

"¿Americano?" he says to the woman.

"Sí," she answers, then launches into something that sounds vaguely familiar but that he can't understand. She is waving the book at him.

"Ju visitín ere?"

"Sí," she says again, smiling, then indicates the books laid out in the stall in front of her and says something else. She seems to want him to pick a book. Pito shrugs and points at one with a picture of a goat on the front. Once Nacho Cañales stole a goat from the back of a *carnicería* and

---

they all took it into an empty lot by the new construction and cut its throat and watched it kick till it was dead and then tried to cook it in a big fire. Nobody really knew how to cook, so Pito only got a few bites that were either raw and stringy or totally black before he gave up and went searching for a place to hide the night through.

The woman picks the goat book up and three others and pays the woman behind the table. Pito watches her hands, watches the change all the way back into the wallet, but there is no way to do it now that she has seen him, has spoken to him.

The woman hands him the goat book.

At first he doesn't understand. *"Cabra,"* he says, pointing to the picture of the goat.

"Sí, cabra." The woman smiles. *"Es para tu."*

She has bought him a book. The turistas do strange things. "Tenguiu," he says to her, and then the one with the short hair calls and she says *hasta la vista* and is gone.

"¡Cabrón!" says Pito, and the woman behind the table laughs.

"To use that you have to be able to read," she says, reaching for the book. "You might as well give it back to me."

Pito snatches it away. "It's mine."

He walks from the mercado, the Arab who sells medicines over the loudspeaker blaring at his heels. "Is your liver sore? Are your eyes yellow, your gums bloody, your sputum greenish and hard?" Pito tucks the book under his arm, walking casually, hoping that the guardia won't see him and say that he stole it.

The beach is a mile long from rocky point to rocky point, a gleaming sickle of white sand fronting a wall of resort hotels. Shelter islands interrupt the surf before it reaches the shore, and the swimming is good once you get past the breaker line. Women with baskets full of turnovers or coconut patties or pearl necklaces trudge up and down, flocking in groups wherever a tourist shows interest. In the early morning there are tourists on rented ponies riding on the wet sand, giving way to local rich kids cruising in dune buggies when the sun climbs higher. There are stands of cabanas with distinctive colors and hotel markings, umbrellas for hire, picnic benches back by the sidewalk where the old people sit. Yellow-crested pelicans swoop inches above the water surface in loose formation. Packs of dogs, lords of the beach now that pigs have been banished, roam freely—sniffing, digging, snarling in display when they encounter each other at some urine-anointed borderline. Boom boxes blast rap and merengue from blankets and fritter stands, bass lines throbbing counter beat to the pounding waves.

Skipper counts off her left knee, finding her rhythm as she weaves through the people who stand like slalom posts at the edge of the surf. She runs in-and-outs, one hundred counts of jog, then stride, then sprint, and what's so great is that the beach just goes on forever– she doesn't have to turn around after every cycle like on the football field back home. It's a speed-work day, which is good because on distance days there is just too much time to think and you know where that gets you. Skipper concentrates on pushing her abs back and up toward her spinal column, keeping her head straight and her knees high. On the jogging leg she shakes her arms and hands out, remembering the lactic acid buildup that knocked her out of the 10K at Vail.

Loosey-goosey, she thinks to herself and visualizes, picturing shore birds skittering weightlessly across wet sand, imagines the protein supplement kicking in as she planes her legs out into a stride, neurons firing, fingers knifing a path through the air in front of her.

Reach with the arms. Point those toes and grab a few more inches. Skipper feels her upper body driving her now, muscle mass supplying the power, leaning forward slightly to keep momentum. The intake situation is a little iffy down here. They cook with lard, eat white rice and white bread, and think green-and-leafies are only for the livestock. At least the meat isn't shot up with a lot of antibiotics.

"I know free-range is supposed to be better for you," Leslie is fond of saying, "but they should keep the chickens out of the living room."

Skipper makes a little grunt with every step as she begins to sprint, forcing the air out of her mouth on the exhale and breathing in through her nose, kicking up spume whenever a wave washes over her ankles. She lifts her knees up hard till she finds the zone, then maintains, trying to make each movement as powerful and efficient as the last, trying to spark the quick-twitch fibers, to burn with a clean flame.

"Think pistons," Jerry, her trainer, always says. "The one coming down drives the other one up. And again and again and again."

The distance days are so much harder, harder even than the morning swim. Skipper knows it's probably just blood sugar, the nitrogen sucked out of her blood and replaced with placquelike, artery-clogging chunks of self-doubt and regret. "You have to learn to think on a cellular level," Jerry always says, but sometimes Skipper's cells are bummed, her synapses sluggish and resentful, her fluids balking at ionic transfer, and it takes an Extreme Effort to push her past into balanced performance again. Free-climbing Devil's Chimney got her out of the last funk. Her arms shook for three days, and Chris smiled and said, "That's not depression, babe, that's sheer terror."

Skipper, on the jogging leg again, takes inventory. The bone spur in her heel has numbed out by now, and the right knee, the one she had scoped, feels solid. Chris calls himself "zipper-knees" because of all his surgical scars and says if the docs had been up to speed back when he was playing he could have gone pro. "Everybody's got a chink in the armor," he says.

Her weak point, inside, doesn't figure much in running. Sure, aerobic work builds up the heart and the lungs and reinforces your immune response, but some organs you can't seem to get at, no matter what you eat or don't eat or drink or don't drink or how many reps of what fat-busting, osteo-restorative exercise you push yourself through. Free radicals. Ideopathic symptoms. Organs that underperform.

Genetic mistakes.

Skipper's breath is a little ragged now as she begins the last set. Weeping is probably good for you. An emotional purge. Like the high colonics they do at the Spa, where by the third day you feel as scrubbed and red and new on the inside as the Korean girls with their pumice stones have gotten you on the outside. Only with the crying there always seems to be more, no bottom to it. Though maybe if you train hard enough, embrace the burn, narrow your focus to the width of a balance beam, you can make yourself like those little twistoflex gymnasts who just never menstruate. No flow. No fat. No hips. No suffering that can't be overcome by work and willpower.

Skipper feels the sweet thick low-altitude air feeding her lungs, oxygen-rich, a bit salty here at the ocean's edge, and hurdles a tiny girl who has fallen, crying, as she runs from the waves. We'll put her in the pool first thing. Steam fogging the solar panels, water nearly body temperature, no abrasive chemicals—it will be like being back in the womb for her. But safe. Under control. Skipper thinks maybe she'll take the first week off, just not train at all, figure out a new rhythm with the baby.

Skipper visualizes her just down the beach, the baby, Estrellita, although they're going to call her Star. She's standing already, perfectly formed, healthy, arms out and waiting, smiling. Skipper lifts her knees, races forward.

Leslie moves ironically toward the water. You've got to be kidding, she seems to be saying, as she watches a wave surge over her ankles, then suck back into the aggresively blue ocean, her heels sinking in fine wet sand. Her shorts are tight around wide hips and loose around skinny, maggot-white legs. Her hair is short, pinched into irregular tufts with cheap plastic barrettes ("Looks like a white pickaninny," says Nan) and she darkens her eyebrows with pencil in a consciously obvious way. Leslie is short, with eyes that never dart but are constantly moving, judging. She has a collection of oversize T-shirts that seem to have been previously owned by fraternity boys and shuffles around on gummy pink flip-flops. She wears no bra and doesn't react when local boys scoot close on their bongo boards to stare at her nipples.

The other women, sunning, watch her lazily.

"She's only thirty. How can she be sick of men already?"

"That's what she said."

"She's a dyke."

"She is not."

"Well, she might as well be with that attitude she's got on her." Nan waves a woman with a basket of turnovers away. "I can't believe they allow these people selling things on the beach."

"Did you see her tattoo?"

"How can you see anything? She won't wear a bathing suit like a normal person. Sits there on the sand in those *shorts*. We had to wear those shorts for PE back in junior high school."

"It's an ankh," says Gayle.

"What's an ankh?"

"Her tattoo."

"Right, but what is it?" Jennifer wears a lime-green bikini. You can count every one of her ribs.

"And where is it?"

"Just under her right butt cheek."

"How'd you see it there?"

"What's an ankh?"

"She pulled her shorts down for me."

"I told you she's a dyke."

"We were talking about tattoos," says Gayle. "Wes has got a snake wrapped around a dagger on his shoulder, so she showed me hers."

"Your husband has a snake?"

"Am I the only one that doesn't know what this thing is?"

Gayle turns to Jennifer. "It's Egyptian. It's a symbol."

"For what?"

"It means you're a dyke."

"Stop. She said it symbolizes life."

"I can't believe they're going to give her one." Nan holds her chin up, head tilted to one side, as if about to pronounce the score she's awarding the last contestant.

"Why wouldn't they?"

"When there's so many of us with husbands who want to adopt? A child needs a father."

"I didn't have one," says Gayle. "Not so's you'd notice."

"It would have been better if he'd been around, though, wouldn't it?"

"No. Things were worse when he was around."

"I had four. Stepfathers."

They all look at Jennifer.

"What on earth was your mother thinking?"

Jennifer shrugs. "She always hoped the new one was going to work out better."

Nan looks back to Leslie, who backpedals to avoid the wash from a late-breaking wave. "I'm just amazed she could keep her smart mouth shut long enough to get through the interviews."

"She's funny."

"She's *strange*, if that's what you mean. With all the problems these kids have, to land a mother like that. . . . Oh Lord, I can't look."

A tangle of scabby, nervous, rat-tailed dogs works its way past the mothers.

"That ought to be a crime." Nan raises Jack Russells back home and goes on about missing her puppies. "My husband gets them fed on schedule and does all the shots," she says, "but they need their momma."

Skipper joins them, limping ever so slightly, hands on hips, breathing hard.

"Good run?"

"Terrific."

"We're just deciding whether they should let Leslie have a kid or not," says Eileen. "Wanna vote?"

"I just hope whoever she gets has no sense of fashion," says Jennifer.

"She works in publishing. I'm sure in New York she looks fine."

"She's what, like a proofreader?"

"Editor. Fiction books. She gave me one she worked on."

"How is it?"

Gayle shrugs. "Kind of racy."

"Like with a woman on the cover with a pile of hair and her bosoms spilling out?"

"No. It's hard to get into, and there's lots of language."

"Language?"

"Curse words."

"Single mother with a career. She'll have to get an au pair."

"Can she afford that?"

"She's in publishing."

"If she *is* a lesbian," Eileen muses, "she won't have to worry. They'll have it organized."

Leslie slogs back from the water, wet just to the knees. She flops on her blanket in the shade of the beach umbrella.

"You could use some tanning lotion."

Leslie waves it away. "I was supposed to be dark," she says, "I'd have been born Puerto Rican."

"Who's going in?" asks Gayle, standing and pulling her baseball cap off. "Eileen?"

"Never learned to swim."

"I thought you waitressed at the Cape."

"Doesn't mean you go in the water. That's for summer people." Eileen has raw Irish skin and auburn hair. She wears a black one-piece suit she bought at Filene's just for the trip.

Gayle heads for the water alone.

"This isn't a beach, it's a parking lot for people."

"It is pretty lively."

"I could do without the music. It's so *aggressive*."

"It's nice to see people who look middle class here," says Eileen, looking around at the crowded sand. "Local people. I thought it would just be the ones with the bodyguards and Mercedes-Benzes and everybody else living barefoot in a shack."

"You can tell who's middle class in a bathing suit?"

"I get a feeling, yeah. And all these colors. Those two boys— same mother, it looks like, but one's black and the other could pass for white."

"That's so unusual?"

"In Boston, yeah."

"I go there," says Leslie, "I see white parents with brown ones, black ones, Asian-looking ones—"

"That's Cambridge. Not Boston."

"Right."

"Cambridge is another planet."

"I suppose there's bound to be problems wherever you are."

"They give my kid any trouble in the neighborhood," says Eileen, "I'll rip their fuckin' heart out."

"Don't let our born-again friend hear you say that." Nan indicates Gayle, swimming parallel to shore.

"I think it's the goddam Jesus H. Christ she objects to, not the fuck-and-shit stuff," says Leslie. "But I don't know what their policy is exactly."

"Does she speak in tongues?"

"Not when she's with me. Not so far."

"They come Saturday mornings and just camp out on your front steps," says Nan. "Usually one black and one white."

"They who?"

"Jehovah's Witnesses."

"That's not what she is."

"Same thing. They proselytize."

"They what?"

"Proselytize."

"Spell it."

Nan lifts her sunglasses to give Leslie a look. "Don't be smart. You know what I mean."

"Lots of religions do. The Pope sends missionaries all over the world."

"He doesn't send them to Topeka. I have never once had a Catholic on my doorstep."

"Well, we've toned it down some," says Eileen. "Ever since that Inquisition thing—"

"And Jews. You ever see a Jew out looking for more recruits? They don't want outsiders."

"Gayle says she can listen to music and go to the movies, so it can't be too heavy, whatever it is."

"Fundamentalist."

"Yeah, whatever that means."

"You seen her husband?"

"No."

"Wes?"

"I saw him when she first got here. She's not kidding about that tattoo. Looks like a Hell's Angel with a haircut."

"Maybe she was a chopper Mama."

They laugh.

"He's the one got her sober," says Eileen. "And she's worried about him running the diner alone."

"She prays every night. I can hear it." Jennifer's room is next door to Gayle's.

"If she scores her kid before I do," says Leslie, "I'll think about converting."

Señora Muñoz does her accounts. The couch in the lobby needs reupholstering. The gas and electric need to be paid. She needs to remember to tell the girls she knows that one of them is stealing soap. She has to decide on the cable TV package. And the one in 214 has started paying in reales and insists on the bank rate instead of the conversion Señora Muñoz offers at the desk. The one in 214 started in 206 and hopped to 210 when it opened up and now has her eye on the corner room 221 if the couple from San Jacinto leave before she gets what she came for. Señora Muñoz told her it was considered a suite and would be more expensive but the mother cornered the couple and got them to write their rate down on a piece of paper which she has waved in Señora Muñoz's face far too many times. They are good business usually, but sometimes she longs for the days before the mothers arrived, when clients came and went without your having to know what kind of laundry detergent they were allergic to.

And now that she has extended herself to attract the mother business, the Ministry decides to reexamine their export policy, caving in to hack politicians waving the flag and a handful of aging radicals searching for a cause. Like her son Buho.

"Mami," says Buho, lugging his tool kit through the lobby, "that one in two-fourteen—"

"You aren't touching the shower, are you?"

Buho has done more damage with his wrench than his student group ever inflicted with Molotov cocktails.

"She complained—"

"She does nothing but complain. Don't do anything till Herminio comes up. And clean your glasses."

Bujo only pushes his glasses back against his forehead and glares at the novela playing on the little TV. "We should take it apart and leave it there for a couple days, see how she—"

"You're not the one she'll be waving her finger at. Wait for Herminio."

The mother in 214 isn't happy with her water pressure. Señora Muñoz could put her on the first floor where it's a bit better, but then there'd be no warning from the clunk of the elevator that she was on her way to register another complaint.

"I've never stayed in a hotel where—"

"I suppose it's pointless to expect, but—"

"You have *got* to do something about—"

Bujo wipes his hands on his pants. "There's no reason we should be kissing their asses."

When Señora Muñoz asked Herminio to take Buho on as an assistant it was so she could tell the judge he had a full-time job and he'd have pay slips to show. She didn't need another one in jail, not after Raúl in the Castillo eighteen months and then the exile and him in Madrid now with his new young wife, the son of a bitch, embarrassing himself with a girl who could be his daughter while I'm here listening to yanqui mothers whine about the air-conditioning. The men play their games, pissing off the military, making their noise, and who has to pick up the pieces? Who has to order the linens?

"How is he doing?" she asked after the first week.

Herminio shrugged. "He works."

"Is he any use?"

"He is still very young, señora," said Herminio and left to clean the grease trap.

"They're our clients," she tells her son, who has had his face plastered on the walls of police stations and army barracks. "It's how we make a living."

"Selling babies."

"We are a service."

"A service for rich yanqui bastards who—"

"You would be happier if all the clients were from here?"

"Thieves. Fat corrupt sons of bitches—"

"When I die you can invite all the *sinvergüenzas* who live in El Fondo *and* all their fleas to come live here for free. Until then, we provide a certain class of food and lodging to those who can pay for it. Clean your glasses."

• • •

Buho bangs his tool bag against the counter as he leaves her, stomping into the elevator and jabbing the 2 button. She is so fucking proud about the location and the sparkling-clean lobby and the city moving the public bus stop two blocks away just because she asked, but no pride in race, no pride in country, and it's that attitude, that internalized inferiority complex that Fanon wrote about from Algeria but that applies here in spades, that keeps us at each other's throats instead of confronting the real enemy. Sometimes Buho imagines an army of the orphans, poor, unwanted, nameless, organized and motivated and pointed in the proper direction. What couldn't they accomplish with that energy, that concentrated anger? Instead, we're shipping them off to the industrialized North, another raw material to wear hundred-dollar sneakers and mispronounce the name of the land of their birth.

Buho finds 214 open, one of the girls, Asunción or Resurrección or Inmaculada or one of those mumbo-jumbo church names, staring out the window with the fucking novela playing in here, too, as if there has been a state decree that no inhabited space shall be without *Las Lágrimas de Una Madre* yattering in the background, on penalty of death.

"*¿Qué tal?*" says the girl, barely turning her head, and Buho shuts the bathroom door between them, sits on the toilet lid, and lights up a joint to kill the time till Herminio comes and shows him what to do. Water pressure my fucking ass.

Asunción watches the children at recess in the school courtyard that faces the rear of the Posada. There is one ball being kicked, but mostly they chase each other, crazy with energy. A few just run by themselves, from building to fence and back, or in frenzied spurts that take them nowhere in particular. Others link arms and spin and spin and release to go crashing into other frantic children. Asunción tries to work in one of the rooms facing the rear at this hour, hoping to watch them for a while.

She picks out a little girl who would be the right age, smaller than the rest, who stands shyly at the periphery, smiling, hopping with excitement now and then when the action reaches a certain intensity but never quite joining in. The little girl keeps her hands in her pockets. The little girl has braids that her mother must spend a long time fixing every morning. The children scream for the joy of having voices, the children bounce off each other, shake the metal fence to make it talk. Asunción watches the little girl who would be the right age and hopes she has a friend.

Nan is not so sure about the place they choose for lunch. "You ladies are braver than I am," she says, as they enter. Lacquered trophy fish are mounted high on the walls around them. Fishing nets loop down from the ceiling, and a display of spear guns hangs behind the bar.

"It looks like Hemingway's rec room," says Leslie. They sit at a round table near the portholes that face the street.

"What's seafood again?"

"Mariscos."

"And the difference between grouper and snapper?"

"Is there one?"

"I'd like a Mojito," says Nan, to the girl who comes over from the bar. "With lime, not lemon."

"They know how to make them."

"I don't see any limes on the counter."

"¿Una cola?" says Gayle.

"Ella quiere tomar una Coca," Leslie corrects her.

"What'd I say?"

"That you wanted a tail."

"I'm hopeless."

Leslie and Jennifer order daiquiris and Eileen asks for just water.

"You didn't tell her bottled," says Nan, after the girl is gone.

"It's a restaurant. It's in the guidebook."

Nan shakes her head. "It's your call," she says. "Personally, I plan to get out of here with my plumbing intact."

"You think the crushed ice in your drink is from bottled water?"

Nan ponders this. "Doesn't the freezing kill everything?"

"Or maybe it's the alcohol."

"You'll find out, won't you?"

Leslie realizes they're one short. "Where's Miss Congeniality?"

"I think she was off to run another marathon before lunch."

"Or swim a couple thousand laps."

"I wonder if she keeps smiling underwater?"

"I had a body like that, I'd be smiling too."

"She likes to keep fit," says Gayle.

"And Hitler liked a parade. Woman is obsessed."

"Only difference is we just talk about our fat asses, she does something about it." Jennifer has narrow boyish hips and no ass to speak of.

"We could order for her, you know. Pick the leanest, least appetizing thing on the menu—"

"What's the movie where they replace all the housewives with these perfect-looking clones?"

"—And her husband looks like a guy in a jeans ad."

"You've seen a picture?"

"Yeah. Two of them hiking in the Rockies, glowing with health."

"Nothing wrong with that."

"He sells sporting goods."

"Footballs and baseballs?"

"Hiking gear. Kayaks. Stuff you climb mountains with. They make a lot of money."

"She's very sweet," says Gayle. "Upbeat."

"She'll have the kid in one of those backpacks, carry it up Everest."

"She's been here longer than any of us, but she's still got a positive attitude."

"I trust her as far as I can throw her."

"That's 'cause you're from New York."

"That's 'cause I'm from planet Earth," says Leslie. "Someday one of her microchips is gonna misfire, you'll see the real Skipper."

"That's her given name, you know."

"That was Barbie's little sister, wasn't it? Skipper?"

"She'll open her mouth and this thing with six heads will come out—"

"There's been a few nasty things to come out of your mouth."

Leslie bows to Nan. "Thank you."

"I'm gonna let her do her thing to me."

"Thing."

"Her discipline?" Jennifer seems to be asking them if it's okay. "That she teaches?"

"What, Pilates?"

"No. "

"Alexander Technique?"

"That isn't it. It's Eastern."

"Feng shui."

"You do that to houses. There's some movement involved and some, like, energy release and some physical manipulation."

"That's how they get you—the physical manipulation. You come back a size two with dimples and good bone structure."

"Where do I sign up?"

"I like to look at her." Gayle smiles, showing a few missing teeth. "You see what God can create if he's got a mind to."

Skipper comes in breathless with several plastic bags stuffed with herbs. "Guess how many seafood places called El Pescadero there are in this neighborhood?"

"Grab a seat," says Leslie. "We ordered you the bacon cheeseburger."

"Is it two-thirty?" says Jennifer, looking at her watch.

"Uh-huh."

"So in Virginia it's—?"

"Two-thirty. We're in the same latitude. Longitude? The same time zone."

"I've got to call Henley."

Jennifer steps outside to use her cell phone. They can see her through the porthole, punching the numbers.

"Poor thing."

"Yeah. House in Newport, estate outside of D.C., they got a boat bigger than my apartment."

"They almost split up."

"Join the club."

"You almost split up with—?"

"No, but that's life, right?" Eileen shrugs. "It happens."

"Not the best time to be adopting a child."

"Maybe it's what they need."

"Something else to disagree on."

"Some*body* else."

"Most kids grow up shuttling between houses these days."

Nan snorts. "Not where I come from."

"I forgot. Land of Milk and Honey."

"It's irresponsible."

"Maybe we should rat her out to the Agency."

"I would hope whoever provided their references—"

"Had the good sense to lie when necessary."

"They must get some negative ones," says Eileen. "People who say, 'Under no circumstances should these people be parents.'"

"And if you're clueless enough to ask somebody who'd write that to vouch for you," says Leslie, "you deserve to be screwed."

"You make it sound like a conspiracy," says Gayle.

"No, it's a game." Nan has her glasses on, frowning at the menu. "Why you think they've got us down here for so long? They're gonna make us *earn* our babies."

"With her money you'd think they'd have landed one by now."

"I'm sorry, señora, but we do not sell our children in this country. That will be six thousand dollars, please."

"It's not like that," Gayle protests.

"How many questions have you answered about your net worth?"

"That's to make sure you can provide."

"Provide the bureaucrats with their salaries."

Gayle shrugs. "I just wish she could relax a little. This should be a joyful time."

"I bet you two piña coladas her husband'll fly down some weekend, make a donation to Our Lady of Perpetual Red Tape, and off they'll go with a little bundle of sunshine."

"You sound so bitter."

"My daddy called children the glue," says Nan. "The glue that held a marriage together."

Leslie waves for the waitress to come over. "My parents' marriage was more like a hammer. My mother used me to bang dents in my father."

"That explains a lot."

Skipper, quiet throughout, finally speaks. "Leaving Sunday with a baby," she muses. "Wouldn't that be awesome?"

"Henley?"

"It's quarter of three."

"I'm sorry. It took us awhile to find this place and then these phones—"

"What's up?"

"We're having lunch. It's a place called—"

"With the baby. The progress report."

"I haven't heard from them today."

"Have you called them today?"

"I called them yesterday. They said they'd inform us the minute there was a new development. They always say that when I call."

"But you didn't call them today."

"Henley—"

"Do I have to do this? Do I have to come down there again and—"

"You make yourself a pain in the ass and they stick you on the bottom of the pile."

"Or they deliver as soon as they've got something, just to get rid of you."

"There are women who have been here weeks longer than I have. This woman Eileen—"

"I talked to my Korean connection again."

"We agreed to drop that."

"You maximize your options, you maximize your chances of achieving your goal."

"I've heard your seminar, darling. Many times."

"It works."

"We're not dealing with commodities here."

"You don't think so? The same rules apply. There's supply, there's demand—"

"There's a lizard in my room that makes a noise at night."

"They don't have blizzards down there. Too close to the equator."

"Lizard. Like iguana, gecko, chameleon– lizard."

"They don't do any harm."

"This one makes a noise. It keeps me up."

"Ask the desk to get it out of there."

"They'll laugh at me."

"That old battle-ax has never laughed in her life."

"Mrs. Muñoz? I'd never ask her."

"For what we're paying they should catch the thing, cook it, and serve it with ranchero sauce. Look, are you going to be able to do this?"

"I'm fine. I'm all right."

"If I ran my business like they run that half-assed country—"

"The Baby Exchange."

"What?"

"There'd be a Baby Exchange. Men down in the pit, yelling numbers, nursemaids up in the balcony, holding babies. Crying babies."

"Right. Jenny, we've got a three o'clock here, it's after quarter of—"

"I miss you."

"I miss you too. You're being a trooper. Call me if anybody moves down there."

"Honey? The Korean thing?"

"Give me some room to operate, okay? We get skunked in Margaritaville, at least we got a fallback position."

"They say it's happening, it's just the legalities."

"Jenny, these are the people who flunk the test to work for the motor vehicle department. Nothing is certain."

"But if these people you know can really arrange for—"

"So maybe we get an extra baby seat for the Explorer. Henley Junior and Kim Chee. I gotta go, honey."

"I love you."

"Love you too."

"I don't think you can order it that way. "

"I've seen them in the market. Jennifer, we ordered." Nan hates to wait for anybody. "You eat shrimp, don't you?"

"Whatever. I'll just pick."

"We're discussing papaya."

"I'm not saying they don't have the fruit," says Leslie. "It's just that it's a pussy word."

"Pussy word."

"Vaginal euphemism. Beaver, clam—"

"Nobody ordered clams, did they?"

"The lower on the food chain you eat," says Skipper, "the better the nutritional value. But the risk of toxicity increases."

The waitress brings them bread and butter.

"I heard that girls are menstruating earlier but boys reach puberty later than they used to."

They look at Jennifer.

"Why would they do that?"

"I don't know. It was on the radio. I only heard the first half."

"Down here," Nan proclaims, "you have to worry about those syndromes— whether the mother was intoxicated—"

"FAS," says Gayle.

"And drugs– crack and all that—"

"They have crack down here?"

"Where do you think it comes from?"

"And then there's genes."

"What can you do about that?"

"Exactly my point." Nan has put her Mojito aside without taking a sip. "You could have a time bomb ticking and never know."

"What do you know about birth kids?"

"Well, you know both parents, their families—"

"You have any idea how many combinations there are?"

"But it's from a known pool."

"You got any relatives who were crazy? Or had some kind of physical disorder? Or were just dumber than shit?"

"People in my family have six toes sometimes," offers Jennifer.

"On one foot?"

"It's pretty common."

"People have birth kids, they think it's going to be all their favorite qualities combined."

"You get dealt a bad hand," says Nan, "you can always train it out of them."

"Train?"

"Educate, influence, discipline—whatever you want to call it. Raising children. Whatever they carry from their parents– laziness, violence, promiscuity."

"Is there a promiscuity gene?"

"You look at a culture, its problems, some of it's got to be genetic. The people come to the U.S., and in a couple of generations they're more civilized."

"Know how to make fire, discover the wheel." Gayle is pushing Leslie's foot under the table, warning her that she's raising her voice, they're not in Manhattan.

"You know what I mean. They assimilate. They've been trained to be good citizens."

"But if it's genetic, then all their old savage ways are still there."

"Our prisons are full of people who give in to their natures."

"So this training. You roll up a newspaper and—"

"You let children know what's expected of them. You're consistent. If they're born with some kind of disability—racial, cultural, whatever— you make them aware they've got some catching up to do."

"So it's a race."

Nan sighs, exasperated. "Look, we have a capitalistic form of government. If there are going to be winners, there have to be losers. You don't want your child to be a loser, do you?"

"Perish the thought."

"I think you have to watch them and see who they are," says Gayle, "and then encourage the best of what's in them."

"You make them who they are."

"Your parents made you?"

"Absolutely. Now, at some point I took over responsibility, once they'd taught me right from wrong and how the world worked, but by then they'd put their stamp on me."

"I just hope mine is very calm," says Leslie. "The one-neurotic-per-family rule."

"If mine is no good at math, I'm gonna be no help at all."

"I hope she can sing," says Eileen. "I always regretted that. I like music so much but I can't sing."

The waitress brings appetizers, a platterful of glistening hot beef empanadas. Leslie gives Skipper a look, then forks one onto her plate. "Whatever this is going to do to my lower tract, I don't want to hear about it."

The car exhaust is sharp at the back of Pito's throat, plowed aside by heavier gases when a bus or truck passes. By the end of the day he'll have a headache only the paint can smooth over. Pito and Big Garza wave their rags, and when a likely one appears he squirts the windshield before they can wave a finger at him. Most put their wipers on then, and he leaves them without a glance inside, but every few red lights one will submit to a cleaning. There have been a lot of robberies in traffic lately, more and more people driving with windows up, doors locked, and a pistol in the glove compartment. When the water runs out, Big Garza takes the spray bottle to refill at the Fuente de la Paz in front of the embassies while his brother and Pito sit under the shade of the statue horse.

Little Garza turns the pages of the book. "Can you read this?" They used to have Little Garza hold all the money, but the older kids beat him so badly the last time they caught him he just gives up now and empties his pockets. Now Pito and Big Garza split it and all three run in different directions when they're attacked.

"Sure," says Pito. "It's about a goat."

"Will you read it to me?"

"Maybe later." Reading is like a place he's not allowed to go, a place that belongs to other people, people who have things he can't have. When he sees the ones walking to school in the morning, the ones wearing backpacks and laughing in groups, he wants to hit them with rocks, more for protection than for fun, because even when they aren't looking his way he knows it's him they're laughing at. The schools, from the outside, don't look much different from the prison out by the dump where the Scab People live, but when they come out at noon the children are all laughing. Laughing.

"Mira," says Big Garza, coming back from the fountain with the bottle full and a white condom in his hand. "Think we can sell this?"

"Did they use it?"

"If they did, nothing came out."

"What is it?" asks Little Garza.

"If Mami owned one of these," says his big brother, dangling the thing in front of his face, "neither of us would be here."

• • •

Licenciado Buendía opens the mother's file and scans his notes on the case. He can feel her watching him on the other side of the desk. Unblinking reptile eyes, like a snake contemplating a rat it is about to swallow. With most he would only have to pull out another stack of official documents, sigh a bit, and remind them how the Minister hates to be pressured. Even the husbands, flying in for a day or two, full of fire and anger, can be humbled with a Form 1013-C in triplicate ("I'm sorry, Señor, but the Ministry does not accept duplicate copies.") But he can tell that this one, with the cutting eyes and disapproving set to her jaw, will not be so easy.

"Señora, I'm not certain what you wish me to do. Your petition has been filed, the placement procedure is under way—"

"We're paying you."

"And I must comply both with your wishes and the laws of our country."

"All I see so far is another layer of payoffs. We've done all the paperwork, we hand it to you, and you pass it on."

"It may appear that way, but I assure you—"

"They said we had to hire a local lawyer or no dice."

"Yes, that is one of the regulations. If you are unhappy with my performance—"

"It's been more than two months."

"—I can recommend another advocate. But at this point a change might prejudice your case."

Buendía glances at the photo of Wilfredo and Pilar on his desk, both posing in their school uniforms next to one of the Sisters. The Sister does not have her hand out asking for more money, which is a rarity. Books, uniforms, trips, plays—all part of a good education, according to the Sisters. Then there are saint's days and churches to be rebuilt after earthquakes and hungry children in countries whose names he's never heard of, a never-ending stream of requests that the children bring home. Candies to buy, greeting cards, letters from missionaries pleading the latest emergency, and Wilfredo and Pilar still innocent– "Papi, they're starving." Who can say no? And this is only primary school with their teeth just waiting to crumble and their shoes too small every two months and Buendía regrets that he fell into his practice after the golden days, when private adoptions were still legal and a lawyer was a free agent, when the sums exchanged were limited only by the degree of the yanquis' urgency.

"So you've got us over a barrel." The mother sits with arms folded and feet planted, as if ready to block his way should he try to escape the office. "I understand that."

"Please, señora—"

"At this rate the baby will be talking by the time we get it. Full sentences. I don't want to have to undo all of that."

"Undo?"

"These are important months for development. Children learn things—"

"I understand this."

The mother has very light blue eyes and wears her hair short. She wears a leather belly pack and walking sneakers. They start wearing sneakers and pants to the office after the first two visits, no longer so desperate to make an impression.

"Our file," she says, "assuming they haven't tossed it down the air shaft, is in a pile of other applications."

"I sympathize with your impatience, señora."

"All I want from you is to find a way to move it from the bottom of that pile to the top."

Buendía sighs, spreads his arms. "Señora—"

"And if we receive our child by—let's say the end of this week—there will be some kind of bonus on top of your usual—"

"The government forbids us to accept more than the standard—"

"The government doesn't need to know anything about it, do they?"

Buendía always loves this moment. He has practiced his look of dismay in front of the mirror, experimented with the length of the stony silence, perfected the exact tone of voice. "I will pretend that you have not suggested this, señora."

Usually there is the satisfaction of a flustered apology, a husband usually, stumbling to say that, no, that's not what they meant at all, with that stunned, helpless look of a yanqui discovering that there is something below the equator that cannot be bought.

The mother doesn't blink.

"Bonus or not," she says evenly, "it's still your job. You don't want my husband to get his teeth into this. George sued the phone company once, and by the time it was over he'd cost them—"

"Señora, I will make my best effort, but I can promise you nothing." Buendía lifts the receiver from his desk phone, punches the number, and sits back in his chair.

"Posada Santa Marta, " she answers. *"¿En qué puedo servirle?"*

"Es Ernesto."

Buendía watches the mother as he speaks. His notes say this one understands no Spanish, but you can never tell.

"I have a client here," he says, speaking rapidly just in case. "A Señora Nancy Hightower."

"Qué bruja," mutters Señora Muñoz. "A new complaint every morning."

"Her accounts are in order?" Buendía smiles at the mother.

"Rubén wants to poison her, but she's paid up through Sunday." He can hear a novela playing on her TV as she flips through the ledger. "Two months, one week."

"Could you afford to lose her a bit early?"

"Con mucho gusto. But if you can wait till Monday, I'll have the advance—"

"Comprendo perfectamente. Gracias para su consideración."

Buendía hangs up, puts on his look of guarded optimism. "I have made an inquiry."

"I was right here. What did they say?"

That we will give you one of our precious children when hell freezes, he wants to say. You might as well climb back on your broom-stick and return to the North. But there is the commission to consider, and the settlement with Angela that is sucking me dry– it doesn't hurt so much for the children, but to pay for her vacations to San Felipe and put more money in the pockets of that leech of a divorce lawyer—

"No promises have been given," he tells her, drawing it out, "but your paperwork is entering the final phase."

"That's what you told me the last time I got you on the phone."

Buendía adds to his notes that he must tell Araceli not to accept this mother's calls. He presses the button below the edge of his desk that lets her know to buzz him.

"But this is the final phase of the final phase," he says, holding her eyes to let her know something has really changed. "I believe your hopes will be coming to fruition very soon."

The intercom buzzes.

"Dígame."

"Es hora de su conferencia, señor," says Araceli over the box. *"Perdóname."*

Buendía stands and offers his hand to the mother. "You must forgive me. A function at the Ministry."

The mother stands and takes hold of his hand for longer than is comfortable. "We've got a deal, then?"

He is tired of her reptile eyes. "If the Lord is willing." He smiles. "Araceli will see you out."

When the mother is gone, Buendía makes a few more notes in her file. They act like it's a customs brokerage, as if their rattan desk set is waiting crated just in the next room, needing only the rubber stamp of this paper shuffler, this slow-witted thick-fingered bureaucrat, to get on with their perfect lives. They think he is a bandit. The rate the Ministry has set is a joke, and the little that Señora Muñoz shares with him for strongly suggesting the clients stay at her posada—

He punches the number into the phone. It would be amusing one day to see just how high they'd be willing to go, these yanquis with their money and their hurry.

"There is a cash machine in the lobby, señora. I regret to say I cannot accept American Express."

"Ministerio de Servicios Humanos."

"El Gerente, por favor."

"De parte de quién?"

"Licenciado Buendía."

He flips through her file as he waits. The standard questionnaires with the standard responses, carefully coached by the agency up north. They'd prefer a girl but will accept either. No birth defects please, no history of criminal activity or mental illness in the birth parents. Nothing too unusual. But this one, with her staring eyes and her voice like sharp elbows, is not going away. She will make his life hell.

"Ernesto. ¿Qué tal, hombre?"

"Don Gonzalo," he says, trying to measure the right proportion of familiarity and deference into his voice, "I have a favor to ask of you."

The rooms in the Posada Santa Marta are smallish, opening to the balconies, and the walls fuzzy with early-seventies macramé art. Each day finds a wrapped bar of soap and plastic bottle of spring water in the bathroom. There are tiny ants that seep out of the woodwork at night, a spreading stain of them, and geckos that pose motionless for hours, then inexplicably flash to another spot on the wall. The overhead fans wobble and squeak if they're set on high but help keep the mosquitoes at bay. The floors are tile, and a single lamp with a low-wattage bulb lights up when you flick the switch by the door. The sun slants in for most of the day, though, on Eileen's side of the hallway.

"Oh, no, come on in. You can work around me." She is writing postcards when the girl knocks. It's the one she likes, the one who usually does her room. "No problema." You hate to hold them up when they work so hard.

"Con permiso," says Asunción, and pulls the cart up in front of the room, propping the door open with the rubber wedge. This is the one who leaves a little *propina* every week, a few reales under the glass ashtray with *Gracias* scrawled on a sheet of the Posada stationery.

"I'm writing to the relatives," says Eileen. She feels bad that she can't say much more than hello and thank you, feels bad that she chose German back in junior high school which has proven to be such a waste. "Big family. *¿Familia grande?*"

"*Yo también,*" says the girl. "*¿Cuántos?*"

"How many? Nine of us. Four brothers, four sisters."

Asunción holds up six fingers. "We are six. I have three brothers who are gone now— two of them are dead. And the little ones I take care of." She wishes they had taught her some English before she had to leave school. They say if you can speak English and know how to spell and type on a machine it's easy to get a job in an office. And it would be nice to really talk to the mothers.

"Whoever this girl is I'm getting," says Eileen, "my daughter, she's already got a roomful of cousins."

Asunción just smiles and starts in on the bed.

"Listen to me. My daughter." The woman keeps talking. "I don't think I've called her that before."

This mother is her favorite right now. One of the ones who puts her used towels on the sink instead of leaving them on the floor. Who puts the tray outside in the hall if she gets room service. She has nice eyes and a nice voice, this mother, and has a photo of the man who must be her husband leaning against the lamp on her bedside table.

"It's pretty weird, you know?" Eileen sits back from the desk and turns to face the girl. "You don't know who it's going to be, really, but you can't help having these ideas. Fantasies."

Asunción smooths the new sheet down. She wishes she hadn't run out of the pillow mints halfway through her rooms, that she'd held one back for this mother. Somebody has been stealing them off the cart.

"I have this day in my head—it's crazy to do these things, make up stuff, you know—but I've been running it through my head since back when I still thought I could have my own. Just before I fall asleep, day-dreaming, whatever." Eileen frowns. "It's comforting, I guess."

Asunción makes hospital corners, tucks them under the mattress.

"It's early winter, there's snow already—we get some serious winters in Boston. It's a snow day. You don't have those down here, do you?"

"Esnóe?"

The woman mimes something fluttering down from the sky with her fingers, then hugs herself and shivers.

"Una nevada."

"Like the state, right. That makes sense. It's a day when there's no school. She's still little but old enough to go to school a full day—third grade, maybe. I let her sleep late. I used to love that. I come in and she's this little warm bump in the bed and I sit by her for a second and tell her, 'Honey, it's a snow day, I'm going to let you sleep.' You enjoy it more if you know you're getting extra, that usually you'd be up and brushing your teeth. Finally she gets up and comes out in her pajamas and I make cocoa with—you know—those little marshmallows on top. And we talk about what we're going to do that day and you can hear snow shovels outside crunching, the plows rumble by every once in a while scraping the streets, and maybe it's still falling so it stays clean on top of everything. White. And then I get her dressed, all the layers, although now it's less with the polar fleece and she can do most of it herself, but you help because it's a pleasure, her arm on your neck while she balances to put her boots on, no thought about it, you're just an extension of her body."

Asunción passes the mother with the trash baskets, still listening. The mother's eyes look like she'll cry.

"We go to the Common, or maybe all the way out to Jamaica Pond, depending on the weather. She's just bold enough to skate out away from me for a little bit, shaky, but she keeps looking to make sure I don't stop watching her, and she always comes back to lean on me and rest.

There's zillions of kids of all ages zipping around and that makes her really excited, but mostly she wants to be with me, just the two of us. And later—when I take her to Shakey's or Ground Round or whatever seems like a big treat to her and let her order just french fries if she wants as long as she has some of my soup too—she tells me stories—stories about her classmates or stories she's made up or whatever—and we talk there in a booth surrounded by other mothers and their kids and I'm just one of them, you know? And when we walk home from wherever I can park the car, there's the sound of our feet on the new snow, her taking two steps to my one, and maybe if they haven't shoveled the walk like they usually don't I have to go in front, to break the way for her."

Eileen wipes her eyes. "This is ignoring the fact that I'm supposed to be at work, right? That I'm the one with the job."

The girl comes back in from the cart. She sits on the edge of the bed, careful not to muss, and faces Eileen. When she starts to talk, it is as if she thinks Eileen can understand her though they both know she can't.

"I have a baby up north," she says. "Esmeralda was what I wanted to name her. She'll be two years old on the ninth of April." Asunción folds her hands in her lap and looks at her knuckles, raw from the bathroom cleanser. "Maybe she is where they have a snowfall, I don't know. "

Every month or two, when a new group comes in, she picks one of them. The one whose face she tries to see, the one whose voice she tries to hear when she imagines Esmeralda with another woman in the North.

"I was so young and there is still my brother and sister to care for and I have to work. The nuns came out and talked to me and told me it would be the best thing I could do for her."

The girl is quiet for a long moment. "Are you okay?" asks Eileen.

"I hope she was chosen by a mother like you," she says.

They smile at each other shyly, Eileen shaking her head to say *I'm sorry I don't understand* and Asunción shrugging sadly and rising to go do the bathroom.

- -

Jennifer lies on the rubber yoga mat on the floor. Skipper runs the tips of her fingers gently over her skin, starting from the back of her head and skimming all the way down to her heels. "This is better on my table," she says. "It folds up but it's still heavy to carry around."

"I'm not uncomfortable." Jennifer closes her eyes and tries to listen to her body. "Are you manipulating my aura?"

"Something like that. You have to feel where the hot spots are, how the energy polarizes. Everybody is a bit different."

"There isn't any of that deep stuff—"

"Rolfing."

"As long as I know what they're going to do I can prepare myself, but when they dig in and they don't warn you—"

"I don't do anything too intense."

"Good."

Jennifer relaxes her stomach a bit and turns her face to the side. "I think I feel something."

"There's quite a knot in here. Something really emotional."

"I know."

"Would you like me to work on it?"

"Be my guest."

Skipper has put some tranquil music on her little portable CD player, waterfall music, and is wearing loose sweatpants and a T-shirt. She uses the palms of her hands and her fingertips, moving them over Jennifer's back beneath her left shoulder blade.

"Do you do this on children?"

"I have."

"Is it different?"

"Oh, they tend to wear more of their issues on the outside. You don't have to probe as much. And they get a lot of what they need just with— you know—handling."

"You think they can tell if it's not their real mother?"

Skipper thinks a moment, pushing energy with her hands, before she answers. "You're going to be the real mother."

"You know what I mean. Like if I was going to breast-feed—if I had, you know—it would be one thing if it was my own baby, but the idea of letting somebody else's suck on me—"

"I don't think you can know till you actually do it."

"I'm not so maternal."

"You're not a mother yet. Just a candidate."

"I hate that, on the forms. Like somebody is voting somewhere."

"Somebody is. There are three times as many applicants here as they have children. You won."

Jennifer purrs. "Whatever that is you're doing, it's good."

"Great. . . . Now I'm going to ask you to visualize an emotional state. Try to concentrate it in one area of your body."

"Like—?"

"Why don't we try anxiety?"

Jennifer laughs. "How'd you come up with that one?"

"Where are you sending it?"

She concentrates. "Uhm—it's already here—like, at the base of my throat?"

"Turn over, then."

Jennifer turns onto her back. Skipper lays the backs of her hands softly against her ears.

"I'm not so impressed they granted us a placement," says Jennifer, "when you look at some of the others they picked."

"Like who?"

"Have you seen that scar on her wrist?"

"I thought it was a birthmark."

"It's a scar from a burn."

"Loosen your arms."

"She told me when she was little, just a toddler, she was playing by the stove, touching the knobs and stuff, even though her mother had told her a couple times not to. Her mother grabbed her arm and held a hot skillet against her wrist."

"Oh, God."

"And she wasn't saying 'Hot, hot,' she was saying 'You obey your mother or this is what happens.'"

"That's pretty heavy."

"What freaked me was she told it like she was proud."

"Nan?"

"Like 'I don't know about the rest of you, but I had a mother who *cared*.'"

"There's all kinds of mothers."

"You just worry for whatever kid they get."

"That's true for birth mothers too. You get born, you take your chances. There can be all kinds of negative baggage waiting for you out there." Skipper places her palm flat on Jennifer's sternum. "You're holding onto it awfully tight, there. The anxiety."

"Do you think *Henley* is too big a load?" says Jennifer, her forehead knotting. "Naming him?"

"Names aren't so important."

"But he's not going to look at all like his father and he may not be good at or interested in any of the same things, but he'll have this Junior thing laid on him."

"Your husband must have felt strongly about it."

"We looked through the name book when they told us it was going to be a boy, but the only one we liked was Joshua, and there's way too many of those."

Skipper smiles. "We had a Joshua. Back before there were so many."

"You had a little boy?"

"The first one was going to be Annabel if it was a girl, which it turned out to be. I was young enough we didn't ask for an amnio."

"And you miscarried?"

"Uh-huh."

"I read where there's all kinds that end in the first month, before the woman even knows she's conceived."

"This was in the last trimester."

"That's terrible."

"They just said she—they knew it was a she by then—she's not going to be viable but at this point you'll have to carry to term."

"You had to—?"

"It's like a delivery but without the same . . . spirit. Nobody brings a video camera."

Jennifer frowns. "So you know what it's like to be pregnant. Really pregnant."

"Uh-huh."

"And Joshua?"

"He was born with his lungs not properly formed. And with Gabriel it was his heart."

"There was another?"

"Gabriel."

"And they both—"

"Lived."

Skipper lifts her hands off Jennifer, shakes them out. When she starts again she is holding Jennifer's foot in her lap, lightly pressing the sole with her fingertips.

"Joshua lived about two days and Gabriel hung on for a whole week. They were incredible." Skipper's hands are still for a moment. "You're not drinking enough water."

"What?"

"Your kidneys. See this here?" She presses a point on Jennifer's instep. "This tells me you're not flushing too well. Beer, wine, soda—they won't do it."

"I'm drinking lots of juice."

"Good for the rest of you, but you need more water to flush things out."

"I'll try."

Jennifer's shifts her hips. The waterfall music is making her sleepy. She hasn't been sleeping well, worrying, and hates to take pills because she feels bloated and hung over in the morning.

"How do you—I can't—how do you get past that? Losing two—three—?"

"Imagine that you're made of light," says Skipper, holding Jennifer's calves firmly in her hands, closing her eyes, concentrating, "and that you're spreading outward into a black sky. . . ."

The streets are a little wider in the Barrio Dorado. Long cars with black-tinted windows roll to a stop and disgorge sleekly dressed couples. The neon is more tasteful here, sidewalk cafés with squadrons of hovering waiters and classical guitar tape loops that barely encroach on the neighboring restaurants' sound designs– Casa Linda, El Horno, Mi Viejo Rincón, Bocadito's, the new Zumba disco in the old Planet Hollywood building. The beggars sit against the walls a discreet distance from the café doors, rag bundles with an upturned palm sticking out. The mothers navigate through the early diners and late shoppers to El Castillo Blanco.

"This is more like it," says Nan, leading the way inside. Subdued conversation, Peruvian flutes breathily rendering the soundtrack from *Man of La Mancha*, busboys in native ceremonial costumes. A stunningly beautiful girl shows them to their table.

"How many dollar signs next to this in your guidebook?" asks Eileen.

"We don't get into the wine list, we'll be fine."

"I'm treating," says Jennifer.

"Oh, come on."

"No, really, I want to."

"Lunch, maybe, but here—"

"I'm treating. Period." Jennifer puts her hands over her ears as they sit.

"In that case, let's see the wine list."

Skipper opens the leather-bound menu. "What's the word for *broiled* again?"

"Brolado? Abrolado? Where's Leslie when you need her?"

"They must be pretty wiped to face that room service again."

"Or just sick to death of us."

"The Odd Couple. Hey, they have it in English on the other side." Nan holds the menu up. "I knew this was the right place."

"You're in a good mood."

"Went to see the Man today."

"Buendía? Is something up with your placement?"

Nan just wiggles her eyebrows.

"You mean like a bribe?"

"Sums of money were mentioned, yes, but mostly I just put the fear of God in him."

"He didn't seem like he'd scare too easily."

"You have to know how to handle these people. They've got an inferiority complex—Lord knows they got reason to have one—and you have to know what's bite and what's bluster. You don't think every one of us couldn't have finished our business and been long gone by now? They just like to hold your feet over a fire for a bit, make the gringos squirm."

"That's how I felt when they were doing all the fertility tests," says Jennifer. "Like they were inventing new stuff just to try on me."

"I had two operations."

"And nothing, right?"

"It must work for somebody."

Nan snorts. "It works for the doctors. You don't want to know what those bastards put me through."

"They had me on this stuff with nun's pee in it."

"This is a regular doctor?"

"Italian nun's pee. Some hormone from women of a certain age who have never been sexually active."

"It's a racket," says Nan. "They tried to talk my George into some business with his gonads. I thought he was gonna choke the intern."

Eileen seems upset, watching Nan. "So you're saying you did something or said something and now they're putting you at the head of the line?"

Nan winks. "Baked potatoes. London broil. I think we've scored, ladies."

Leslie makes the call. *"Un orden de empanadas de queso para dos, sopa de pollo, lechón asado con arroz . . . sí, sí . . . y una margarita . . . gracias."* She hangs up and turns to Gayle. "Twenty minutes."

"I'll start timing them in half an hour."

"I wonder where the others ended up going."

"In the Barrio Dorado? I bet the menu says things like 'Incredible Edibles.' "

"I wonder if they think we're being antisocial. Getting room service."

"So what if they do?" Leslie sits on the edge of her bed, raising her legs up to examine the burgundy polish job on her toenails. "I'm sure the rest of them have wanted to do the same thing, just to get some time away from *her.*"

"For me, it's just doing everything in a group."

"Oh, come on, if *she* wasn't in the group it'd be fine. Of course, Miss Triathalon there—"

"Skipper is a good person."

"You cut people a lot of slack."

"She is. It's just her exterior is a bit—intimidating." Gayle studies the menu. She sits in the soft chair by the TV set. "Did you order the cheese things? The turnovers?"

"Yeah."

"I eat any more cheese I might never poop again, but they're *so* good."

"I got the opposite problem."

"Still?"

"I've given myself up to it. You just have to scope out where the nearest toilet is in every new place."

"Poor thing."

Leslie turns the TV set on and lowers the volume. She watches the images for a moment. "Their stuff is even worse than our stuff."

"I wish I could speak it like you do."

"You don't need to understand the words to know how bad it is. Stupidity is a universal language."

"She was a communications major, Nan."

"That's news."

"At Kansas State."

"She told me she went to the University of Missouri," says Leslie. "Majored in political science."

They are silent for a moment, thinking.

"What'd she tell you her husband did for a living?" asks Gayle.

"Engineer."

"High school chemistry teacher."

"You're kidding."

" 'My George is a real taskmaster,' " she says, imitating Nan's voice, the tilt of her chin, " 'They get through a year with him, they know that Periodic Table *cold*.' "

"If I tell you something," says Gayle, "you promise not to pass it on?"

"Only if it's really juicy."

"She steals."

Leslie hits the mute button on the TV. "Steals what?"

"Off the maids' carts. I've seen her take a half-dozen soaps, shampoo— and you know the mints they put on the pillow at night?"

"You're shittin' me."

"Fills her pockets with them."

"I suppose she assumes it's her right."

"It's furtive."

"Furtive. I love it."

"She didn't see me 'cause I was halfway up the stairs. She looked both ways down the hallway and then dug in."

"Everything is so cheap down here, why would you—"

"Probably can't help herself. I mean, she seems so in control all the time, but—"

"Most of your serial killers are totally methodical."

"Oh, come on."

"I know you guys aren't supposed to diss anybody in public, but you got to admit she's a sociopath."

"Is that like a psychopath?"

"With a lower body count, yeah."

"Then why are we letting her have a child?"

"Whoah, Gayle, girlfriend—that's a big leap. They make the rules, not us, and we—"

"We could say something."

"To who?"

"To the people at the agency here."

"That would go down really well. 'In light of the persistent and malicious disappearance of our pillow mints, we the undersigned—' "

"So what do we do?"

"I don't know." Leslie shakes her head. "Be really good mothers to ours. Pray for Rosemary's Baby."

"This is serious."

"I know. It's life, though. You wanna know how many submissions we get every year where the basic story is that Mom's a fruitcake? It's a whole genre."

Gayle is not happy. "So we're afraid to rock the boat. Afraid to get the Ministry riled up."

"You know, I think all it is, we just don't like her. It happens. Some people rub you the wrong way, you start to see every little thing they do and blow it up. The kid, whoever it is, will survive." Leslie does not sound too sure. "Is it a half hour yet?"

You have to be careful where you pick to sleep, or the big kids will rob you or try to fuck you or just beat you up for fun. Pito and the Garza brothers always meet at Gordo's store just before he closes at eight and see if they made enough for paint. Gordo likes to pretend he doesn't know what they do with it.

"I don't want you little pendejos spraying shit on the walls," he always says, when he sells the paint.

They run down to the river, where they hide the rags. Silver and gold are the best. You spray a little into the center, then cup the rag over your nose and breathe in hard till you start to float. The back of your head goes first, and if you have a couple of cans to share the rest of you will follow. Pito closes his eyes, and it is like he is floating on a raft down a river of molten gold with a brilliant silver sky above. Then they walk to the stalls or the underpass or the junk-car lot or any of the other sleeping places, bumping shoulders as they weave and giggle. Pito likes to watch their paint-stained fingers glistening in the streetlights, likes to breathe deep and pull the last of the floating color into his brain. The dogs are out then, pest-ridden bands of five, ten, twelve, but after the paint Pito loves them too much to throw anything.

When Nan gets back to her room she sees the doll on top of the TV where she set it. It looks darker than it did at the mercado. She picks it up, feeling the cloth, pulls the dress and panties down to see what it looks like under there. Bleach. Not too much, a solution, but maybe a good long soak for the body will bring the right color out. And just hope whatever is stuffed inside of it doesn't gum up. Nan puts the doll back on the TV and makes a note to get a packet of bleach. The telephone rings.

Sometimes she feels like a delivering angel, sometimes like a car wreck. The kind of accident that changes a person's life forever, that blocks off one pathway and pushes you down another. Doña Mercedes supposes there is some reasoning behind it now, some effort to match the child with the parents. When Abuela first came it was just the whim of the Mother Superior and the holy guidance she called for. Doña Mercedes supposes, hopes, that now there is some effort to take the tiny bit that the little ones have revealed of themselves and the self-portrait presented in the applicant questionnaires and put them together in a way that is better than blind chance. At Christmas the workers each buy a small present and wrap it and put it under the tree with a number on it, and then they each close their eyes and reach into a pillowcase to pick a number and that's the one you get. Doña Mercedes hopes it's better than that.

They told her the little one at the end of the fifth row is going out tomorrow, the little negrita with the dark eyes and the dimples when she smiles, and to get her ready. They won't let them go out with a really bad rash or an eye infection or if their temperature isn't right. It gives the wrong impression. This one is fine, whining sleepily as Doña Mercedes rolls her to check.

Doña Mercedes leaves a note for the morning shift to feed the negrita a little extra and to make sure she's changed by ten when the mother is supposed to be there. The order came through suddenly, which makes her wonder what strings have been pulled.

"Who knows, mi pequeña," she whispers softly, "what is coming for you tomorrow? Maybe something wonderful."

The stainless steel cart with the next feeding is pushed in, plastic bottles color-coded, wobbling with milk. Doña Mercedes cruises between the cribs, empty arms aching to be full.

Cruisers

EMMETT TOSSES HIS BREAKFAST CRUMBS off the jetty and watches the shitfish rise to check them out. Blue-green, almost translucent, they wiggle listlessly in the shade of the hull all day and congregate at the surface near the vapor lights at night. "Shitfish got no 'urry," the locals say. "Just weat for somebody flush."

He hands the plate back to Muriel on board. "I'm going to see if Roderick is there yet."

"He never comes in till eight." Muriel drops the plate into the plastic suds bucket to soak.

"I thought maybe because of this Whitey and Edna deal—"

"He'll probably sleep late. They called him down, it must have been, what—?"

"Four-thirty."

"See if the paper is in yet. And don't make a nuisance of yourself."

They got the Sunday edition of the St. Augustine paper once a week–news, want ads, employment, real estate, and funnies crammed into their little PO box at the marina office. Emmett needled Muriel for reading the obits first.

"There are people dying now," he'd say, "who never died before." Muriel would pretend to ignore him.

They were moored in the section Emmett liked to call the Lesser Antilles, where most of the smaller live-aboards were concentrated and the walk to the security gates and harbormaster's office was farthest. The shadow of the Ocean Breeze Lifestyles complex barely reached them in the morning. The buildings had gone up rapidly, replacing the funky collection of waterfront businesses that had stood since before they'd come to stay. LET THE FUN BEGIN! says the banner they'd strung up on opening day, still hanging over a year later. There are several units left unoccupied. The marina itself is only two-thirds full, peak season a few weeks off, and many of the boats lay sheathed in blue vinyl, owners off the island or sleeping in town.

Bill and Lil are up on the *Penobscot,* though, Bill prepping the cedar decking while Lil pries open a gallon of goldspar satin.

"Ahoy. "

Lil nods. "Morning, Emmett."

"Still working this varnish farm, eh?"

Bill, grimly sandpapering the foredeck, snorts something like a hello. They were in their late fifties, small, sun-baked to a tobacco-stain brown with nearly identical short-cropped gray hair.

"You're at it early."

"Got to stay on top of these babies," says Lil. "Lot of nasty stuff floating out there." Emmett had only seen them take her out once, and then just for a two-hour shakedown. Lil had been a registered nurse and was still handy with a remedy if you had something more than a headache, while Bill had taught high school and had nothing good to say about it.

"You folks up for the ruckus?"

"Slept right through it. Bill heard voices but thought it was those party people in the motor cruisers."

"There were a dozen of them out there. Lights, stretchers—"

"We were dead to the world. Some wild stories were flying in the Crow's Nest this morning. But you know rumors on this island."

"It was the lights woke me up, not the sound," says Emmett. "Of course, Muriel says I'm deaf as a post."

"I should be so lucky. This one"— Lil jerks her head toward the

Scavenger, a day sailer owned by one of the locals—"has got his radio on all weekend. Rap music or whatever their version is called here. Makes Bill grind his teeth."

Bill wraps fine-grade sandpaper around a wooden dowel and goes to work on the mahogany trim. He and Lil wear the same brand of t-shirt and shorts, Topsiders, and matching hooded windbreakers when they sit out at night. Emmett wonders if they swap clothes.

"I never figured Whitey and Edna—"

Lil lays out her brushes. "I know. Edna was telling me just last week that they were looking into a condo here."

"My wife is convinced you can't live on a sportfisherman," says Emmett. He can see the tuna tower of the *Silver King*, Whitey and Edna's old Bertram, over the forest of masts. "Suppose they'll auction it right away. Unless they've paid their mooring through the year."

Lil frowns, staring at her varnish. "Condos. They must have been desperate."

"Well—storm season comes around, some folks like solid ground under their beds. What do you hear about this Cedric?"

Cedric was the tropical storm curling in from the Atlantic, possibly mutating into the first hurricane of the summer.

Lil glances out over the channel. Clear blue sky, flat water. "It'll blow itself out. Peaked too early."

"It does hit, it's gonna ruin your finish."

Lil shrugs. "Best way to protect the wood." She chooses a brush, riffling the bristles with her thumb. "No, you buy into that condo life, you're ready to throw in the towel."

"They've put up some real luxury boxes in the last few years."

"The ones we looked at, that Pelican Cove outfit? They'd blow down like a stack of cards."

Bill grimaces. "Pelican Cove."

Lil jerks her head toward her husband. "Says he'd just as soon ride it out in the marina."

"There's gonna be a big one hits this island sooner or later, Cedric or no Cedric. I can't say they've knocked themselves out preparing for it."

"Cyannot stop de wind, mon," mutters Bill, mimicking Roderick's island lilt. "She come, she come."

Lil dips the edge of her brush into the varnish, careful to avoid dripping as she starts to apply it. "We've been thinking about Curaçao."

"Dutch people."

"A lot of them speak English. And the prices are right."

"What's a rum collins?"

"Less than here, I can tell you that."

"I suppose. Muriel and I talk about Mexico now and again."

"Mañanaland."

Emmett shrugs. "The peso just keeps falling. Our checks could go a lot further."

Bill wipes the section he's just sanded with a damp cloth. "Mexico," he says. "One good case of the trots and you're history."

A fishing skiff with a pair of locals aboard chugs around the reef of auto tires that serves as a breakwater and heads for the fuel dock.

The marina had been nothing much when Emmett first tied up here twenty years ago, rickety unpainted wood crusted with gull droppings. But as the cruisers and their money grew in importance, the mosquito fleet was driven to a shallower harbor farther west and a French corporation built the new jetty and facilities. Now ramshackle boats like this might wander in illegally to sightsee among the yachts or hustle up charters, but when Roderick was on duty they didn't dare tie up.

The man working the outboard waves lazily to Emmett.

"Golden Years." He smiles. "Bringin' the chat round."

A lot of the locals call him by the name of the boat, and Muriel endures being hailed as Mrs. Golden Years. "Could be worse," he likes to tell her. "If we had that catamaran on C Pier you'd be Betty Bazooka."

Rut Adams is up on the fly deck of the *Squire*, nursing a Bloody

Mary and training binoculars on the new arrival at the far end of the marina.

"Anything to report?"

Rut brings his binoculars down, his eyes taking a moment to adjust.

"Emmett. Caught me spying."

"I don't suppose they spend their time looking at us."

It was just there one morning, looking more like a space-age hotel than a boat, dwarfing the Cheoy Lee and Broward hundred-footers in the Land of the Giants. A forty-plus sportfisher was perched like a toy on the aft deck and the heliport had been used once so quickly nobody saw who jumped in or out of the chopper.

"They got manned submersibles on that thing—those Jacques Cousteau things? Decompression chamber in the lazarette, satellite dish, large-format screen like a movie theater. Got two Jacuzzis, personal trainer, cook with a full staff—"

"You saw all this?"

Rut shakes his head. "Archibald, the local fella who comes around with the crabs? He's been on board a bunch of times. Got a thing going with one of the maids. Filipino gal."

"I've still never seen the man," says Emmett. "Just people running around in uniforms setting things up."

"He's been here once or twice."

"Imagine being the center of all that. You get a whim to go out and dozens of people jump into action." Emmett has walked on the pontoon beside it once, pacing off at least eighty yards, staring up at his reflection in the tinted plexiglass cabin panels. Nothing stirred aboard. Muriel calls it the Mother Ship and says it's crewed by bulb-headed aliens. "So what's he look like?"

Rut clears his throat, recalling. "Swarthy fella. Remember the one Nixon used to hang out with? Relleno—Refugio—"

"Rebozo."

"Looks like him."

"Drug money?"

"Not enough security hanging around. I don't think he's Spanish of any kind. Not an Arab either—Arabs don't dive."

"They don't?"

"Hell, no. My guess is he's some Greek, owns one of these international dot-com outfits. Making money out of thin air."

"What you think it runs him to keep it floating?"

Rut always knows what things cost or has an educated guess. He stands on top of his big Hatteras, calculating, face glowing red with his first drink of the day. "Damn if I can even imagine. Meggy was here the other day"—Rut's wife, Meggy, lives in their cliff house and only visits on weekends— "her Daddy owned half the state of Delaware, and even *her* jaw dropped when she got a look at it. I'd say crew and staff alone is a good fifty–sixty grand a week."

Emmett whistles, looks back toward the massive yacht. "A thing that size, hardly know you're on the ocean."

"You sail people." Rut grins. "Wrestling a hunk of canvas and puking your guts out."

"Dacron," says Emmett. "Things have progressed a little."

"If there's no wind you're still fucked. Hey, what's the deal with Whitey and what's-her-name?"

"Edna."

"Edna."

"No details yet. I'm hoping to track Roderick down."

They both look toward D Pier, to the yellow tape cordoning off the *Silver King* in its berth.

"I think of him sitting out there every evening in his fighting chair, knocking one back."

"G and T," says Emmett.

"That what it was? I'm a scotch man myself. I could see him from up here—he'd raise his glass, we'd toast the sunset."

"A real gentleman, Whitey."

"Health problems?"

"Not that I know of."

"That age, it can go fast."

"They brought in a black marlin last month. Whitey was in the chair. Fought him four–five hours before he made his last run. Boated him, cut him loose, but he just floated sidewise on the surface so they circled around and gaffed him in before the sharks could gather. Good seven, seven and half feet. You can't swing that with health problems."

"Fish like that will take up a lot of wall space."

"They'd caught it before."

"What?"

"Edna said that when they got it on board they recognized the marlin—scars, the shape of its dorsal. They were sure of it. Couple years ago in the Dry Tortugas."

"That's one for Ripley."

"She said Whitey was pretty upset about it."

"Killing the fish?"

Emmett nods. "Either that or that it was the same one. He was always saying, 'I like to beat 'em, not beat 'em to death.' "

"Stick a hook in your lip, drag a quarter mile of line through the ocean for a couple hours, what's he think is gonna happen?" Rut shakes his head. "Moody bastards, fishermen. That Hemingway—"

"Whitey never cared for Hemingway. He liked the dog fella."

"Dog fella."

"Call of the Wild, White Fang—"

"Jack London."

"Loved him."

"He wrote about boats?"

"I guess so."

"London. Think he drowned himself. Or drank himself to death." Rut kills the last of his Bloody Mary. " 'Death, where is thy sting?' "

"He died of TB." Chase Pomeroy steps out on the *Rockin Robin* in the next slip, rubbing his eyes. "Or some shit like that. Sailed to the South Seas and brought back all these really gnarly diseases."

Chase is a currency trader still in his thirties who has recently traded up from a little Sea Ray to a Sunchaser Predator.

"That thing get airborne?" asks Emmett, eyeing the boat.

"It'll move." Chase climbs on top of the cabin and lies on his back, covering his eyes against the sun. "Make the Caymans in under three hours."

"What's your hurry?" Rut complains about Chase speeding in the channel but always comes on deck when he brings a new girlfriend around.

Chase shrugs. "I wanted to float with the current, I'd find some Haitians and build a raft. What can you do in that thing, twelve knots, max?"

"It depends." Rut's face gets redder. "You hear the brouhaha last night?"

"Saw it. I was at Zooma till two—dead night, lot of dental hygienists off a cruise ship—then I hit the Daquiri Shak with Ricky G till it closed. We got back from the Dak, and there's the whole sorry excuse for a police department and the even sorrier excuse for a rescue squad."

"They couldn't rescue a turd from a toilet bowl," says Rut. "I ever get in the shit out there, I'm calling Key West and take my chances on the wait."

"They asked us for ID. You imagine that? Ricky goes up to the captain—whatever he is, the one in charge—and says, 'You know me, I used to bang your sister when she worked in my restaurant'."

"That must have cleared things up."

"Ricky's slipping payoffs to every one of these guys, what're they gonna do?"

"You see anything?"

"Lotta lights, lotta local constabulary. I think the old folks were already out of here by that point."

Emmett nods. "You heard anything more about the storm?"

"Just that it's supposed to be coming." Chase shifts his arm away from his eyes to squint up at Rut. "I'm taking this out today, pollute the environment. You see Stephanie—"

"That's the new one? Redheaded gal?"

Chase nods. "Yeah, with the wide butt. Tell her I'll be at Zooma by ten."

A trio of frigate birds sail over the marina, gradually losing altitude and seeming to pick up speed as they swoop down into the channel. It is already hot. A film of diesel oil swirls in rainbow colors around the pilings and a single turtle paddles between the moored boats, head just breaking the surface.

Emmett likes to thinks of the marina as a community, maybe a few more transients than usual but with reliably suburban rhythms. A bit of bustle at sunrise, morning errands, buckling down to serious work by midday, and then the relaxing slide to cocktail hour. He likes to hear the hardware rattling as the boats rock in their slips, the squeak of rope and cleat, the sharp luffing of plastic boat covers. He likes to hear the motors coughing into life, thrumming as they pass on the way out, likes the smell of polyurethane and Deet. Emmett likes the long tines of the jetty with their evenly spaced slips, hundreds of boats with distinct outlines and personalities moored side by side, the blazing primary blues and reds and yellows of gear, the stunning white of fiberglass and Dacron. He liked the gulls and pelicans in the old days, too, but the feeding and dumping regulations have had their effect and they only pass over now, heading for the smelly chaos of the locals' wharf.

Roderick is talking with Ricky G, who sits looking disoriented at the fore of a shiny new Beneteau. Ricky is wearing a shirt with a Day-Glo parrot fish design and has marks from fiberglass deck beading on one side of his face.

"Looks like somebody passed out on the deck," says Emmett.

"I needed to rest." Ricky never seems to shave yet never has a full beard, sporting a perpetual morning-after stubble. "These people are up in Vermont or something."

"What if I trespass you, sleep on Ricky bar some night?"

"I've pulled you out from under the table more than once."

"Never 'appen beyond closing time. Surprise me them authority don't 'carcerate you while they here last night."

Emmett steps closer. "Listen, Roderick, what—"

Roderick puts his big hand up for silence before he can say more. "Mr. Alphonse already vex me wit' instruction. I got nothin' to tell till official version has been spoken."

"Were you here?"

"Drag me ass out of bed, got to open every gate in creation." Roderick shakes his head. "Why they don't weat till sunup, spear a mon his sleep?"

"It was an emergency."

"Nothing in that boat that wouldn't keep till sunup."

"Remember the dude two Christmases ago," says Ricky, "washed up by the old turtle works?"

"Accidental causes."

"That's what they always say when they don't know shit. Didn't know where he came from, what boat he was off of, nada. And nobody ever claimed him."

"Plenty of that on this island."

"But the watch he had on, the guy was obviously a tourist—"

"Black mon drown," says Roderick, "authority don't inquire. White mon drown they declear mystery."

There is a pause as they all watch the blond divorcée from Sarasota and her teenage daughter in matching bikinis pass on the parallel pier. Ricky moans quietly.

"I could go either way with that."

"Them womens kill you, Ricky. Rum has sap all your powers."

"I heard a rumor," says Emmett, "that it happened three days ago. Whitey and Edna."

"No way. He came in just yesterday." Ricky tended bar at the Y-Ki-Ki, which he co-owned, and spent so many of his waking hours shooting the shit behind the counter that he never had a tan. "About four. Sat at the end, three G and T's, paid his tab, and left."

"You didn't talk with him?"

"There were these Belgian girls, I was feeding them Yellow Birds—you know, with the amaretto? They were starting to loosen up, so I didn't pay much attention to Whitey."

"Whitey always drinks his cocktail on his boat," says Roderick. "Why is he paying double to you?"

"Psychology's not my field, man. I just pour 'em what they ask for."

"How'd he look?"

"Like he always did. Like he just stepped off that battlewagon of theirs with some twenty-foot sea monster in tow. He had that squinty-lookin' smile—"

"Muriel called him the Ancient Mariner."

"He wasn't so ancient."

"Couple years older than me, and I'm getting on." Emmett turns back to Roderick. "I think as a resident of this marina, I deserve—"

"I give you a groundation and everybody want to ax me same story."

"You tell Emmett here," says Ricky, "and the news will *fly*."

Roderick just smiles and starts away. "Weat for official story. Then I tell you what part is a lie."

When Emmett last talked with Whitey he'd been fine, upbeat even. They ran into each other at the local grocery, the one a mile walk from the marina but half as expensive as the Captain's Larder at the Ocean Breeze complex.

"Only thing she'll eat anymore," said Whitey, when he caught Emmett checking out the four loaves of white bread and dozen tins of ham spread in his basket.

"I thought you liked to cook?"

"Used to. Used to do a three-course layout in that little galley of ours. Baked bread, pies. Now, it's just—you know." Whitey shrugged. "It's another meal."

Emmett nodded. "Mine won't have anything to do with fixing dinner. Twenty-five years of feeding the kids—"

"Yeah."

"So I just fire the old hibachi up."

"Grilled what—was it amberjack last night?"

"You can smell it."

"No problem. Just don't let the day man catch you."

"Roderick and I have an understanding." Emmett pushed his items forward on the counter to make room for Whitey's case of bargain gin. "How the fish been treating you?"

"Oh, fair." Whitey and Edna didn't keep much of what they caught but went out almost every day. "Punk Loomis got into a bunch of wahoo the other day off the east tip– we might try that."

"What are the locals catching?"

"Infectious diseases."

They laughed. As more kids drifted down from the States there were fewer and fewer locals working in the bars and restaurants, and Ocean Breeze advertised that it had 'fully professionalized' its staff, which meant most of the black faces were gone. The little market was one of the few places Emmett still rubbed elbows with people born on the island.

"It had to happen sooner or later," Whitey said. "That 'no problem, mon' thing only goes so far and then you need some service. It's something we thought about a lot before we made our commitment here."

"But the culture—"

"Nobody comes here for the culture."

There was a carnival once a year that Emmett tried to avoid, people passed out in unusual places, and a couple of local bands that played loud enough to be heard over the water several miles away. What amazed Emmett most about the island was that it was populated at all, with no fresh water and almost nothing edible grown in the interior. European sailors had tried leaving pigs and goats on it for provision, but they quickly died of thirst, and cane and sisal plantings hadn't done much better. The locals were descended from the workers on these destitute plantations and escapees from slave ships that ran aground in the early 1800s.

"All dem other crop feel," Roderick liked to say, "but tourist business been very good to we."

"You circle the globe between ten and twenty-five degrees above the equator," said Whitey, laying a sack of limes on top of the gin, "one port isn't much different than the next."

"So you're here for a while."

"Oh, we're here to stay. Like it says in the brochures," Whitey winked at Emmett. " 'It's always smooth sailing in our island paradise.' "

The Schmecklers are behind the pilothouse of their big Frers headsail ketch, spreading engine parts on a tarp. Emmett knows the father and son are Fritz and Stefan but can never remember which is which.

"Part still hasn't come in?"

"Customs," says the father. "They steal it."

"One focking injector." The son stares down at the disassembled machinery. "They don't know what it is, but they steal it."

They are tall and wide-shouldered, relentlessly enthusiastic, with thick beards bleached by the sun. The first day they sailed in, Muriel thought somebody was shooting a beer commercial.

"You were a friend of the diseased?" asks the father.

"Diseased—?"

"The one who is dying."

"Deceased. Whitey—yes. They were neighbors, sort of. D Pier."

"Your boat is?"

"The *Golden Years*? Island Packet cutter?"

"I have seen this."

"Nothing compared to your rig, but we call it home." Mrs. Schmeckler, Greta, smiles as she steps up from the cabin to shake a mat out over the starboard side. "Whitey and Edna were eight or nine slips down from us."

"They were having some problem?"

Emmett considers. "I got the impression they were living their dream. Down here in the sun, chasing fish, nothing on the horizon but more of the same—"

"Our dream now is to circle the world in the *Liebenstraum*," says the father. "It keeps us moving forward."

"And when you finish?"

"Then we start on another dream," says the son. "You have been to Havana?"

"Havana, Cuba? No, I'm—we're Americans."

"We go there next."

"Could be some serious weather coming."

"If this cylinder is not fixed," says the father, "we will grow old here. Become native people."

Emmett thinks it's a joke but he's never sure with the Schmecklers. "There are worse fates."

"Men have woyage for centuries without a motor," says the son. "Maybe we go on with only our sails."

"Don't think it's likely you'll find a Mercedes injector in Havana. Pretty lean times, what with the embargo and all. And berthing this baby without an engine in a strong wind—"

The father smiles. "Sailing is easy, ja? Only the landing is hard."

It had been another perfect day, maybe two weeks ago, heading northeast in a bracing dance with the wind, hull slicing through the swells, a half-dozen gulls coasting in their wake. Muriel had an instinctive feel for trimming the sails and they barely spoke anymore, one anticipating the other's next move, making a leisurely ten knots into a slight breeze.

At first Emmett thought a cloud had drifted in front of the sun— a sudden chill, a dimming. Then he felt the hole inside of him, expanding. There was nothing on the horizon in any direction, nothing. But it wasn't fear or feeling small in the vast ocean. He had always preferred cruising *to* somewhere, somewhere they'd at least stay overnight. A destination. Going out and coming back to the same port, no one waiting for them, only the mute variables of tide and weather to define their passage— he felt suddenly disoriented, tempted to let the wheel go, to turn off all the systems, sit back, and see what would happen. The feeling didn't last more than a few minutes. Blood sugar, maybe, or just some random fan-tods. He told Muriel to come about, and she gave him a look but didn't question. The trip home was just as spectacular.

Larry is nestled in a pile of life preservers at the base of the mast on the *Zephyr*, pecking at his laptop. The power cord loops over his bare feet and disappears down into the cockpit.

"When you were crewing a ship in the old days," he says, without looking up, "you hung out at the sailors' bars till a couple likely ones drank themselves stiff, dragged them off, and threw them in the hold till you were a full day out of port. Now I'm on the fucking Web."

"What happened to your girls?"

Larry hit the marina three weeks ago with a pair of girls in their twenties, whom he'd introduced to Emmett as his galley slaves.

"Bugged out on me."

"The both of them?"

"They came as a team. I saw the skinny one, Kim, in town yesterday. Hanging all over one of those boogie board guys with the blond dreads. Bitch just waves—'Hi, Captain Larry!'—like she and her dumpy little pal haven't totally screwed me."

Larry is in his early fifties, salt-and-pepper beard, a regular at the Y-Ki-Ki since his Catalina sloop limped down from the Bahamas. He was gradually heading for Tahiti, he said, once he got the right crew on board.

"You know, there's a couple young fellas on the island know their way around on a boat," says Emmett cheerfully. "Skip Andersen's boy there, Nicky, and the one that works at the bait shop– Jay? Jordan?"

Larry shakes his head. "Only room for one hardtail on this bucket."

Emmett shrugs. "You're the skipper."

"They do that passive-aggressive thing? My wife was the queen of that. She could say 'Oh, don't worry, it's fine,' so it came out 'You blew it again, you insensitive piece of shit.' "

He seems more agitated than usual. At first, from the bile invoked when he spoke of his ex-wife and her evil lawyer, Emmett thought Larry's divorce must be recent, the wound still raw. But he'd been single a full eight years, cruising for five, a computer-dating Ahab chasing a wet dream.

"Even if they don't learn jack about sailing," he says, "these young ones get to practice their routine on me."

Emmett keeps smiling. "So is there some kind of computer shape-up where all the able-bodied sea ladies advertise?"

"Something like that. But you hire one, they bring their whole damn sorority along. If this wasn't too much boat to single-hand, I'd be off this rock by now." He looks up to Emmett. "You hear the scuttle on the old couple?"

"Roderick won't talk."

"What does Roderick know? He didn't go inside the boat."

"You did?"

Larry logs off, closes the laptop, and sets it beside him. Emmett sees now that his eyes are red, his hands trembling slightly.

"I saw the old guy, Whitey, there at Ricky's place just yesterday afternoon. Then last night I couldn't sleep, so I get up, take a walk around the jetty—"

"This is late—"

"After three, at least. I get down at their end of D Pier and I hear the radio. Just weather reports and shit, somebody giving the update on this Cedric."

"Edna was a real weather junkie," says Emmett. "We'd be sitting here, she'd tell you it was raining over in the Sea of Cortez."

"Fairly useless information."

"She explained the whole hurricane thing to me once. Most people think it's like straight wind pushing you over? But really you're being pulled, sucked in to fill a vacuum. Like going down a drain." Suddenly Emmett doesn't want to know the details, dreads the responsibility of passing the news to others. "All that noise and activity," he says, "but inside there's this big nothing."

Larry frowns at his hands. "The thing is, it was *loud*. The radio. I passed by, but on the way back I figure at that hour, not a light shining on the boat, they must have spent the night in town and left it running. So I'm gonna do the Good Samaritan thing."

Emmett suddenly feels a little dizzy. He looks across the channel. Something, not clouds exactly but a different kind of sky, is coming together in the north.

"You hesitate to step on somebody's boat without an invitation. Especially the live-aboards."

"You just don't do it," says Emmett, upset. "It's an invasion of privacy."

"I'm feeling pretty fucking invaded right now," says Larry, "if you want to know the truth."

"We haven't actually seen Edna for a while," says Emmett, stalling.

"No. I don't suppose you have." Larry wiggles the power cord with his toes, thinking. "You know that shark gun he kept by his chair when they went out for big stuff?"

"Short-barrel forty-four."

"About as much wallop as you can get from a rifle. You can imagine, point-blank range, not shooting through water—he was just down on the saloon couch, the rifle was still between his knees. And the wife—the blood on the pillow and sheets was all dried. He must've caught her sleeping."

Emmett sees a trio of jellyfish working their way along the pontoon, no color, no edges, just a slight lack of focus in one part of the water. "Was she on her back? Looking up?"

"Yeah—"

"So she could have been awake. Knew it was coming, even."

"Like some kind of mercy-killing deal?"

"Why not?"

Larry considers this. He is shivering a bit, the shadow of the Lifestyles complex covering them both. He shrugs. "Who knows what the fuck goes on in people's heads? I figure she was already gone three–four days when I sat with him at Ricky's. I asked what was new, and he said they were thinking about tarpon."

"That's all?"

" 'We've been thinking about tarpon.' "

They are quiet for a long moment, a breeze picking up and tinkling the wind chimes on the back of the converted tug two slips down. A sucession of hippie-looking people come down to use it on some sort of time-sharing deal. Muriel calls it the Love Boat.

"I hauled my ass back here and got my cell phone, tracked down the cops. I didn't go back in a second time, just gave them my statement. I'd forgot to turn the damn radio off. Took the locals an hour before they figured it out." Larry looks out past the breakwater. "The fella calling in said he thought this Cedric might turn into the real thing."

Emmett nods. The channel water has a little chop to it now. The frigate birds have disappeared.

"The way I feel, just let it blow," he says. "Be good to clear the air."

Terminal Lounge

OLD OVERHOLT APPEARS AS TOMMY is stocking ice. Rattle and crunch of the cubes into the bins, look up—and he's there.

"I never see you come in."

"You're a busy man." Old Overholt settling onto his roost.

"I'm just on," says Tommy.

"Time for my medicine."

Tommy sets up a rye and Sprite, the first strong whiff of the evening as he pours. He had a guy behind the counter once, Conrad, when he was managing Bottoms Up. Got fried every night but you never saw him take a nip. "It's the fumes," he'd say, Conrad, grinning too much near last call, "they go where you can't pee them out."

Tommy lays the drink in front of Old Overholt. "You, sir," he says, "are a drinking man."

"From a long line."

"Some nights in here, they get going with the daiquiris and coladas and all, I could be making smoothies at the mall."

"I'd no sooner put fruit in my liquor than I'd put it in my coffee." Overholt makes a face as he takes a small hit on the rye. "My father used to drink this straight."

"A different breed."

"My grandfather, worked in a tannery, he'd drink a gallon of beer at lunch. For the nutrition, he said."

"It's a grain, sure."

"He had skin like leather, my old man's old man. From the chemicals."

Tommy places bottles of the hard stuff in their holders thigh-high behind the counter, pressing speed pourers into place. When they bought the old train station, Donna redesigned the interior but left the bar itself to him. "This is my operating room," he'd tell the customers, "my cockpit. You could blindfold me and I wouldn't spill a shot's worth."

"So how's things, Tommy?"

"Chuggin' along."

"That's good. For those of us who have been *derailed*, so to speak, it's good to see a young fella making his way in the world."

"Not so young."

"You get my age, anything under fifty is kindergarten. How's your better half?"

"Fine. She's fine."

It was a jumble of benches and smashed tile when they bought it, an iffy proposition even with the rehab loan from the city. But Donna had three brothers in construction and a real knack for designing things. The old timetables on the walls, the steam engine photos, all the polished wood—not bad for a cocktail waitress who flunked art in high school.

"You should think about it for a career," Tommy would tell her. "There's a lot of businesses out there crying for a theme."

"I've got a career," she would say, elbow-deep in accounts and receipts at one of the tables. "Keeping you from pouring our investment away."

She did the books, Donna, poking her little calculator with a single lacquered fingernail and shaking her head. "It doesn't add up." That was her favorite phrase. "It doesn't add up."

Spacy Stacy floats in and perches at the far end by the jukebox. Tommy lets them play with the box till eight, when he puts the tape program on. Stacy swivels, feeds the juke, and punches a few numbers. A reggae song begins to play.

"Calypso music," grumbles Overholt. "I thought that died with Harry Belafonte."

"He's not dead."

"Rum drinkers down there. My old man's brother Jack was a navy man. He swore by that dark Jamaican stuff."

"They used to give them a grog ration every day, the British Navy. Rum mixed with water."

"You're a compendium, Tom. What were the proportions?"

Tommy shrugs, heads down toward Stacy. "I suppose it varied. Captain smelled bad weather coming, he might have watered it down some."

"The source of many a mutiny." Overholt bangs ice cubes against his teeth, polishing off his rye. "Drinking water would kill you in those days."

Stacy is somewhere in her fifties, skinny arms sticking out of a big Hawaiian shirt, wispy blond hair fading to gray, freckled sun-cured skin. She gives Tommy a big, forlorn smile.

"Hiya, handsome."

"We're out of bananas, Stacy."

"Mai tai."

"Is that gonna be it tonight? 'Cause if it gets busy—"

Tommy doesn't mind mixing the complicated ones when it's not frantic, but he only has two hands and Shawn won't be in tonight.

"Make enough for a couple," says Stacy. "Maybe three or four."

"You sure?"

"One of those moods."

Stacy has been disappointed in love, as she has told Tommy in great detail several times. A good passenger, though, adds a bit of color to the place with her shirts, doesn't get sloppy. He's never seen her go home with anybody.

"Cedric loved this song," she says, eyes closed, nodding toward the jukebox.

"I know."

"Donna around?"

Donna makes Stacy nervous. Donna makes a lot of the passengers nervous, though she doesn't really work the tables anymore. Something about the way she seems to be watching every pour, measuring. "You're the cruise director, Tommy," she tells him. "I'm the cashier."

"She'll be in sometime later."

Stacy pushes her hair back, an armful of shell bracelets clacking together. "You two are an inspiration. It's so hard in this world."

Tommy mixes the rums and the syrups, the curaçao, and gives it a good shake.

"And then, if you're interracial, it's like everybody's got an opinion. Everybody's in your business."

Tommy pulls an old-fashioned glass from the chiller and pours one. Stacy takes hers without garnish.

"They can't stand to see you happy."

"There's a lot of resentment in the world." He places the drink in front of her.

"He was a beautiful man, Cedric. Sweet. But they poisoned his mind."

Tommy gives her a sympathetic smile and moves to the other end of the bar. He pushed her once for information, for the end of the ballad, and she pulled out a photo of her with Cedric on the beach in their party days and made him admit they looked like a perfect couple.

Tyler is settling in, pulling his tie off, shaking his head over the latest insult.

"Tyler. How they treating you?"

"I feel like hammered shit." He knows Tyler from back in the eighties, part of a pack of corporate raiders who hung at Bottoms Up when one of Tommy's responsibilities was checking the bathroom stalls for coke ODs.

"What can I do for you?"

"Rusty Nail. Use the good stuff."

Tommy reaches for the single malt on the back wall. "What's the Market doing?"

"Fucking me. From a height."

Tommy doesn't know if Tyler is a first or last name. He comes in after work a couple times a week and hits it pretty hard.

"What's that blue thing?" he asks.

"Blue thing?"

"The Outcast of the Islands there," he says, nodding toward Stacy at the far end. "What's she working on?"

"Mai tai."

"Jesus." Tyler grimaces. "Looks like what they give you to check your GI tract."

"You've had that done?"

"My ex. She had stomach complaints." Tyler tests his drink, closing his eyes appreciatively. "Turned out to be pure bile."

Tyler's fellow traders had moved on to a place called the Closing Bell, but lately he came to the Lounge to be among less familiar faces.

"And how are you doing, Tom? How's this place panning out?"

Tom grins, holds out his arms to encompass it all. "I'm living the dream."

"That's terrific."

"We're bringing in a bigger crowd every night."

"An up cycle."

"Bars don't have the roller-coaster thing your racket does. People take the ride a couple times, feel at home, you'll never lose them."

"If anybody gets to beat the game," says Tyler, "I hope it's you."

Tommy has seen a lot of them like Tyler. Not even his age yet and already whipped by life. Either you let it get to you, defeat you, or you hunker down, feed the engine, and barrel on through. The Lounge was really going to take off one of these days. It had been building up steam, all the signs were there, I mean leave the tracks and *fly*. No matter what certain negative parties might think.

Amber is on tonight to run the floor. Tommy is pouring himself his first, a finger of Glenlivet, when she brings a wad of new singles to the register.

"Donna in?"

"She'll probly drop by later. You need something?"

"Just my schedule."

"You can talk to me."

"I'll wait."

Amber and the new kid, Bethany, are all right, into the spirit of the place, and do pretty well on tips without feeding the passengers free ones or coming on like lap dancers. Amber especially has a great sense of the room. Tommy had instituted the Quarter-to Rush, pulling the steam-whistle cord at fifteen to the hour and giving the staff fifteen seconds to pick up one of the line of shots waiting for them on the counter. The other passengers liked to see the floor staff hustle through the crowd for their payoff, and a shot an hour was about the right amount of lubrication to keep them loose, keep them motivated. Amber could snake hers in passing, somehow always there within reaching distance, and throw it down on the move without breaking stride. The deal was, of course, that Tommy would polish off whatever was still there on the pine after the fifteen seconds were up.

"Unclaimed baggage," he would say, shaking his head as if suddenly discovering the shot glasses in front of him. "Can't leave that lying around."

Amber could stall a table of drunks to give them some recovery time, or whisk a pitcher still a third full from the middle of a bunch of frat boys and manage to leave them thinking they'd gotten a free refill by the end of the night. She'd been bugging Tommy for a bigger cut of the tips.

"I'm carrying some of these people, Tommy. This even split—"

"Is what you got back when somebody was carrying *you*. It works out over time, Amber. Every once in a while you got to leave some money on the table."

When Tommy pulls the cord for the first Rush the train is just leaving the station. The before-dinner drinkers are in for a quick one, the Mighty Sparrow is chattering on the box, and after he knocks back his own shot

Tommy can feel the floor starting to move under his feet, that trick of the senses where it's not clear if the platform is moving or the train, the ground never quite where you expect it when you put your next foot down.

Bethany asks where Donna is when she comes up for hers.

"She might be in and she might not," says Tommy, checking out her face jewelry. It used to gross him out, especially the nose things that looked like boogers, but now he thinks it's kind of sexy, like the whole bare-belly thing and the ones with the tattoos in the small of their backs. "You card that bunch by the door?"

"They checked out okay."

Tommy hates wearing his glasses and can't read print on a driver's license without them, so he puts the girls on it. "Look like they're fifteen, max."

Nick and Nora come in then, Nick with the junior wise-guy chain hanging down and his shirt open a couple buttons too many and his tanning-salon bronze skin, giving his little chin jerk of a greeting to Tommy as he slides onto the stool. Nora has brought a package into the place, already wobbly on her heels. Nora is maybe five years older than Nick and does the full-frontal makeup thing, her nails always matching her eye shadow and her hair tortured into tight little ringlets that look like they hurt. She sits hard and looks not quite at Tommy.

"L.I.T.," she says.

Tommy looks to Nick, who just holds his hands out as if to say, Don't ask.

"I should ask for a doctor's report, serving one of those."

Nora is usually a white-wine gal. She doesn't acknowledge the joke.

"Gin and tonic," says Nick.

Tommy turns to assemble the ingredients for Nora, splashing gin, vodka, rum, and tequila into the blender, measuring out white crème de menthe. Nora was a clerk at Public Works, and one day Nick was behind with his utilities and came in person to squawk over the penalty. They'd been coming in together for six months or so, lots of knee hockey on the stools till there was a booth free and they could put their heads together. They were always out the door, Nora stuck to Nick like a barnacle, by half past ten. Tommy dumps a can of sour mix in, fills with cola to the line, and flicks the machine on. He prefers working with a shaker, the whole Chiquita Banana rumba of the movement, but there isn't time when the Lounge is filling up.

"I don't see why not," says Nick, as if continuing a conversation.

"What're you, kidding?" Nora avoids her own eyes in the mirror, won't look at Nick.

"It's how we started. Why not—"

"Go out with a bang."

"Don't be that way."

"What way should I be?"

"You never had any complaints."

"Right."

"I mean we're both adults. We came into this thing with open eyes. I don't see why we can't—"

"Because you're marrying some cunt tomorrow, that's why."

"Watch the mouth." Nick looks to Tommy as if for moral support.

Tommy lays the drinks in front of them. "One Long Island Iced Tea for the lady." He smiles. "One G and T for the gentleman—and I use the term loosely."

Nick is not amused. She isn't the only one he brings in—Nora—but with the others he doesn't linger. Just a leg opener at the bar, maybe something stronger if he can get them to go for it, and then out. A clean operator, though, never a scene. There have been a few in the Lounge already, slaps and shouts, engagement rings thrown, that one crazy Puerto Rican girl, Dominican, whatever, waving one stiletto heel around like an ice pick while she stalked the poor shlub she was mad at with the other one still on, a hobbling little cyclone of fury. And the one with Donna— which was highly unprofessional of her—but that was family business and there was no breakage. Tommy's mother threw plates, God knows with plenty of reason, and he would make a joke of it with Mike Delahanty from the apartment downstairs, who could hear everything.

"Wasn't too bad," Tommy would say. "Three plates, a coffee mug, and a cereal bowl."

"You should buy the plastic ones," Delahanty would say, smug, as if his father hadn't gone out for the famous pack of cigarettes and never come back. "You can pitch a double-header with 'em, they won't bust."

The stools were all taken now, each passenger with a destination in mind, the whiskey sippers, the imported-draft drinkers, the ones who upped the ante with each round ordered and the cautious ones who tapered off. A few might miss their stop, lulled by the ride, but most pushed back from the counter right on schedule. Brewster, who never slouched or rested his elbows on the counter, was a Grey Goose martini man, just that single silver bullet and then home to the wife. Zigliewicz, Mr. Z from the Department of Human Services, drank Manhattans, constantly pinching the bridge of his nose, as if testing it for numbness until it told him it was time to go. A few, like Overholt and Spacy Stacy and sometimes Tyler, were there for the whole ride.

"Baseball," says Tyler, working on his second, just sipping now, "you hit sixty home runs one year, whatever the record is, you've always got that. Maybe the next year you lose a step, eyesight diminishes, can't hit the curveball—"

"They send you to Paducah." Overholt proclaims it like a sentence of death.

"You're out of the game. But that accomplishment, that record, they can't take that away. My racket, you have a shit day, a shit week, it's like you've always *been* shit. It erases what you've done in the past."

"You've done that well? The Market version of sixty home runs?"

"Not my point. My point is there's no *closure*. Every day you start from scratch—"

"A Sisyphean task."

"He at least had a big rock to push against. All I've got is the damn telephone, some numbers."

"You got to bank your best years."

"My *ex* got to bank my best years. It's like putting Babe Ruth's first wife in the Hall of Fame."

"Athletes are an exception. The rest of us—"

"The rest of us are only as good as our last twenty-four hours."

"There's a depressing thought" says Tommy replacing Overholt's drink with a new one, a bit heavier on the Sprite. "You make your fortune a drop at a time," Pete Koenig, who he broke in under at the old Wharf Rat, used to say. "The drops add up to drams, the drams to pints, the pints to barrels, and pretty soon you're swimming in it." Not that he shorted anybody seriously or switched labels. Tending bar was psychology, not chemistry, and they could always buy it at the liquor store and pour their own if they had a complaint.

"The numbers will always catch up with you." Tyler was a tireless purveyor of statistical doom. The rate at which the ozone layer and rain forests were disappearing. The odds in favor of plane crashes. The probability that you already had prostate cancer. "You study the actuarial tables, it's never a question *if* they catch up, only *when*."

"We're all born behind the eight-ball." Overholt, holding his rye up to the light to appreciate its color.

"And the people I'm surrounded with. You ever watch seagulls?"

"Spiraling aimlessly at the mighty ocean's edge." Overholt has been known to stand and recite from memory.

"I see them in the landfills on the way to work. They call it a flock, as if they cooperate with each other, when it's only just a mob of predators out to feed their own faces and to hell with the other guy."

"A cutthroat business."

"But even seagulls only want what the other bird has in its mouth."

"Beak. Winged creatures have a beak."

"They never attack another gull just to see him go down. I swear I'd chuck the whole thing in a minute, but at my age—"

"You're a stripling."

"In your twenties, you make a lateral move, no big deal. You can shop around for a few years. Employer looks at me on his carpet, thirty-eight with my hat in my hand, he thinks one thing: This guy crapped out. Couldn't cut it."

"You wear a hat?" Overholt looks around for evidence.

"An expression."

"Used to be an American man would not venture forth with his head uncovered. Newsboy cap, pearl-gray fedora—an entire industry was devoted to it. Haberdashery. Be glad that's not your game. You wouldn't have a job left to be disgusted with."

Tyler makes a trembling fist, squeezing till his knuckles go white. "That's my stomach, six-forty-five every weekday, when I roll out of bed."

"We seek transcendence," says Overholt, "but we settle for numbness."

"Transcendence."

"To rise above our worldly lot. To soar."

Tyler unclenches the fist. "I work on the eighty-fifth floor, got a window, look down on the whole city. But I never feel like I'm soaring."

Tommy grabs Stacy's pitcher and heads down to fill her up again. He looks forward to a shift behind the counter. Almost always. The physical rituals, the smells, the sounds, working the alley like a matador. "Never work doubles with a guy with a fat ass," Pete Koenig used to warn him. "You'll spend you're whole night climbing over the son of a bitch." The Rat was by the shipyard and you dealt it straight and fast. There were fights now and then, Pete watching with the practiced eye of a ring judge till he'd give Tommy the nod to call the cops. Or not. Maybe one fight a week, a lot less than the Anvil and the Spike down the block, the gay crowd going through a heavy-metal and leather phase. When those would spill out on the street the shipyard guys would bring their drinks and watch, offering encouragement and instruction. Pete would stay inside, consolidating the stock, till they came back. "Who won?" he'd always say. "No decision," somebody would reply. "The referee was watching their asses."

"He never hit me," says Stacy, watching the blue liquid rise in her glass.

"That's good." Tommy never asks for context on the ride. A conversation is a compartment you stroll through on the way to the next one, moving forward without a finite beginning or end.

"The next one, the one he took up with after me—well, I heard stories."

"Terrible thing, to hit a woman." Not that I haven't been tempted.

"That wasn't the kind of person he was, Cedric. If something happened later, after me, it must have been provoked."

"Sure. You can push a man just so far."

"She was black, of course. Maybe he figured life would be easier, he'd stop feeling like a target. They see you happy, and it infuriates them."

"Lights out on the jukebox, Stacy." Tommy switches the tape machine on under the counter. You step across a line, and—no, violence is not the way to go, but it's understandable. There are limits.

Tom Jones comes on, singing that it's not unusual. Corny, but the passengers like it a little corny, lyrics they can recognize, nothing too up-to-the-minute. Not too heavy with the percussion, people have to hear themselves think, not too folksy. It isn't Starbucks in here. At the Rat when he started they were still playing Sinatra and Tony Bennett and Jimmy Roselli wall-to-wall every Columbus Day. His grandfather's music. Tommy doesn't hear the lyrics anymore, it's just part of the mix. He does feel the bass line, though, the rhythm like the clack of railroad ties as they pick up speed, and there is that tiny blur now, motion blur, when he swings his head fast to look down the bar, all the stool sitters taken care of, Amber coming up with an order, Donna still not at the register.

"They poisoned his mind against me and he never recovered," says Stacy.

Tommy wishes that more of the happy ones were coast-to-coast passengers. It's fine, of course, the grousers, the bitter pills, the walking wounded, they soak up the product like sponges and it's part of the deal to provide them shelter and consolation. But he longs for a stretch— because it was always impermanent, a few weeks, a few months—a stretch of golden times when your bar was the center of something joyous and energetic, when people smiled the minute they stepped inside and couldn't wait to see who was here and what was up. There'd been a while like that at Dunnigan's, before the shooting, almost a full year at Bottoms Up before the coke took its toll, and then there was the long summer he was just out of school when they went to the Crock and Bull for at least part of every night and felt like living legends. It had become their club-house through no desire or effort on the part of the owner, a crabby old Polack with a train wreck of a nose, but they met there and brought girls or girls just showed up because that's where they were and where life was happening, Tommy and his friends holding court like young princes of the city and every fucking thing was possible. Jimmy Testa, whom they called Two Ton and who died early from the heart thing, passing out on his stool one night, then waking up to win two hundred dollars arm wrestling, then passing back into a stupor with the twenties stuck under his wet, fat face. Len Spitz laughing so hard the beer blew out his nose. The Walsh twins double-teaming girls from out of the neighborhood, switching shirts in the bathroom to see if they could tell the difference. Tommy himself, breaking the speed record for a whole pint of Guinness while the old micks shook their heads and complained about the waste of it. Now and then a crowd like that would come into the Lounge, good *craic* lighting the place up for a few nights, but they never stuck. Mostly they were only there for a couple of rounds, then away to the next place. Tommy had sent some of the kids, Rusty or Shawn or the skinheaded one, Rick, out to scout the other places in the area on slow nights, to report what the action was, what the scene was. He'd started Wings Wednesdays to compete, though Donna hated the smell, and karaoke on weekend nights and the Quarter-to Rush and the Happy Hour-and-a-Half on Fridays. Every night was different and the Lounge was gaining momentum, new passengers coming on board all the time, but it never felt like the *center* of anything. Maybe cable TV was to blame. The mopes came in nearly every night, though, and Tommy struggled to stay buoyant, to keep it rolling, keep the mood conducive, while they grabbed a hold and tried to pull him to the bottom.

"You ever think, Stacy," he says, knowing it's a mistake, "that it just wasn't meant to be?"

She studies his face a long moment. "Were you ever in love?"

"Sure." For all the good it did me.

"There's your answer."

A space opens up as One-Beer Bartlett steps away and a kid with his hair waxed up like a cartoon character, somebody with their finger in a light socket, takes it.

"Rob Roy," he says. "Skip the cherry."

"Coming up."

"Shawn coming in tonight?"

Tommy glances at the kid in the mirror as he pours scotch.

"We used to work at Squeezers together. I'm still there."

Pete Koenig called it "riding the line." A professional courtesy. A barman came into your place, dropped the name of his, and he was on the cuff. It was understood you drank free if you should wander onto his turf, which, on your nights off or between shifts, was highly likely. The fraternity extended all over the city, with a few unwritten rules about never ordering anything with more than two ingredients and not hogging a prime seat during busy times.

"Shawn won't be in," says Tommy, leaving the drink as he moves away. "That's two-fifty."

Who, above the age of eighteen and with hair on his dick, would want to drink at fucking Squeezers anyway?

They'd met at the Grotto, where Planter's Punch was always on special and Yma Sumac tortured the scales on the sound system and Donna had it all under her thumb. She made the men who came in feel like they'd joined her private club, remembered faces, drinks, always a "Welcome back" on your second visit, a "Where've you been hiding?" if it had been more than a week's absence.

There was an air of the unachievable about her, but they came anyway to drink and watch her work the room, always in some silky Asian thing with a high collar and a slit up the side. "I'm not leaning over with my tits hanging in their faces like the fucking Saint Pauli girl," she'd say, a point of pride though her breasts were too small to do much hanging— nice ones, no complaint there, but small—and those slits went way up high on her leg. Blond hair and green eyes almost slanty with the Slavic cheekbones, a knockout in the Dragon Lady outfits. A great attraction, and friendly enough to the barmen, but she really only got interested once he'd let it slip he was saving for his own place. That he was a serious person and not just another one-for-you-two-for-me jackoff drifting through the scene. She'd come over in the slow hours and diss the management, who truly didn't have a clue—it had been the Cave and then the People Pit and then the Lava Landing and now the Grotto—as if people wanted Styrofoam stalactites and jungle music while they got juiced. She'd worked at as many joints as he had and paid attention. She'd lay the green eyes on him and he'd open up and tell her things he'd never spill to the other guys behind the counter, his idea of a special place that was more like home than home, where people for generations would say "Your father and I met at the place," or "The place was where the whole deal started," or "Remember that incredible night at the place?" The micks, the ones just over from the old country, called it *craic,* rhymes with Jack, and in Gaelic it meant all the good things people went to a pub for, a shifting pocket of fun and excitement, elusive as a rainbow's end. Donna had her ideas too, about hiring, the decor, the music. They'd picked the tape loop for the Lounge together, song by song, excited in those early days, and sometimes if it was one of his favorites he could get her up to slow dance for a few verses, alone together in the half-transformed room, swaying together like movie stars.

"You should be off with your asshole buddies there, having a bachelor party." Nora to Nick.

"I'd rather be with you." Nick, short on imagination but with the stamina of a starving coyote, to Nora.

"I'm touched."

"I mean it. After what we've had together, there should be some kind of—you know—send-off. Something appropriate."

"Appropriate."

"I mean, just because my whatever—my nupital status—is about to change, doesn't mean we can't—"

"Yes it does."

"What, honestly, is the difference? If I hadn't told you about this thing—"

"If you'd lied to me—"

"Sure, but you wouldn't know it, see, so it would make no difference."

"That I was banging a fucking liar."

"The mouth, Nora."

"A fucking married fucking liar."

"You're something, you are."

"Yeah, I'm something, but it's not a fucking married—about to be fucking married—fucking liar."

"Mouth like a sailor."

"I'm sorry I'm not enough of a lady for you."

"You're—look, you're terrific. I wouldn't of spent the time on you I have if you weren't, but things happen. Life goes on. And that's no reason we can't—"

"Yes it is."

A pause. Nick studies her, a professional once-over, like an axman waiting for a tree to topple. She won't look at him. He glances at her empty glass.

"I buy you another drink?"

"Why not?" She glances to Tommy, eyes not quite locking with his. "Hit me again. L.I.T."

Tommy starts to say something about pacing herself, or maybe coasting awhile with something full of tonic, but she's up, steadying herself as the bar lurches toward her, straightening, then navigating the path to the LADIES with small dignified steps.

"Man got to pass through the Gates of Hell to score a little pussy," says Nick, pushing two glasses forward, "Do me again too."

"Congratulations on your happy occasion," says Tommy, smiling hard. Pete taught him never to step into a cross fire, never to back a man into a corner he'd have to punch his way out of. "Bring the bride in sometime, I'll pour you both a free one."

By the Quarter-to-Nine Rush they are at full steam, careening around the corners, Amber and Bethany too busy chatting up a table of advertising honchos to deal with their shots, so Tommy has to put both away. Only Lester, out from the kitchen smelling of french fries, is there to join him. Lester never misses.

"Looks like a good night, boss. They really got me hopping back there."

"Try to keep one foot on the ground."

Lester brings his own in a metal flask and tries to pace himself through a night, so far managing not to set anything important on fire. Cooks. Never had one who wasn't a lush.

It's too early for any of the guys to be in, Casey from the Devil's Triangle, Alex from the Bent Elbow, Suds Gallagher from the bar at Pompey's Steakhouse, Johnny Giacomo and Weasel Wesley from the Pump House, the crowd from Mr. Wonderful. The front line soldiers. The things they put up with, the service they put in, of course you're gonna stand them a few rounds. This is not the problem, this is not the difference between red ink and black, whatever she might think. Tommy's favorite place to drink now is Dennis Riordan's little hole in the wall by the old Post Office. Ballads in the box, no TV, dark wood wherever you looked, and every whiskey worth drinking behind the counter. An amber glow, Tommy thought, every time he stepped in after a long night's pouring in the Lounge. An amber glow all around and soon it was in you as well, warm and dark and liquid, like floating in the bottom of an oak barrel. And Dennis was a total pro, setting the pace, if you could call it that. There were no clocks in Riordan's.

Here, you had to keep the engine stoked. There was the rent to pay, the interest on the loan, all of Donna's expectations and anxieties to be fed. He often felt like the fireman on an uphill locomotive, humping shovelful after shovelful of coal into the maw of the boiler, sweat hissing as it plopped on the loose embers at his feet, desperate to beat gravity with steam. A roaring mouth to feed. When what he really wanted to be was the genie in the bottle, the one who smiled and made everyone's wishes come true, the grumps and the hopers, the novices and the old men in overcoats, the lunch-pail working men and the dot-com whiz kids in sudden free fall. You had to be some kind of exceptional prick to be left off Tommy's wish list.

"So, Shawn," says the kid with the hair sticking up. "Is he—?"

"Not coming in." Tommy doesn't slow as he passes. "Shawn isn't working here anymore."

Puzzled look. "Since—?"

"Since I said he doesn't."

A sports argument has erupted at the entrance end of the bar and they're waving him over. The Joes, who he knows only as Joey V and Joey G, for *vodka* and *gin*.

"Lombardi's best Green Bay team versus last year's Patriots."

"A bunch of punks."

"Punks who won the whole deal and could run circles around those old Packers."

"In their prime—"

"In their prime they were small and slow."

"There was half as many teams as today– the talent was concentrated."

The Joes always bring a debate in from the street but will never sit next to each other, often talking across two or three complete strangers, hoping to hook them into the controversy.

"Their front line gives away eighty pounds per man. They couldn't budge my guys."

"Your guys? When did they get to be your guys? You hate the fucking Patriots."

"That doesn't mean I wouldn't bet 'em big time over Lombardi's best. What do you say, Tom?"

Tommy always tries to qualify his answer, to define terms in a way that lets both parties win.

"Depends on how they officiate," he says. "Old-school rules, what was allowed back then—I'm talking Butkus and those people—a lot of it today wouldn't be a penalty, it would be *assault*."

"No shit." Joey V.

"Can't argue that." Joey G.

"But the guys today, it's like the Bionic Man—the weight training, the performance drugs—and the rules protect them more. None of this "If it's caused by contact with the ground, it's not a fumble." Old days, in the pile-ups, you held on till you saw zebra stripes and people stuck thumbs in your eyes. Green Bay's linebackers got to Brady, just once, they'd pull his head off. And there goes the Pats' offense."

"There's reasons for those rules."

"Yeah, to protect the pussies they got on the field these days. And to protect the NFL's investment."

"Neither team, playing in the other's era, could win," says Tommy. "You put a modern soldier in the Roman arena, he'd end up with one of those pitchfork things up his butt."

"Tridents."

"And you hand Spartacus a modern combat rifle, like with the infra-red video scope and the computerized bullets, stick him in a free-fire zone—he's dead meat."

"That's how I always thought of you, Tom. A man out of his time. You should have run one of those saloons with the sawdust on the floor and the barrel of pig knuckles on the counter."

"With sleeve garters."

Tommy is not sure he's being flattered. "One thing I wouldn't have," he says, "is any crème de fucking menthe behind the bar."

The engine is really thrumming now, every voice raised full volume, the tape blasting, and it's hard to hear the girl all in black who shouts over the shoulders of the stool warmers.

"Somebody upchucked by the urinals."

"Upchucked."

"Puked. My boyfriend just told me to tell you."

"I need this information?"

"People should know. So they don't step in it."

"A public service announcement."

"Hey, it's your floor."

Yes, it was his floor and he was far too busy to be mopping it. He would have sent Shawn in to deal with it but Shawn wasn't in, was not going to be in. If the passengers couldn't figure out which urinal not to use that was their problem.

He goes on automatic pilot as they plunge deeper into the night, Tommy reading lips more than hearing orders, mixing, clearing, wiping, stuffing the wet green bills into the drawer, measuring by the feel of it, ice cubes bouncing, the noises with a constant Doppler-effect tail on them, Amber too frantic on the floor to fix the hair plastered with sweat on her forehead. Tommy checks her out more than once, dodging through the crowd on the rolling floor, working her smile, looking good, but no, she was too young or maybe he was too old, and there were those dollar signs behind the eyes, like Donna. Donna, who'd deal it out of a measuring cup if you put her back here, when you had to be a dreamer, had to be a romantic in this business, or it turned hard and phony as a Vegas clip joint at six in the morning, girls limping off shift with their mascara chipping away like old stucco. It wasn't about an ounce and a half of this and a half ounce of that, it was about Alabama Slammers and Burning Blue Mountains, about Blood and Sands and Brave Bulls and Crazy Nuns and Flying Scots, Highland Flings and Irish Mist, Zombies and Kamikazes, White Spiders and Tequila Sunrises.

It was about Sex on the Beach.

Tyler has his tie all the way off now, a red one, wrapped around his forehead like an apprentice samurai, discussing Archimedes' Principle and that different vessels need different amounts of liquid before they'll float—displacement, that's what it's called—and he's one drink away from leaving the dock and Overholt is trying to remember what it was that his own father, who always wore a hat till he sank to living on the street and drinking what was that stuff, that wine—

"Ripple?"

"No, not that."

"Thunderbird?"

"My mother drank that. With ice in it. No, this was made only for them, the street alkies, you'd trip on the bottles when you went down there. On the label—Night Train Express!"

Overholt slaps the bar with triumph.

"You should know that one, Tom, working here. On the label it was a steam engine going hell for leather with a big black cloud of smoke trailing over, and my old man drank it till they scraped him up and put him in the drunk ward and then he couldn't smuggle it in, not a sip, and he dried up to nothing and died."

"A ship over on its keel, beached, aground, is a sorry thing to see," adds Tyler, on a parallel track. "But a rising tide—that's it, Tom, fill it to the top—a rising tides lifts all boats."

Before it's over, Nora is hanging on Nick, a half head shorter than she is, as he escorts her out the door. Her liner has washed down her cheeks and her eyes are swimming, and Nick is cooing to her, as best as he can through the effort of half carrying her, 'It's all right, baby, it's all gonna be fine, you'll see" and Stacy is crying a little too, dabbing at each new leak with a cocktail napkin the way she does, and Tommy tells her he'll drink a glass of her tears if she'll smile for him—their usual routine together—and she beams one up at him, a real dazzler of a smile and you see what Cedric was risking his ass for and Tommy pours himself a couple fingers—maybe two fingers and a thumb—of amber glow and says this will have to do for the tears, you've chased them all away. She's finished all her blue stuff and sits rocking side to side with her eyes closed, humming "Jamaica Farewell" with no regard to the song running on the tape loop, and what you wouldn't give for that kind of loyalty, carrying her torch through all these years for a guy who never hit her, unlike Donna, Donna throwing bricks under his wheels, saying it doesn't add up, the marriage, the bar, pulling him down, slipping around with fucking Shawn—fucking Shawn, of all people, who used to work at Squeezers and couldn't pour an honest round of drinks to save his life! But hey, the machine rolls on, there's no stopping it, and if that's her choice to jump off just when the grade gets a little steep, miss a couple payments, big fucking deal, there isn't a saloon in town doesn't come up short now and then, the banks know that or they ought to, for Christ's sake, and so should the credit people on the phone, but there's other ways he could swing it, so don't even wave, leave her there by the side of the tracks, receding, already receding in his mind, and the amber is starting to really glow now and it doesn't hurt to smile, if that's what he's doing, no time to look in the mirror with a piña this and a brandy that to mix, she's getting very small back there as the tracks ahead open up, always opening, the lulling clack beneath the wheels measuring time, and who needs clocks or cares if the Quarter-to Rush goes off this time at half-past, not raising the neck of the bottle between each shot but filling them in one sweeping pour, and he becomes vaguely aware of Overholt up on his feet, orating the way he does before he calls it a night, his voice all italics and regret.

"*The cowboy lay on the barroom floor,*" Overholt declaims, chin lifted, one hand steadying himself on the bar, "*having drunk so much he could drink no more. He went to sleep with a troubled brain— and dreamt that he rode on a Hell-bound train.*"

Only that— then a salute to Tommy, a bow to the stool warmers on each side, and when Tommy looks back, distracted for a moment by a woman who is not quite Donna moving toward the LADIES, he is gone.

Tommy feels them all looking at him then, wanting something, needing something, and he doesn't know if there will ever be enough to fill that need, so he turns his back on them to face the gleaming wall, magic liquids in colored glass, and smiles or continues to smile, not so much dizzy as uncoupled from gravity as he feels it begin to lift up, just like he always said it would, the distance between him and her, between the promise of the engine and the crushing weight of what is hurtling behind it growing, growing, if you don't ever stop, it can't catch up with you and then the amber glow is coming from inside him and the whole thing is airborne, leaving the silver rails to soar upward, upward, long-tailed comet into the black night above.

Above The Line

IT STARTED WHEN HONDO WILCOX set himself afire and landed in Intensive Care with IVs sticking into him every which way. I rode with Hondo in the old days eating his dust in a couple Budd Boetticher pictures after the War. Had him a kind of permanent sneer, the kind of dark good looks that smiling only makes worse, so he got hired to whup up on peons and sodbusters and backshoot the hero's best friend. Couldn't ride worth horse pucky, so I'd sometimes double him in the long shots, especially when he'd get shot from his mount. My specialty was the fall-and-drag, but I could get picked off pretty much any way you asked for and never got my head kicked in.

Hondo was smoking where he shouldn't ought to, some unfiltered lungbusters he'd smuggled in or traded for, and it got loose with his palsy and fell in his lap. We're all in Rec Therapy putting them through disco aerobics and he's back in his room with the door closed, screaming. By the time we get there he's burnt a layer of skin off his legs and the sprinkler system is doing its version of a submarine picture, the part where the depth charges bust all the pipes. So we got the ambulance out front and wet linen to yank off the entire ambulatory wing.

When Hondo comes back, he's not so good. I've seen it enough at the Home, the look they get when all that's on their minds is the last roundup. It isn't so much peaceful as *narrow*, like they got their eye on something small and fixed in the distance and won't bear any distractions.

He was like that when his family come to visit and the grandson couldn't take it, so he's out into the hall and sees me pushing the breakfast cart.

"It's nice," he says, "they let you help out."

A good-looking kid, skinny. Thirty–forty years ago they'd've done something with his nose, give him one of those names: Rock. Tab. Rip.

"I don't help much," I tell him. "I work here."

"Oh. I'm *sorry.* I thought you . . . you look—"

"I look like I should be out to pasture like the rest of the fossils in here."

"I didn't mean anything."

"Relax. Gimme three–four years, I'll be on the other side of the enema bag."

The kid smiles a little. He's uncomfortable, thinks he should be in with the rest of the family catching Hondo's Mount Rushmore act. He's got his hair slicked back the way Dan Duryea wore it for his polecat roles, and he wears one of those jackets where the sleeves don't come much past the elbow, like the tailor didn't finish.

"You know my grandad?"

"Hondo? Used to stare up his horse's business end some forty years ago."

"In pictures?"

"If it wasn't in pictures you wouldn't find Hondo closer to a horse than the two-dollar window at Santa Anita."

"You were in pictures? What's your name?"

"Son Bishop."

"*The* Son Bishop?"

Now I was never *the* Son Bishop and never will be. Not that there was another one. Except for the stunt work I don't think I was ever on the screen with fewer than three other fellas, and that through a cloud of dust or gunsmoke. I'm one of them that clear out of the bar when the lead man and the black hat square off, one of them that thunder down the main street shooting pistols over their heads or ride into formation when the bugler sounds charge. When Babs Stanwyck or somebody like her says, "Meet the boys," I'm one of the boys. I rode with the Jameses, the Youngers, the Daltons, and the Wild Bunch. I died with my boots on. Directors knew me as *Hey, you* or *That bowlegged son of a bitch,* as in "Yak, have that bowlegged son of a bitch fall off and roll toward the camera on this take."

"If there's a Son Bishop was in pictures," I tell Hondo Wilcox's grandkid, "I'm it."

He pumps my hand. "The old stunt guy, right? Wow."

I can't imagine Hondo would ever have mentioned me, even if he remembered who I was, so I figure the kid must watch way too many old movies. My immediate problem being to get two dozen cheese-food omelets unwrapped and still tingling from the microwave onto the bed trays of the nonambulatory men's wing, I nod and begin to push away.

"Nice meeting you."

"I must have seen *Six Black Horses* fifty times," he calls.

"That's terrific."

"I'm a big Audie Murphy fan."

I worked with Audie a bunch, nice polite kid—we all thought of him as a kid, though he was about my age at the time. Like this one, who comes running down the hall to catch up with me.

"Ira Levinsky," he says.

"Don't believe I ever worked with him."

"No, that's me. My name. Grandad's too."

"Ira?"

"*Levinsky.* Hondel Levinsky. The studio had him change it."

"I shouldn't doubt they did."

"I had it changed back when I was twenty-one. It's tough enough to make your own place in the world without somebody's shadow over you."

Now they barely remember Scott Brady or Rod Cameron or Rory Calhoun, and they were the *gi*ants in the pictures I did. Hondo Wilcox was pretty far down the credits even at the time, and any shadow he casts is a mighty slim one. I don't share this with Ira Levinsky.

"So, you still active?"

"Active?"

"In the business."

I look around me. Mrs. Winchester, who drew storyboards at Fox, is struggling down the hall with her aluminum walker. When she gets to the nurses' station, she'll turn around and work back to her room. It takes her the whole morning.

"I don't know as *active* is the word I'd use."

"See, what it is," says Ira, "I'm producing this Western and we need an old guy, wise-grandfather type, who goes out on his last cattle drive."

My swan song in the picture business was a vampire-cowboy epic in the mid-sixties, starred a fella who later had his own TV series—which they show reruns of all the time on the set in the sunroom. Italian people made it down in Sonora and I played an Indian chief. No lines, three grunts, one fall.

"I *am* old," I tell him. "I got that part nailed."

"Can you still sit a horse?"

"A moving horse?"

"Well—yes."

"How fast is it moving?"

"It's—you know—he's the grandfather. The young guys do all the dangerous stuff."

Don't get me wrong. I don't have stars in my eyes, never did. It's just the health plan, see. The kind of pictures I was on, Republic serials, fly-by-nights, bring-your-own-horse jobs, I never built up much on the official records. And the health plan they got now, maybe I could get home care if I fall sick, or maybe qualify to get in here instead of some roach motel down in Long Beach. I'm at that time when you got to look ahead, you don't have family. You got to be hardheaded.

"Do I have to fall off?"

The screen test is quite a kick, in that I hadn't done one since my very first job. That was for old Charley Wade who ran the stunt people at

Monogram. He put me up on this man killer they kept for rodeo scenes and then commenced to spitting patterns between his boots, which was his way of laughing, while the horse knocked planks out of the fence with my shins. I got clipped pretty good behind the ear when it flung me through the rails, and I come up sitting a yard away from Charley as if I planned it.

"You were on the circuit?"

"Yes, sir. Broncs and some roping."

"You punchy yet?"

"No, sir. I don't generally land on my head."

Charley nodded and spat between *my* boots and said, "He'll do," which was his version of a seminar.

For this one Ira had told me not to shave, so I figured it was one of those ravioli jobs where you can't tell the white hats from the black hats, 'cause they both been dipped in bear sweat, and what few words there are don't match up with the lips. The director is an English fella in a safari suit with this big lion's mane of silver hair, and they do the test with me on horseback on a soundstage up in the Valley. They don't have the real wranglers on yet, so it's this poor scared-rabbit production assistant who's got an old nag they've doped up to keep her from bolting to the other side of the wall where they're shooting one of those TV shows with fifteen little orphans being raised in a house by a former professional wrestler. The horse has that zombie-eye look the folks at the Home get a half hour after evening meds, and when the boom swings his pole at her to catch my dialogue she starts to back up. I do what I can, but I suspect at this point you could yank her teeth out without much reaction.

The English fella thinks for a minute, pushing his knuckles into the spot between his eyes like he's listening for a message from another galaxy. "I'm going to give you one word," he says. "Grizzled."

And then the boy who dragged the horse in starts throwing lines at me while the nag's head drops lower and lower. I think the longest speech I had before this was "Git yer head down, it's the Kiowa!" and here they got me rattling off five–six sentences in a bunch. I get through the two pages they give me, and then Ira and the English fella, whose name is Cedric, and this other fella, who is the casting director I think, come up and start to talk about me as if I'm not there.

"I see possibilities," says Cedric.

"There's a quality," says the casting fella.

"The look is right."

"It's the right *genre.* We're definitely in the West."

"But there's something a bit off."

"Is it the voice?"

"The age is right. I despise that rubber-and-glue routine."

"We're definitely in the West. I smell bacon frying. Flapjacks."

By now the nag has done what nags will do, right on the studio floor, and it don't smell like flapjacks.

Cedric closes his eyes and starts to mash his forehead again. "It's a question of *rhythm,*" he says. "A man of leather and dust, a man of the vast herds—"

"Grizzled," I venture. He opens his eyes to stare at me.

"Props!" he bellows, and the boy who led the mare in and threw me my lines jumps up, looking around. There is nobody but him. Cedric grabs him and says something in his ear, not taking his eyes off me. The boy runs off.

"Bishop," says Cedric. "It seems you have an extensive background in the cinema."

"I been in a load of pictures," I allow. "Never had to say much, though."

"Unspoiled. Marvelous."

"A fresh face," says the casting fella.

"He's a natural," says Ira.

"This would be quite a coup," says Cedric. "For both of us."

The boy runs back with a tin of chewing tobacco and peels it open. Then he offers it to me. The others go back to their chairs.

"I'd like you to *spit*," says Cedric, hitting the *t* so it sounds like an insult, "after you deliver each of your lines." He smiles. "As I said, a question of *rhythm*."

The boy with the tobacco, whose name is Stuart—or Poor Stuart as I start to think of him—is still offering it up, nervous to be near the nag's head, which has dropped to half mast. She starts to sway.

"Buddy," I say to him, "you take a twist of that and jam it up under her bottom lip. Mind your fingers."

Poor Stuart looks at me like I told him to breed with a chicken, but he stuffs half the tin in there and I take a pinch for myself and he backs off. The nag's head comes up right away. We go back into the lines then, only now I got to gob on the floor in between.

I never much cared for the chewing habit, makes me queasy, but I done my best Hank Fonda as Frank James, and Ira starts to giggle and the casting fella and Cedric exchange little looks and the nag swallows her wad and starts snorting and moving forward, backing the boom operator up till he's got to telescope his pole.

"Outstanding," says Cedric, when there's no more lines left. "Very raw, very man-against-the-elements. The suits will be mollified."

"Can I get off now?" The horse was starting to sneeze and crab-walk, and a few of the smaller kids from the program next door had come around to peek.

"Bull," said one to his fellow orphans. "Mr. Ed is in black-and-white."

The shoot was in northern Wyoming, where I hadn't been since my rodeo days. The company had taken over a chain motel off the interstate for their headquarters, and the little girl who drove me from the airport would slow down and stare out the window every time we'd pass a bunch of antelope, which made for a long ride.

"It's just like in the song," she says.

"The song?"

" 'Where the deer and the antelope play.' "

"Right. You keep making that trucker behind us downshift, darlin,' you're about to hear a discouraging word."

"Only one thing I hate so far," says the girl, speeding up a little. "No Thai food."

They'd brought me in a couple days before my first scene so's I could get what Cedric called *acclimated* and it's a good thing. Now, I expected as how I might be the oldest person on the set, but when I come into the motel lobby it's like there's an Eagle Scout convention in town. None of us in the trade in the old days looked that young even when we *were* that young. Boys and girls wearing a lot of combat gear and tool belts, carrying walkie-talkies everywhere, even though the shooting hadn't started yet. They were all so polite and expeditious getting me checked into my room, so excited about everything, I could tell they didn't have the first clue how to make a picture.

That night I'm in Wardrobe, a room looking out onto the little swimming pool, when Cedric and Poor Stuart walk in. I'm in my skivvies waiting for the wardrobe girl to find a pair of jeans that don't bag so much in the rear.

"Bishop," says Cedric, his version of a hello. "You're familiar with the Arthur Miller classic?"

"It's a golf tournament?"

"The *play. The Death of a Salesman.*"

"I heard of it."

"Don't let it influence you too much."

The wardrobe girl brings me a pair of boots while I'm waiting for the jeans. "These should fit," she says.

"Willie is very flawed, very human, but he is by no means a *wanker,*" says Cedric.

I catch on that he's talking about my character, whose name is

Willie Bowman. Willie owns a little half-assed cattle spread and has two grandsons, Britt and Huddie, who he wants to pass it along to.

"Willie doesn't have the wrong dreams so much as an unfortunate haplessness in bringing them about. Feet of clay."

I wish my own feet were made of something besides flesh and blood once I jam them into the boots the girl give me. My circulation isn't much to begin with these days, and the boots choke off whatever is left.

"How they feel?" says the wardrobe girl.

"They'll be numb soon enough and it won't matter."

"What size are your feet?"

"They were nine and a half a minute ago, but unless I get these off real quick—"

Cedric goes on about Willie while Poor Stuart and the wardrobe girl drag me across the room by my heels trying to pull the boots off. The upshot is that neither of Willie's boys can fill their old man's shoes and Cedric orders Poor Stuart to fill mine for a couple days to stretch them out. They got to rub soap on his socks and shins to get them on and when he leaves he's got this little smile on his face, like somebody trying not to whimper.

In the morning they take me out to the stables to pick a mount. The head wrangler is named Emmaline, which is a new one on me. In my day, wranglers had names like Buck or Tex or Sagebrush and ever 'one of them could pee standing up. They just call this one Em, and she's got a pretty face and arms like a hod carrier. She's got twenty animals or so, none of them too sharp-looking.

"Snapped 'em up at an auction," says Em. "They don't bite or kick much, but that's all I can say for them."

I pick out a chestnut mare who's holding herself away from the others, like she don't care to associate with riffraff.

"This one I call Lefty," says Em, while she lays on a saddle for a trial run. "She'll drift sideways on you a bit if you don't keep her honest. May be blind in one eye."

I climb up. It has been awhile, a long while, but it kind of feels good to be up on a real horse again.

"They ast me did I have experience with movies and I ast them back did they have experience with animals, and so we settled for each other," says Em. "Your boys come in before. The actors? Took the two biggest."

"They ride?"

Em thought that over a second. She had a way, a kind of dry manner of saying things, reminded me of old Charley Wade. "Oh, they stayed on all right," she said. "Their *aim* wasn't much, though."

I put Lefty through her paces and can tell somebody's used her for roping at some point. She's got scars on her chest like she went through some fencing, and a chunk is missing from one ear, and she shies away if you come at her from the right side. A used horse. I ask Em to put her aside for me.

"You done this before, huh?" she says.

"A ways back."

"There anything I ought to know?"

Em looks like she can take care of herself. Straight yellow hair that just hangs straight down under an old cowboy hat, denim shirt with the sleeves cut off to show her muscles, bright green eyes that make you kind of jumpy if you look at 'em too long.

"Well," I tell her, "at some point your animals are going to foul up, and that English fella is gonna start to scream. Don't say what's on your mind. Your best bet is to make like you're too damn backwards and ignorant to understand a thing he's talking about."

"Oh," she says, nodding her head. "I thought it might be different in the movies."

Em shows me the herd, which is a bit of an exaggeration as they only got some thirty head. There's at least five cowpokes with speaking parts in the script, plus a vaquero who gets trompled in the first reel, and me and my two boys, which makes about three animals per man.

"Little paltry for a drive, isn't it? You sure they don't have more coming?"

Em shrugs. "I laid out the upkeep per head to them, and this is how many they said they could afford."

"In the black-and-white days we used stock footage for all that. There was one stampede I was in on they must have slugged into a hundred pictures."

"The script called for longhorns," says Em. "But it cost too much to get 'em up here."

A couple grips drove up then to figure out the rigging on the chuck wagon and one of them turns out to be a female, which is another new one on me. Little bit of a thing, curly hair, looked like the girl on the raisin box only she's wearing a brand-new King Ropes cap instead of a bonnet. Name is Mickey, and I catch both me and Em staring at her while she climbs around that wagon. Em has met her before. The big lug with Mickey is nicknamed Popeye, and he keeps hefting the wagon tongue in one hand and doing weight-lifter moves with it.

"You a wrangler?" Mickey asks me.

"Used to be," I say.

"You got any idea how this thing works?"

"We can figure it out," Popeye mutters to her.

"The rigging part is simple," she says. "It's the horse part I'm not so sure of."

Em steps forward then and allows as how she can show them right now, and I fade into the background. Em brings a pair of likely looking suspects over and has Mickey pat them and get used to them and Mickey is all smiles, so I figure I got these gals' number, and Popeye wanders around lifting saddles and wagon wheels and bales of hay and eyeing the cattle like he might just lift one of *them* all of a sudden. He gets bored with that and ends up sitting on the ground tossing dried cow chips against the barn.

"*Popeye,*" says Mickey.

"What?"

"That's cattle poop."

Popeye gets up quick and starts wiping his hands on things real frantic and looking for water to wash them off in. Mickey laughs like it's the funniest thing she ever saw. She's got a great laugh, Mickey, dimples, pretty smile, the whole nine yards, and even Em is grinning the tiniest bit when she turns away to me.

"Cowboy humor," she says, in her dry way.

Now, I was on some low-budget horse operas in my day, but none of them was what you'd call half-assed. People knew their jobs. You had a list of scenes to shoot and you went out and you shot them, and if you didn't make your days they got somebody else who *did,* real quick. We didn't shoot nights, of course, and they were only B pictures—you didn't do extra takes for acting—but we were *professionals.*

This saga I'd landed in was more like a slow-motion stampede than a movie shoot. They had barely enough actors and crew and livestock to make a Gene Autry serial, but Cedric was after something a little more Cinemascope. Ira was a nice boy but he was only attached because he'd sunk a lot of money he'd made as a bankruptcy lawyer into the picture and went around saying how this was his first time on a movie set. The camera crew was a slew of Russians who'd just walked off the boat and kept talking in Russian during the sound takes, the soundman looked like Buddha with a beard and liked to hang his radio mikes on the actors first thing in the morning, then eavesdrop on them all day long, grinning under his headset like a damn Chinese monkey, and the various boy and girl scouts with their walkies acted like there was a war on, shouting a lot of garbage about the A-team and the battle zone and bogies at ten o'clock.

At the end of the first day they were two days behind.

It was just establishing shots, some cowpoke stuff around the ranch set, but once they had me in my trailer after makeup they only came for me once, to say it was lunch. Poor Stuart hobbled up in my boots and tells me if I cared to dine inside he could bring a tray over.

"I'll get in line," I tell him. "How's it going?"

"Cedric and Misha are fighting." Misha's the Russki who's shooting.

"They just started."

"They just started *shooting.* They've been fighting for a week. Misha says the light is feminine today, and this is a masculine story."

I peek out at the sky. "Looks pretty butch to me."

Poor Stuart shrugs. "Maybe it's a language thing. And the horses keep looking at the camera. Whenever they start to roll, all the horses turn their heads and stare into the lens."

"They never been in pictures before. Someone shoots off a couple rounds between their ears, you'll see some real action."

At lunch a little Elisha Cook type with a red nose who's the publicist brings the boys over to meet me. Britt is being played by a good-looking blond kid named Jordan, who I'm told was a teenage heartthrob on the television a few seasons back, and Huddie is being played by this real serious type who says he wants everybody to call him by his character's name, so I don't bother to remember his real one. At my age your head is crammed with so many names it's hard to fit new ones in. Jordan is shadowed by a slab of beefcake I figure is his bodyguard or stunt double but is introduced as his personal trainer.

"Iron Ike," says the beefcake, crushing my hand. "You pump?"

"Pump?"

"*Lift.* Weights."

"Not if I can help it."

"Never too late to start."

"So you were in the silents," says Jordan.

"I was pretty silent," I tell him, "but the other folks got to talk."

"You know John Wayne?"

"He shot me off a few mounts."

"Way cool. Well, see you around the campus."

Huddie has been staring at me the whole time, and when Jordan and his gorilla and the publicist step away he starts in.

"The way I see it, Britt wants to kill you," he says.

The kid is serious, dead serious. The only more serious person on the picture is Poor Stuart, but he's out walking size ten feet in size nine boots and has an excuse.

"He's the firstborn, he's got that oedipal thing going, you're a threat to his manhood. With me—well, your daughter died because of me."

It dawns on me that he's talking about our characters. "She did?"

"In childbirth. It's not in the script but I asked Cedric, and he liked it for backstory. You've always held it against me, though you tried not to show it. And I'll do anything to please you."

"Oh."

He shakes my hand again and fixes me with that intense look of his. "I rented some videos," he says, before he goes off to spend some quality time with his horse. "I admire your work."

At lunch I sit with Em and her boys and the grip and gaffer departments. Em's boys are local ranch kids who look a hell of a lot more like cowboys than the actors they've hired except they're all wearing T-shirts with names of rock-and-roll bands like *Armageddon* and *Liquid Discharge* stenciled on the chest. They're a little shy of the crew, who seem like a pretty nice lot. The crew take turns telling worst first-day stories, and Mickey is clearly one of the guys to them, joking and swearing and joining in when they start to gripe about the food, which is cordon blue compared to the hash they used to sling at us in the old days.

Now, I got nothing against a female working with the riggers. No reason one couldn't pull it off. But I got to tell you it set a little strange with me at first. On the old Westerns there was maybe the script girl and makeup and hair, and that was all, she wrote. You had your schoolmarm and black-eyed Mexican beauty, but that was actors and they don't count. It was just us fellas, and that was the atmosphere and the talk and a lot of the fun of it. Getting paid to eat pussy was how Charley Wade described the job, and all of us that'd done real work outside the pictures pretty much agreed with him. The riggers and the juicers and the wranglers and the bit players like me all knew each other and drank together and swapped lies and girlfriends and got each other hired when we had any pull. Women were a constant subject of conversation, but you sure as hell never saw one of them humping sandbags off the grip truck.

"I say one of us counts the horses every morning," says Mickey, poking her Salisbury steak with her fork. "Make sure the caterer isn't cutting corners on us."

"What are they eating above the line?" asks Popeye.

We all look toward the table where Jordan, and Cedric, and Ira, and Misha are eating.

"Shrimp scampi," says the key, who is so miffed at the food we got he's working on his second plate of it. "Except for what's-his-name, the younger brother. Huddie. He got bacon and beans, special order."

"Naw," says the best boy, "I read in *People* he's supposed to be a vegan."

"Not on this show, he's not. Wants to stay in character."

"I heard the grandfather is some old guy they found in a nursing home, used to be in, like, Roy *Rogers* movies," says Mickey. "Can't act a lick."

Em winces, but there's nothing she can do. It's the first day, so none of the others are wise either.

"They tried every character actor in Hollywood over fifty," she goes on. "You know, Richard Farnsworth, Wilfred Brimley, Jack Palance, those guys. Even tried, like, country singers– Willie Nelson, Johnny Cash. Nobody'd bite for scale."

The crew guys shake their heads.

"When I worked with Roy," I say quietly, "he *was* a country singer– Sons of the Pioneers. I forget the name of the picture, but they had me wearing chaps as wide as a brood mare's heinie and those things would *flap* somethin' fierce whenever I'd walk. Every sound take, you'd hear the director shout out, "Somebody tell that bowlegged son of a bitch to stand *still!*"

There's a little moment of silence, Mickey turning red in the prettiest way, all the riggers frozen in mid-bite.

"I thought you worked with Em," she says finally. "I'm sorry. I didn't know you were *talent*."

"No talent involved, darlin'. What they needed was *age,* and that I got in spades."

"I'm really sorry. They—you know—actors, the above-the-line people, they don't usually eat with us."

"Don't worry about it."

"She didn't mean nothin'," says Em.

"I know. Don't worry about it." I reached across to offer my hand. "Name's Son Bishop. I been in lots of pictures, but this acting game is a new wrinkle to me. I'd prefer to steer clear of Cedric and that crowd if I can. Make me kind of nervous, which I don't need on top of all the lines I got to remember. As long as I don't put a damper on you folks—"

Mickey shakes my hand. "You mean can you eat with us? Oh, sure. I mean, that'd be great. Really."

And then she gives me a smile makes me wish I could hire on as a rigger and be on the other end of whatever she's carryin' all day long and there's Em next to me staring at her thinking the same thing, I can feel it. Mickey's the age my grandaughter would be if I had one, and these days with the young girls I just admire 'em from an artistic point of view. But sometimes you get a smile like that where you can see all the way down into the woman behind it, and it don't matter how old you are. You just *wish.*

At the end of the day, Cedric and Ira and the AD meet for an emergency production confab while most of the crew reconvenes at the Happy Trails Lounge back at the motel. We are just on time for the Happy Trails Happy Hour, which precedes the Nightly Sound Stylings of Miss Vernell Paige, whose photo is displayed on a sandwich board by the entrance. The Russians are at one end of the bar, drinking noisily, while at the other are the grips and gaffers and some strays from other departments.

"Let's face it," says the best boy, a skinny kid with wild hair who looks like he's taken a few too many volts on the job, "We've signed aboard, and it's the *Titanic*."

"It's the first day," says Mickey.

"Right. And it should have been easy. No acting, nothing but MOS shots, but we don't shoot squat."

"Did you listen to that camera?" says the boom. "Sounds like a B-52 taking off. No wonder the horses are spooked."

"What is it, an old Arri?"

"We should be so lucky. I think it was manufactured in Poland or something."

"A Panachevsky."

"It's the first day," Mickey repeats. "They got time to get ther shit together. Besides, when are we going to get another chance to work on a Western?"

"Wonderful. I get to pull cable and step in horseshit at the same time."

The publicist comes in with Teddy Milton, who you've seen in a million pictures and TV shows and is near my age, though he's had some nips and tucks done on his mug. We've got one old doll at the Home, skin tight as a snare drum, but look behind her ears and you can see how many times she went under the knife, like rings on a tree stump. Teddy is playing my pal Charley, who sits on the chuck wagon and ladles out nuggets of prairie wisdom now and then. I'd never seen him in real life before, without makeup– you don't get that complexion drinking French fizzy water. He seemed to have had quite a few already.

"Pleasure to meet you," he says. "Any snatch potential on this picture?"

Mickey is on a stool right beside him but he doesn't notice or doesn't care. Maybe he's more used to women on the crew than I am.

"The last one I worked on was so bad," he says, "I had to fuck the script girl."

This is a line I've heard connected to various leading men back in the forties, which is probably the last time Teddy got laid and didn't pay for it. Mickey doesn't bat an eye, so I decide not to be gallant.

"I'm sort of retired in that department," I tell him. "I'm afraid you're on your own."

Teddy sees that he's standing with a bunch of beer drinkers and heads over to the Russian side, where the hard stuff is being poured. Happy Hour officially ends then and Vernell Paige comes on. She's nightclub-blond and might have been a real looker at one point, but is pushing fifty, though I wouldn't venture from which end. Her voice is better than you'd expect for a motel lounge out where the sky is not cloudy all day, only her piano player thinks he's a stylist too and keeps changing tempo in midstream. Vernell smiles even bigger then and turns to look at him, singing louder in the tempo she started out in, and there's this little tug-of-war for a couple bars and sometimes she wins and sometimes he does. Her act is stuff from my era, ballads and old show tunes, songs with a melody. My side of the room kind of ignores her while the Russkis keep shouting for her to sing rock and roll. Mickey and I are the only ones who applaud after a number, and she's only being polite. Pretty soon the room starts to fill up with young girls, made up and dressed to kill, only this is Wyoming so maybe it's only dressed to wound. They come in and scan the room, look disappointed, then sit around in twos and threes, tossing their hair and watching the door.

"They're waiting for your boys," Mickey says to me, in a break between songs. "Starfuckers. At least that's what they're hoping."

Poor Stuart hobbles in a bit later to tell me call is five-thirty. They must have decided that sitting around in the dark with nothing to shoot for an extra hour would get them back on schedule.

"Listen, Stuart," I say, "take those things off before you cripple your-self. You can tell the teabag there I demanded you give 'em to me. Wanted to sleep with them or some garbage like that."

He winces a little smile. "I don't think I can get them off."

So I listen to Vernell do "Blue Skies" and "Stormy Weather" while Popeye and the best boy take Poor Stuart into the gents and separate him from my boots. There's a lot of that in her act, Vernell—one song contradicting the one before it, "That Lucky Old Sun" leading into "Stars Fell on Alabama," or "Hit the Road, Jack" following "Won't You Come Home, Bill Bailey?" Not that anybody else in the place notices, what with the grips bellyaching and the young girls watching for Jordan and trying to look bored and the Russians yelling "'Hound Dog!' Sing for us Hound Dog!'"

I come up to Vernell after her first set. "That was great. You got a hell of a warble there. Puts me in mind of Keely Smith."

From the look in her eye I couldn't have come up with a better one.

"Really? Thanks so much." She looks over her shoulder, where the pianist is doing calisthenics with his fingers. "I'm part Indian too," she whispers, "just like Keely. Arapaho."

If you looked close you could maybe see it, back under all that blond and makeup. Before I could say anything else, I felt myself being nudged aside. It was Teddy, showing all those teeth that must have set him back a bundle, doing his debonair act. He took Vernell's hand the way Rex Harrison used to do it.

"Amazing. That was"—and here he closed his eyes like he hadn't been rehearsing what he was going to say for fifteen minutes,—"that was *vintage*."

I don't need so much sleep these days, but five o'clock was still pretty much of a shock to the system when it come around.

Jordan was grumpy in the van from the motel, and Teddy was hung over and fell back to sleep. Iron Ike worked one of those hand-grip things and talked to the kid driving about multivitamins. Huddie had spent the night out in the bunkhouse set. Now, the rancher's son wouldn't have been sleeping out with the hired hands, but he said it was part of his *process,* so there he was when we pulled up, frying dough in a skillet from props over a little cookfire he'd made behind the Port-o-Sans.

"Grampaw," he says to me, first thing. "I got a question."

"Do I answer as me or as the character?"

"Uhm—as you, I guess."

"Shoot."

"What did they use—back when—to wipe themselves?"

The way he asks, it's like the fate of the world is in the balance, so I don't laugh.

"Back when I was working or back when there was cattle drives and such?"

"In the Old West."

"Well, I heard corncobs were real popular. Dried ones. Kept 'em in the outhouses."

He nods and is off to pester the caterer. I swear if I'd said sandpaper he'd be after the carpenters.

I do my first acting that day, if that's what you want to call it. Cedric has me spitting chaw in the middle of sentences as well as at the beginning and end of them, and Poor Stuart is backpedalling around holding up cue cards 'cause they're sure I won't be able to remember the lines, and they got Mickey running just under camera range, holding a white card to bounce light up into my mug. The problem with this is that between her and the boom and the dolly there's nowhere to gob but *on* the white card, so they have to bring a clean one in every couple takes.

"Bishop," calls Cedric after the first few, "keep in mind that this is your *realm.* Shabby, *mean,* sordid even, but your realm nevertheless. You are *king* here. When you spit, you spit with *authority.* Jordan, a little more hangdog, please. The sense that there's somewhere else you'd rather be."

"That's what I told my agent," cracks Jordan, and everybody but Huddie laughs. When we start up again, Huddie's got a wad big as a softball in his cheek, and Cedric calls cut after two lines.

"Dear boy," he says, "what *is* that in your mouth?"

"Chaw," says Huddie, though it's hard to understand through the load he's packing.

"I know we spoke about your desire to please your grandfather, to be like him in every way, but we mustn't be so *literal.* Your diction leaves something to be desired as it is."

Huddie looks like he's letting them yank an arm off, but he does spit it out. We get back into the scene, and about the third go I realize I don't have to do much else but talk to these boys the way I feel in real life, 'cause just like in the picture they don't know shit from Shinola and I'm too old to be the one teaches them the difference. Cedric calls "Cut and print" at the end of that one.

"Whatever you just did, Bishop," he says, already heading off to the next setup, "please don't think about it too much."

At lunch the riggers and juicers all said nice things about my acting, and I think a couple might have meant it. After eating, I sat with Em, watching a bunch of them play basketball on a hoop stuck on the side of the grip truck. Mickey played too and held her own, darting around in her little sleeveless T-shirt. Even had her a jump shot, like the college gals on TV.

"You think she's sleeping with any of them?" says Em, out of the blue.

"I only been here a day and a night," I say. "It wasn't posted on the call sheet."

"She's not married."

"Doesn't wear a ring anyways. Though you might not, doing grip work."

"I suppose you know the deal with me," says Em.

I look at her– strong good-looking woman, but sure, I suppose so.

"It's nothing I got a problem with," she says, "but sometimes you can get—you know. Left out."

I don't know what to say so I just nod. And I get this twinge that maybe I'd like it more if Em was playing Jordan's part. Hell, I'd leave the ranch to her any day.

"If she ever says anything about me, one way or the other," says Em, "let me know, okay?"

During the wrap that day, the grips pretend the white cards I've gobbed all over are those inkblot things that shrinks use to tell if you're loony tunes or not.

"I see a spider," says the key. "A spider eating a grasshopper."

"I see a cannibal eating a missionary," says the one they call Bungie.

"I see us all eating Salisbury steak again," says Mickey. "See? There's the canned mushrooms."

"I see our horse wrangler," says Popeye. "I see her eating Mickey."

"Fuck you." says Mickey.

By the third day we settled into a kind of rhythm, falling only a page short of what was planned most of the time. When Jordan wasn't giving Ira grief over his lousy hotel room or early call or cheesy-looking costume or less than starlike entrance in the picture, he spent his time in his trailer with Iron Ike, doing who knows what. He'd come out to act and, after lunch, to watch the crew play ball. They never asked him to play, and he never gave a hint that he wanted to, but he'd stand there watching behind his sunglasses till the AD yelled that we were back in. Huddie found a local fella working as an extra who had an old pistol collection, so every lunch they'd walk out and blast away at fence posts with live ammo. Since Misha and his Red Army had taken to wearing cowboy hats and sitting together every day, this left only Cedric and Ira and Teddy Milton at the big shots' table. Ira looked like he hadn't slept since we started and haunted the set, saying, "It's going great, huh?" and "Have you seen the dailies? Dynamite stuff!" to anybody he made eye contact with.

I looked in on the dailies once– they put them up in one of the motel conference rooms, and it was the only entertainment available other than Vernell Paige and her dueling pianist. All I could tell was that the Russian was a poky son of a bitch but he knew how to shoot and that watching myself was a big mistake. You look in a mirror all your life and get used to the mug on the other side, but it doesn't prepare you for what a camera and a big screen will do. I'd never had a close-up before, and now I saw the reason why.

"You're doing great," Mickey says to me one morning, while she's putting a silk together and I'm muttering my lines to myself. "Everybody's really knocked out by your stuff."

"Cedric doesn't seem too impressed," I tell her. "All he does is grind his knuckles into his head."

She shrugged. "Brits. They're all repressed, can't show their feelings. Inside he's probably ecstatic."

In the afternoon he was so ecstatic he bounced a copy of the script off the back of Misha's head, and we wrapped early so Ira could try to patch things up between them.

I think it was the third week of principal I come into the Lounge and feel right off that something is different. Verrell has got the upper hand on "All of Me," staring the pianist down with her most vicious smile, the Russians are toasting each other, and Em and most of the American crew are nailing down their usual stools. I see the trio of local gals Bungie started calling the Barnacles 'cause you couldn't scrape 'em loose with a cold chisel, and they're looking daggers over into a corner where—lo and behold—there sits Jordan with Mickey. One gander at what she's wearing and how she's hanging on whatever story he's telling about himself, and I know it don't look good for our side. I sit with the fellas, and damn if they don't say a thing about it or look her way for a full hour. Everybody does a pretty good impression of Cedric and Misha by now—Cedric's brain-massage technique and the way Misha says *lightning* instead of *lighting*—so they're busy with that until the lovely couple stroll out of the Lounge and we can all exhale.

"Girl's gonna get her ass handed to her," says the key.

"She should know better."

"Must be going to show her his mirror collection."

"Just what we need in the business, another hyphenate," says Bungie. "Grip-Starfucker."

I hung till the bitter end that night 'cause Em was drinking serious gin and not saying anything. Most of the crew had cleared out by the time Vernell closed with "I'll Be Seeing You."

"He's not even nice," Em said to me finally. The song and the way

Vernell sang it and the lost look in Em's green eyes just about done me in. She shook her head, trying to figure out how such a thing could come to pass. "Boy needs a damn *apple box* to climb on his horse!"

At lunch the next day Mickey disappeared into Jordan's trailer, and the ball game was a hell of a lot quieter and rougher than usual. Iron Ike was wandering around, looking uncomfortable to be outside that time of day, occasionally dropping down to rip off fifty push-ups or so.

"Comes with the territory," he said to me with an embarrassed little smile, nodding toward Jordan's trailer. "Whatta you gonna do?"

That was the last I seen of Mickey on the set for a while. I'd catch her lugging sandbags from the truck now and then, or sometimes just sitting alone on the tailgate with no job to do. Siberia, we used to call it. Somebody with a temper—Jimmy Wong Howe was famous for this when he was shooting pictures—would take a disliking to one of the crew, and you'd have to hide them far away from the action so's they wouldn't get fired. Jimmy was a tough little guy, been a prizefighter, and I once saw him can a guy for looking at him funny. The grips had banished Mickey to Siberia– at wrap one night I saw four different riggers pass her without picking up the other end of the scaffolding she was dragging. She never showed at Happy Hour after work anymore and the tone of the party changed. The Barnacles give up on actors altogether and paired off with fellas from the art department, and one night some of the local hardtails come in drunk to pick fights with the movie people for monopolizing their women. Popeye separated one gentleman from his front teeth and Ira had to post bond for him. It doesn't take long to become a vital part of the community.

I was used to the acting now and could take it pretty much in stride. Huddie had been sleeping on hard ground under a bedroll since the first night, staying away from things he figured a cowboy on the trail would never do, like change his clothes or bathe. The kid was *rank*. Even his horse didn't want to be anywhere near him, and Em had to assign two of

JOHN SAYLES

her boys to hold it still whenever Huddie needed to mount up. This didn't please him any, as real cowboys got in the saddle without help—except for Jordan, of course, who'd have been happier riding a stepladder.

Em's nightmare came at last, the first big cattle drive scene. The herd had been penned up till then, milling around in the background, but the minute they wandered out onto those high plains that just don't end it was clear we were several bricks shy of a load.

"Is *boolshit!*" says Misha when he sees them. "I'm not shooting."

This was Misha's usual response to the first setup of the day, so nobody took him serious. They laid some track and put the crane together and Cedric explains to Em's boys, who are doubling some of the actors playing drovers, where he wants the stock to go during the shot.

"Twenty dollars," says Bungie to the dolly grip, "they turn onto the track and knock the fucking crane over."

The dolly grip looks at the cattle, wandering every which way while Em's boys are huddling with Cedric, and shakes his head. "Yo, Popeye!" he calls. "You want to push this one?"

It's noon when we start to work it out, and the result is what you'd call underwhelming. The whole bunch of us are past camera in ten seconds, even with the dolly move. They haven't built anything to steer the herd back to first position after the cut, so there's a major roundup after every rehearsal.

"Not enough cattle," grumbles Cedric, after we've slogged through it the fourth time.

"More cows!" shouts the first as if somebody's hiding a couple dozen head somewhere. Nobody moves. Cedric and Ira and the first go into their huddle, and the energy on the set wanders away along with half the stock. The gaffers start tilting their reflector boards to bounce sun onto their tans, Jordan dismounts and starts playing with Mickey's T-shirt, making her giggle, and everybody tries not to get downwind of Huddie. I ride Lefty over to make a suggestion.

"It's none of my business," I start, "but you string 'em out a bit, back up and stick your hundred mil on the camera, dump some Fuller's earth in their path and run a few head right past the lens, it'll bulk this herd up some."

Cedric looks at me like Jack Palance used to when a sodbuster got on his nerves, then picks up his bullhorn.

"Excuse me, everybody," he calls, to get their attention. People turn their horses to look. It gets quiet.

"Bishop here would like to direct the rest of this film."

Lefty looks away as if she's embarrassed.

"We're waiting," says Cedric. "Any more brilliant ideas, Bishop?"

"No, sir, I suppose not."

"Well, then," he says to the others, "shall we set up another?"

Which is exactly what Jack Ford would've done, except he'd have said *"Mr. Bishop."*

By four o'clock they're doing everything I said but the Fuller's earth.

With the Cold War back in full swing between Cedric and Misha, there was more waiting than usual on the set, and most days Em would come hang with me and talk horses. I've got to say the gal knew her business and had a way with the animals. One day I seen her back a greenbuck stallion up a ramp and into a trailer, just talking low and switching sides on him now and then. She had her boys keep the stock clean and fed and ready to roll on a moment's notice, and now and again I'd see her up on one of the younger horses, teaching it something with her knees. Her dream was to have a spread and sell Appaloosas, which is kind of the ranch-girl version of becoming Lana Turner.

"If you're going to be lonely," Em said once, when we were talking about it, "you should at least have work you like to do."

All the father and son stuff in the story had got me thinking, and one night I left the Happy Trails with three beers' worth of nerve and rang my boy in Denver.

"Wesley."

"Who's this?"

"Your old man."

It's been a strange dance between me and Wesley over the years. I'm more of a forty-year misunderstanding than a father to him. His mom and me split when he was two, and since then whenever he needed a father or I needed a son the other wasn't interested.

A long pause. Then, suspicious: "Hi."

"How are you?"

"Fine. You okay?"

"I'm on a picture."

"A movie."

"Right. Up in Wyoming."

"Uh-huh."

Willie, the one in the classic, couldn't have gotten a colder shoulder from one of his customers. There is way too much time between what I say and what he says next, like in a rough cut where the editor's been too cautious. Punch it up, I think.

"I figure I'm this close, maybe you could come up some weekend, see your old man be a movie star."

I have a shit-eating grin on my face, voice too bright, overacting. There is a very long pause, Denver blank at the other end. *Get a spot on your hat*, I think, *and that's a tragedy.*

"You're *acting?*"

"Yeah. Getting paid for it, too. Crazy world, huh?"

"Where is this?"

"Northern Wyoming, down from Sheridan. It's a cattle drive picture." Another pause.

"Well, I'll see," he says finally. "Might not be able to get away. Acting, huh?"

I gave him the directions then and went back to the Lounge. Vernell was singing "Body and Soul" right to Teddy while her pianist did all this Liberace business behind her, playing the keys like a chef decorating a wedding cake. Vernell backed up with her microphone and sat next to the accompanist, smiling at him, laying her free hand gently at the back of his neck. Whatever she did next knocked him up the keyboard a full octave, and all his trills and tinklings disappeared like *that*.

At the bar the guys were rerunning their favorite Jordan horror stories. The day before he'd left us sitting a full hour while he debated Cedric about whether or not his character would keep his hat on during the vaquero's trailside funeral. We ended up doing a couple takes each way, lost magic hour, and heard Misha go through the Russian vocabulary while he kicked a hole in the soda cooler at craft services.

"Now if I was sleeping with an actress—" said Popeye.

"On some movie where there *were* any actresses."

"Right. If I were sleeping above the line, with an actress—"

"She'd have to be pretty desperate," said Bungie. "Like really old or something."

"Up yours."

"Hey, I'm just trying to imagine your scenario."

"*If* I was sleeping with an actress, disappearing into her trailer every afternoon, hanging with her after wrap, bringing her her fucking tea and honey on the set, how would you guys react?"

A moment's reflection. Vernell segued into "Cry Me a River."

"We'd give you unrelenting shit," said the boom.

"You give me unrelenting shit now."

"This would be *really* bad. We'd make the crew van leave early, so you had to ride with the sound department."

"*Oooooooh.*"

"We'd get the desk to cancel your wake-up calls."

"We'd gaffer-tape your door shut at night, then call and tell you there was a fire in the motel."

"Nice friends," said Popeye.

"You guys are a bunch of shits," said Em.

"I slept with an actress on a show once," said the best boy, who'd been quiet up to this point.

"Which one?"

"What show?"

"On *Cold Cuts?* She was one of the victims."

"That narrows it down to about thirty."

"The one who gets the corkscrew in the back of her skull?"

"The one in the wood chipper?"

"The one he does with the staple gun?"

"Naw. Remember there was that scene where we had to rig the camera inside the trash compacter?"

"*Her?* She didn't have any lines."

"She didn't even get scale."

"Hey, she was an actress, all right?" The best boy looked sorry he'd told them.

"Wasn't she the one who didn't shave her legs?"

"With the hair on her back?"

"Who looked like Ernest Borgnine?"

"You guys are a bunch of shits," Em repeated. She had her ten o'clock buzz on and was looking morose.

"Of course we are," said Popeye. "It's part of our *job*."

Em snorted. Once a night she'd say something to defend Mickey and always made a point to say hi to her on the set in the morning. Mickey actually had said something about her to me once, though I decided not to pass it on.

"Don't you just love Em?" she'd said, shaking her head in admiration while Em hooked up the chuck wagon. "She's such a *cowgirl*."

Em walked out when Popeye made a crack about Jordan coming in saddle-sore every morning.

Vernell finished with her teary rendition of "The Man I Love," then walked right over and latched onto my wrist.

"Come on to my room, Son," she says. "We got to talk."

The fellas made some noises about that and she pulled me out of the

Lounge. She had her own room only a couple doors down from the lobby, and it was like being inside a photo album with four walls. Everywhere you looked there was head shots and publicity pictures, mostly girl singers from the forties and fifties– Julie London, Joni James, Doris Day, Helen O'Connell. One wall was all sisters—the Andrews Sisters, the Boswell Sisters, the Lennon Sisters—and another was devoted to pictures from Vernell's career, starting with her in a little Annie Oakley getup singing at a microphone a foot over her head.

She parks under a shot of Keely Smith herself, Louis Prima peeking over her shoulder like a chubby Italian devil. "I call this my Wall of Fame. Some day *those* pictures:—she pointed to the shots of herself—"are gonna be with *these* pictures."

"Well, you got the voice for it." I couldn't offhand think of any famous singers who got their big break when they were fifty, but here I was with my first big acting part at this late date, so I kept a rag in it.

"You need to tell me some things," said Vernell, "about Teddy."

"I don't know the fella that well—"

"Is he married?"

Teddy spent most of his time on the set listing once-famous actresses he'd had, often in my direction, since I was the only one on the set who remembered any of them.

"Son, you remember Betty Gayle?" he'd say, and I'd have to make a noise and he'd go on about what happened between them by the fountain at some Brit scenic designer's place up in Montecito. He had backed off some after I reported that one of his conquests was now a patient at the Home, liver spots, store-bought choppers, and deaf as a post.

The other thing he did on the set was wish he had a drink.

"It's about that time," he'd say, tapping his watch and winking at me. It could be anywhere from ten in the morning to five minutes before wrap. "Gettin mighty dry out here on the lone pray-ree. Mighty dry."

"He never said if he was or wasn't," I told Vernell. "I think he'd of mentioned it, though."

"He wants me to go back with him. To Los Angeles."

I liked her, Vernell. She slugged her way through two shows a night with an assassin at the piano and a roomful of customers who couldn't care less, and she never lost her energy, never gave up on her act. A pro.

"He's an alcoholic, Vernell."

"You're not going to talk me out of this, Son," she said. "There's a good man under there somewhere, and I aim to smoke him out."

She told me the rest of it then, how she'd been a young woman singing on the circuit when she did a jingle for this fella with a car dealership in Cheyenne, and it was romance at first sight. He had a wife and kids, of course, nine of them, being a Mormon and a potent kind of a fella. His brother worked for the motel chain, and for twenty-some years she was a kept woman, seeing the car fella on weekends and playing lounges all over the West.

"Good places," she said. "Nothing too far from the interstate."

The car dealer had died last August, and now the brother with the motels was making goo-goo eyes, like he'd inherited her in the will.

"It's time to move to the next plateau," said Vernell. "But I'm sure as hell gonna get a ring this time."

When I got out of there I was pretty low, thinking about my boy and what a mess I'd made and what your life must be to see Teddy Milton as a ticket to better times. I didn't get halfway down the hall before Spook Riley pokes his head out from *his* room and catches me coming.

"Son?" he says. "You got a minute?"

Spook had just flown up to play my brother Ben, the one who lit out for the California gold fields and made a pile, who appears to me in a mirage while we're crossing some salt flats without water. Spook is about my age and has been doing theater for most of his life, "In the hinterlands," as he calls it. Never done a picture before and they're shooting his only scene tomorrow.

"It's the dialogue," he says. "The casting people called me, they didn't say a thing about the line load."

"You got one speech."

"It's a whole page."

"Well, it's a picture, Spook, so you get to stop and go. You just have to remember a few lines at a time."

I'm on the chair, and Spook, whose real name is Spencer, sits on the edge of his bed. He's got these eyes, round with round lines under them, makes him look like an old scared rabbit, like Uncle Wiggly with a wolf on his tail.

"I can't remember my street back home most days," he says. "I been in here trying to bring back the name of my second wife. It's just not there anymore."

"You won't need to know that tomorrow."

"I haven't worked for two years. Made up some credits—*Life with Father*, Terre Haute, Indiana—who's gonna check?"

"You want me to go over the lines with you?"

He pulls out a little tape recorder. "Could you lay them down for me?"

"Shouldn't you do that yourself?"

"My own voice throws me off," he says. He hands me the tape machine and his sides of dialogue. "Just say them real flat. No acting."

While I read the lines onto the tape, Spook stared away out his window into the parking lot, watching the car lights come and go. Somebody is crying loud, probably drunk out of their mind. I finished and found the button to turn the thing off. Spook looked at me like he'd forgot who I was.

"Maybe if they keep the camera on one side I can have an earphone on the other."

"Sure. I'll put in a word with the Russian."

He took the tape recorder and looked at it like something mysterious was kept inside, then looked up at me.

"People don't die in motel rooms," he said, "do they?"

After that I need some fresh air to clear my head. I walk out into the lot and it's Em, sitting on the tailgate of a pickup, crying her eyes out.

This wasn't your quiet, bitter tears, or your little can't-help-it sniffles, this was flat out boo-hoo-hoo weeping, Em bawling out tears and gasping in air to load up for her next burst. She turned her head away from me at first, but let me sit by her and put my arm around her for a long time. I don't know what she thought about it, her being such a cowgirl and all, but it sure made *me* feel better.

We get to Spook's scene about three o'clock the next day.

Cedric wants to shoot it as a master, of course, Ben rising up in front of me from the sagebrush we've carted in, sacks of gold slung over his back. Poor Stuart comes back from the trailers with the look he gets when Jordan is holing up there wasting everybody's time and it's going to be his job to dig him out.

"And where is our apparition?" asks Cedric.

"In the trailer. He's not—"

"Stuart, we try to keep your duties within your rather limited capabilities," says Cedric, warming up. "Fetching tea, carrying my chair hither and yon, escorting the artists to and from their havens—"

"He's not breathing."

This shuts Cedric up, not an easy thing to do once he's on a roll.

"You're telling me he's dead."

Poor Stuart has gotten careful about how he delivers bad news. "He's not breathing," he says.

Cedric mashes his knuckles to his forehead. "We could have shot it this morning," he says softly. "We had to wait for the bloody *sun* to come out."

Misha takes offense and walks off in a huff. This is not his country and he takes no responsibility for the weather in it. I climb down from Lefty.

"Let me take a look," I say. "It could be he's a heavy sleeper."

One of my jobs at the hospital is what we call postmortem care, so I do what needs to be done for Spook while the crew shoots inserts of cattle hooves trekking the prairie. He went out easy, lying on his back with his eyes closed like he's asleep, dressed in his San Francisco dude costume, his W-2 form sitting on the edge of the little trailer sink. He'd only gotten to the fourth digit of his Social Security number before he wrote a question mark. In his kit bag I found enough pharmaceuticals to dose a regiment of geriatrics. Liver pills, kidney pills, heart pills, blood pressure, all prescription stuff. The guy was a walking time bomb.

The second AD is standing by the steps with the sign-out sheet when I step down.

"Is he really dead?"

"You better get Ira," I tell her.

The decision is made to keep shooting, and everybody is quiet and jumpy on the set while Ira runs around dealing with the bureaucracy of a dead actor. We shoot a scene where Britt and Huddie have a fistfight at a water hole. First Huddie won't let the stunt double stand in for him, which puts Jordan on the spot and he says he wants to do his own slugging too. The coordinator throws up his hands and looks to Cedric, who looks at the sky and observes as how the sun is sinking rapidly into the West.

"If the artists insist," he says, "we can only attempt to capture their brilliance."

The crew start taking bets while the coordinator gives the boys a little lecture, and then they go at it.

It made me think of kids who start their toy trains running at each other full speed. They know it's wrong, but they got to see how hard the smash will be.

The first minute or so of the tussle the boys keep it under control, spitting out some of their lines and eyeballing each other. Then Huddie pushes when it's not written and Jordan goes ass over teakettle into the water. There is a smattering of applause from the crew till Cedric gives them a look that would blister paint.

"This is done?" asks the Russkie operator, still on the eyepiece.

"Keep rolling," says Cedric.

Jordan is back up, mad at Huddie and madder at the crew, and he knows Mickey is there watching, which never makes him any calmer. The boys really get into it then. Neither of them can fight a lick but they got murder in their hearts so it works, sort of, punching and scratching and wrestling and falling in the water, buttons ripping off, hats gone, the continuity girl having cardiac arrest behind me scribbling details down and suddenly blood, lots of it, on them both. It's quiet, but for the two of them. Ira stands next to me with his mouth open, looking from the boys to Cedric and back, Insurance claims dancing before his eyes. Jordan is bigger than Huddie and has more to lose right now, and it ends like in the script with him on top of Huddie, pounding him in the face, and Huddie's head is under water half the time. I look to Cedric and the limey son of a bitch is *smiling*, and that does it.

In the dailies it looks like we worked it out for weeks. I wade in and push Jordan back onto the bank and drag Huddie out by the scruff of his neck and yell that they're nothing but goddam spoiled babies without the sense God gave a fruit fly. That here they been given a job some people would kill for—all you got to do is put one foot in front of the other and *do* it, for Chrissake—and they start every new day thinking up new ways to waste everybody's time and if I'd known I was throwing in with such a band of greenhorn amateurs I'd of said hell with it and stayed home. Then I look into the lens and tell Cedric if he don't tell Boris there to turn the damn camera off I'll stick it up his limey ass. Sideways.

"Cut," says Cedric then. "Print that one."

The part not in the dailies was just as much fun.

Cedric is walking in little circles and rubbing his hands together. "About time we had a little *passion* in this horse opera," he says. Then he turns to Mickey, who is wiping blood off Jordan's face.

"Young lady," he says, "what is your name?"

She just looks at him.

"Which department are you employed in?"

"Grip," she says, looking flat at him.

"Then I suggest you go find a bulky object to lift. You're in our shot."

"He's *bleeding*."

"Impressive, isn't it? Very Method of him. But I need to *keep* him bleeding until we finish our little melodrama by the water hole. So if you'd save your Florence Nightingale turn for later in the gentleman's trailer, we might be able to proceed."

I could feel the crew turning around me, the way they do in the mutiny pictures when their best buddy gets flogged for no good reason. All the fun of watching the actors pound the stuffing out of each other was gone. For the last hour only the Russians talked, whispering under their cowboy hats.

It was a Friday, and at wrap there stands Wesley next to the girl who first drove me to the motel. There's an ambulance flashing its lights behind him. Wes looks older, kind of shaky.

"They said on her walkie-talkie that somebody died on the set," he tells me, without saying hello. " 'The old man,' it said. We followed the ambulance half the way here." Wes shrugs, embarrassed. "I thought it was you."

The fellas in white carry Spook to the ambulance on a stretcher, a furniture pad laid over him, then Jordan and Huddie and the second AD climb in the back after the body. Huddie had three teeth chipped, and Jordan's knuckles were open to the bone.

"You came," I said to Wesley. "That's great."

"I thought it was you," he said again.

We had a two day weekend ahead, so it was pretty lively at the Happy Trails. I wasn't ready to be alone with Wes yet, so I brought him in to introduce to the outfit.

"Son and son," said Bungie. "Far fucking out."

"Quite a scene there today, Son," said Popeye. "Thought you should have let the little one drown."

"I saw a DP hit a juicer with his viewfinder once," said the best boy. "Swung it around like a bolo. Thirteen stitches."

"Never work a show with a Brit and a Russian," said the boom.

A chorus of amens.

"Never sign a flat deal with an Israeli producer."

"Never waive turnaround in Alaska in the summer."

"Never work a show with two stars named Corey."

"Never eat the salad if it's got yesterday's seafood in it."

"Never stand near a Tulip crane if the focus-puller's fat."

"Never work a show," said the best boy, "where the gaffers are uglier than the grips."

Mickey stepped in then, looking worried. The crew mostly got busy with their drinks.

"He's got to stay the night," she said. "The cut on his hand might be infected."

Nobody says boo so I step up. "This is my son, Wesley."

She gave us a little smile. "Your dad's doing a great job." She turned to the crew then, picking out Popeye. "Sorry about today," she said. "I shouldn't have been in the way."

"No skin off my ass." Popeye stared into his beer.

"I don't want the department catching heat because of me."

"Cedric's a dick," said the best boy quietly. "He was out of line."

It was the nicest thing any of them had said to her in weeks. Mickey nodded and left the bar.

"So, did you know this guy pretty well?" asks Wesley later, while Vernell is chasing the piano player through "It Was Just One of Those Things."

"Who?"

"The man who died. The actor."

I been trying not to think too much about Spook. At the Home, we have two or three go out every week. If it's on my shift I wrap them up and take them on the last ride while Milagros at the desk phones *Variety* with the details. Death is our harvest, and I wander around like an old orchard pig waiting for the next ripe one to drop. But on a movie set—

well, it's different. It only happened to me once before, another cattle-drive picture, when little Tommy Hurley's mount stepped in a gopher hole and half the herd run over him.

"No, I didn't," I tell Wesley. "He'd just flown in from Kansas City."

He goes off to bed early, Wes. We're still so awkward with each other, it's work. But we make a plan to meet in the morning and maybe ride some.

I used to take him to the movies. He'd be sitting on the front stoop of his mom's house down in Playa del Rey, on account of she didn't even want to say hello, and sometimes he'd run and jump in the car before I'd get it into PARK. Then we'd go to the show– the Surf, I think it was. He was a quiet serious kid and it was hard to talk, so the movies let us sit by each other for a couple hours without having to say much. The main thing I remember, he always wanted to know if the character was going to die or not, like I'd already seen the picture. We'd be in the first reel and the star would grin or make a joke and Wes would look up at me and ask, "Is he going to die in this?"

No kid wants to put his money on somebody he knows isn't going the distance, but Wes was extra sensitive about this. Usually I'd shrug or say, You never know. There was one Custer picture we went to he asked it so much, every time a new trooper got introduced, I had to take time out to explain the word *massacre*. The Seventh no sooner laid eyes on that Indian camp than Wes was gone up the aisle.

Never did see the end of that picture.

When he got up in his teens there was years at a time I didn't see him, maybe, just called on his birthday so's he could sulk over the phone, and then even that fell away. When folks asked, at the Home or whatever, if I had a family, I got in the habit of saying no.

The next morning it was postcard weather, blue skies, big sun. Misha was in the lobby grumbling, taking it personal like all shooters do. Wes was up before me and we had breakfast at the motel and then went out to Em's setup. A couple of her boys were there, looking hung over.

I took Lefty and gave Wes one of the likelier young horses. We took off cross-country with the sun at our backs.

We'd canter, then walk, then canter, then walk. Wes could ride some, though it's not something I ever taught him. I can tell it's something he's proud to show off to me, and he starts to loosen up some once the interstate is out of earshot.

"I used to think you really were a cowboy," says Wes, while the horses are at a walk. "When I was little. I thought the movies were like documentaries."

"I don't know how you ever picked me out from the crowd."

"I didn't." He's come out to be a good-looking boy. Got some range on him from his mom, strong jaw. Young Joel McCrea, maybe. Little bit of gray on the sides, but he's got all his hair.

"I'd pick one of the actors and make up my mind that was you," he said.

"Oh."

"Hey, I saw the movies a lot more than I saw you. My favorite to play you was that guy, the one who was in *Wagonmaster*."

"Ben Johnson?"

"Naw, the other one."

"Harry Carey, Jr."

"Right. Him."

"I'm flattered."

I didn't say it to Wes but I'd had my own fantasies about him, nothing I ever did anything about, but whenever I felt real guilty they were some comfort. One of them was this, out riding with him, like the one with Alan Ladd and his little deaf boy. Only now Wes is a man of forty-two, forty-three and I've aged clear past Alan Ladd and straight into Walter Brennan.

We'd meant to just ride out an hour or so, but then we saw the low treeline following Crazy Woman Creek and headed for that, and the horses drank alongside us and we rested some and then crossed it. The Westerns never done that much for me, being in them took the shine off the magic, I guess, and I always preferred big-city detective pictures. But I did like that shot where horses cross water. They tried to have one in every picture, sometimes right under the credits at the head, and here we were with our mounts kicking up spray in the sunlight, their heads up and noses open like they know how pretty they look. Wesley's got a big grin on his face like he's thinking the same as I am, and then we're through the scrub on the other side looking smack at the Bighorns rising up in the distance.

I point north. "Up there is where George Custer and his boys got their tickets punched."

"I know. I might take the kids up there next summer."

I got two grandsons, little ones since Wes got married so late. His wife has sent me a snapshot or two but I never seen them in person.

Without saying anything about it, we just keep riding west toward the mountains. It's mostly open range there, rabbits and even a couple prairie dogs flushing out in front of us, the little deer standing their ground in a cluster till the last moment then busting apart like pool balls on the break, scattering fast, then re-forming and running together. And the antelope, there's nothing prettier than how they spring and float, every fourth or fifth stride, white rump sailing in the air. And there's something else up ahead.

"A rider," says Wesley.

Just a dot ahead, traveling the same way as we are but not as fast. It's getting later and my old bones are saying we should turn back but Wes is fixed on this rider, something to catch up to, and he pushes his mount ahead.

"A rider on the range," he says, smiling.

It's forty minutes' pushing before I can see that it's Em we're moving up on.

"I thought I was the only idiot who come out here anymore," she says, when we pull alongside.

"This is my son, Wesley."

They shake hands from horseback.

"You a stunt rider like your old man?"

"Salesman," he says, shy. "Sporting goods."

Em nods, looks at the sky. "It's late to turn back," she says. "I've got some people I'm going to see. I bet they'd like more company."

So we turned south, walking the horses, and Em told Wes about the Johnson County war and who done what to who, pointing directions as if it all took place just over the rise, and then we ride, just easy 'cause the horses are tired and I'm worse, till we come to this sheep outfit where Em is friends with the people.

They are glad for the company 'cause they don't get too much, folks whose people come over from Basque country way back when and don't ask me what their name was, 'cause even after the fella said it twice and spelled it once I still couldn't get a handle on it.

"Your kid's a nice guy," says Em to me, while we're washing up before dinner. "Rides pretty good, too."

"That's none of my fault. He didn't grow up with me."

"My dad used to take me out riding all the time," says Em, face blank while she's drying her hands. "Till it come to what it come to. He—you know—he doesn't approve."

Dinner was lamb, which you could have figured, and Wes and I were so hungry we hardly talked while we stuffed the food down. The folks who used to be Basque turned out to be like Em's unofficial aunt and uncle, and they bragged some about when she was state-champ barrel racer and some about how her father was doing, tiptoed around that while Em stared at her plate, and I figured then that she hadn't talked to him in three–four years.

They put me in their son's room who was away at college, and I went out like I was poleaxed. I'd been riding some on the set, building up my strength, but I hadn't spent a whole day in the saddle for near twenty-five years.

It was some satisfaction that Wesley looked just as decrepit as me the next morning, walking with little stiff steps and holding on to backs of chairs to get across the kitchen.

The rancher couple, Ed and Lila was their first names, put out eggs and bacon and biscuits and gravy and cinnamon rolls the size of wagon wheels, and no matter how much damage we'd done to their lamb and potatoes the night before, Wes and Em and me wolfed the lot of it down. Riding, you'd figure the horse is doing all the work, but it's not true. I thought of the stuff I shovel into my patients at the Home, of the Cup-a-Soup and frozen dinners I run through the microwave in my little apartment, and realize somehow I've left the Land of the Dead and wandered back among the living.

"Jump aboard," I say to Wesley, when I see him hesitating by his mount, rubbing his hips like he wants to call a cab. "The pain gets dull after the first couple hours."

There's a scene in the movie I'd been worrying about, where Willie is riding with his boys and the Indians are trailing them and he's got to tell the boys what to do with the herd while he goes back and makes a stand in the box canyon they're coming out of. They all know he's not likely to come out alive but are putting a brave front on it, and in the script it says how tears start rolling down his face halfway through his speech. Now I got to ride and remember all my lines and then this crying thing, which is what real actors can do, while I'm just a broken-down old stuntman.

Well, the day comes and they got the camera rolling on a crane in front of me and Cedric with that look on his face like how'd I get into this mess? and on either side of me there's my movie boys, one of 'em's a Hollywood snot and the other smells like goat pee on a hot day and the crew are trading these looks, like this is gonna be a *long* one, fellas.

But I got the lines down cold.

And the very first take I get to thinking, right while I'm saying the dialogue, thinking about riding back with Emmaline on one side and Wes on the other, us hardly talking and not needing to, and how I felt riding in between them on that beautiful day across Crazy Woman Creek to the Powder River and I know they're not mine, neither of them, really, but it *feels* like it, I can just about remember how proud I was when Em handed me that barrel-racing trophy, and Wes—hell, Wes and I rode many a trail together and I taught him to fish and lookit how tall and strong they both grown up and don't the waterworks start up all on their own right about where it says so in the screenplay.

It's quiet when I'm done with all my words and Cedric says *cut.* I can't really see him through the tears, but he looks like the convict in the pictures right when the word comes from the governor. He's not gonna fry after all.

"Enough of that," he says. "Let's get our cutaways."

When I put him on the bus to the airport, Wesley allowed as how it would be good for his boys to meet their grandfather. Maybe this Little Bighorn trip, if they took it.

"That'd be fine," I told him. "Just let me know." He had me put my John Hancock on a couple publicity photos I give him. *Yr Grandad, Son Bishop.* First autograph I ever wrote.

The last two weeks we were shooting on the Mexican village set, which meant they brought in the dark-eyed Mexican gal who the boys have their fight over. Actually, she was Greek or Lebanese or one of those Arab countries and grew up in Cleveland, and was quite a looker. Movie-star beautiful. The day they first brung her to the set for makeup tests the whole crew was buzzing, and then she come out on the set in her señorita getup with the bare shoulders and Cedric could barely keep his tongue in his mouth.

"Ah," he said, taking her hand. " 'Ripeness, ripeness is all.' "

As Huddie was still pretty ripe himself at this point, the Mexican spitfire—Irene was her name—put her sights on Jordan. The first day they acted together there was a scene where she finishes her dance and plops down in Jordan's lap, and that's where she settled for the rest of the day, take or no take.

"Poor Mickey," says the best boy, watching with me from the sidelines.

"Actors," I tell him. "It's just how they get worked up for their parts."

The next day at lunch break Mickey comes out of Jordan's trailer with tears streaming down her face. She walks past the crew table, the above-the-line table, the Mexican village extras table, past the set and the honey wagons and out onto the prairie. Nobody says anything till Em gets up and trots after her.

"Mickey just got her walking papers," Popeye starts in. "Should've seen it coming."

"Thought she had a run-of-the-show contract," says Bungie.

"She didn't read the starlet clause."

"Opens the trailer door and there's Chiquita Banana, pullin cable."

"And old Jordan, he's got his hundred millimeter out—"

"Juanita's playing with the focus ring—"

"And here's our girl at the door with two trays of Chicken Marengo."

"Is that what you call this?"

"Some *grip* at the door—"

"And Rosita's already got a grip on his boom pole—"

"Got her clamp on his C-stand—"

"And it's good-bye, Mickey. Back where you belong."

They were quiet for a while, and then Em come back.

"How's she doing?" asked Popeye.

Em was pissed at all of us for being men and being in on the conspiracy. "How do you think?" she said. "Somebody ought to teach that boy a lesson."

We ate quiet again, till Bungie broke the ice.

"So which is the Marengo part?"

Mickey didn't come down to the Happy Trails that night but nobody talked about her. Teddy was with us, drinking tomato juice and complaining about this Twelve-Step program Vernell had got him onto, and she was singing her salute to the States—"Georgia on my Mind," "Moonlight in Vermont," "The Missouri Waltz,"—and the fellas were trying to come up with a title for the picture. It said DEATH OF A CATTLEMAN on the slate and the call sheets, but Cedric had decided that was "a bit spot-on" and announced a hundred dollar reward for whoever come up with a better name.

"We could name it after the two sons," said the boom. *"Finky and Stinky."*

"Butch Cassidy and the Scum-Pants Kid."

"The Levinsky Trail," said Bungie.

That was good for a laugh. Ira had aged ten years in six weeks and was so desperate he was even asking the extras whether they thought the picture was any good or not.

"Blood on the Saddle."

"Blood on the Trucks."

"Blood on the Chuck Wagon."

"Teddy on the Wagon," said Teddy.

"I got it," said the best boy. *"The Cowboy and the Grip."*

We consider that, wondering where Mickey is and how she's feeling.

"Naw," said Bungie. "People won't go if they know the ending's a downer."

It was the next day after lunch, the fellas playing grips against gaffers at the hoop on the side of the truck. They could see Mickey over on a pile of sandbags where she'd been moping for the whole break, and Popeye whispers something to the best boy. Mickey's been kind of watching the game and kind of pretending not to, her back to the star trailer where Jordan and Irene are holed up. On the next play the best boy starts to ooh and ah and limp around.

"My ankle," he says. "My fuckin' ankle."

"You're not hurt," says Popeye. "Let's go."

"I can't, man. I think I sprained it."

"Pussies. Juicers are such pussies."

"Up yours," he says, and sits down on the side.

Popeye makes a big show of looking around then—and I thought I was a bad actor. Finally he pulls the string.

"Yo Mick! Mickey!" She looks up. Who me?

"We need somebody. Putz-brain here thinks he's hurt. You mind?"

She stands up, not sure at first.

"Come on, they're gonna call us back in in ten minutes."

She takes a step forward. "You want me to play for the *gaffers?*"

"Yeah," says the dolly grip. "It's all right to switch sides once in a while. Long as you remember where your loyalties are."

Popeye bounces the basketball over to her.

Em comes up by me while they're playing. Mickey is in the flow of the game like she never missed a day.

"Look at that," says Em, admiring. "Another three inches and she could kick ass out there."

Nobody's really sure who actually done the deed, but I got a look at Em when it happened, and she's the only one didn't laugh or seem surprised. If you see the movie, it's the scene where Jordan's character, Britt, has said the words over my grave and turns to the other hands, jams his hat on his head, and says, "All right, boys, let's get these cattle to market!" You know how they made a big deal in the write-ups about how when he turns into the close-up you can see on his face he's not all that sure of himself? That was the point where he felt the cow flops, fresh ones, somebody'd lined his hat with between takes.

"Inspired" was the word Cedric had for it.

"Cowboy humor," Em says to me in that dry way of hers while Ira is trying to coax Jordan back out of his trailer and the whole crew, Russians included, are dancing around slapping each others' hands like the basketball fellas do on the sports channel.

"It'll nail 'em every time."